The High Priestess: Persephone's Return

VAL TOBIN

ISBN: 978-1-988609-22-5

DEDICATION

To Bob, Jenn, Mark, Chanelle, Savannah, Jack, Ian,
and Scully

Books in the *Tales from the Unmasqued World* Series

The Fool: New Beginnings
The Magician: Infinity's End
The High Priestess: Persephone's Return
The Empress: A Promise of Rain

ACKNOWLEDGMENTS

Thank you to Alis B. Kennedy, PhD; Wendy Quirion; Val Cseh; John Erwin; Michelle Legere; and Diane King of The Hedge Witch (www.thehedgewitch.com) for beta reading, professional advice, and suggestions. Developmental editing by Tahlia Newland tahlianewland.com. Thank you, Tahlia.
Thank you to Kelly Hartigan (XterraWeb) editing.xterraweb.com for her superb line editing and proofreading.
Thanks to Patti Roberts of Paradox Book Covers & Designs for the amazing cover.

CHAPTER 1

Burn already, damn you. Jaycie Nevil squinted at the palm of the hand she held before her until it blurred. Despite her laser focus, it refused to give off even a tiny spark. Tears sprang to her eyes, and her teeth gritted, but she refrained from snarling out her frustration.

While the day hadn't darkened on her and Cora Osler, her companion, it hadn't brightened either. What she wouldn't trade for a flash of light. Although only a student mage, she ought to manage at least a soft glow. She sucked in a deep breath, preparing to make one more attempt.

"Stop. You're exhausting yourself for no reason," Cora said.

Jaycie exhaled, dropping the hand to her side.

"What else is there to do?" She glared at the other woman, who ignored the animosity and eased onto a nearby rock, her goddess gown puddling around her. Her dainty feet, adorned with golden strapped sandals, peeked out from beneath the white, gauzy folds.

"Rest. Gather strength." Cora propped an elbow on her knee and rested her chin on her hand. Long, dark brown ringlets cascaded over her shoulders.

Jaycie forgot her surroundings and drank in the woman's beauty. But only for a moment. Then reality came crashing back, and she let out a childish wail.

"I can't. I'm so sick of walking and getting nowhere. Why won't you help?"

Cora sighed and shook her head. "Sit, child."

It wasn't an order, but the commanding tone made Jaycie drop to the dirt. Hugging her shins, she pressed her forehead to her kneecaps and closed her eyes.

The ground was neither cold nor hot. Everything in this place was a drab and dreary neutral. Sometimes, she considered that fortuitous, but other times, she'd have welcomed a change in any direction. Where was the terror Cora had claimed awaited them this way?

"I understand your frustration."

Without looking up, Jaycie said, "Do you?" Based on what she observed, nothing about the situation panicked or frustrated Cora. Why should it? She belonged in Hades.

Jaycie silently cursed her boyfriend and unborn baby's father, Chase Spenser. He'd summoned Cora, his birth mother, from the spirit world to learn her identity. While an excellent idea, it'd backfired. When he sent Cora back to the spirit realm, she'd dragged a pregnant Jaycie through the doorway with her just as Chase slammed it shut. Not only had he closed the door he'd opened to bring Cora through, but he'd also sealed every opening between the worlds.

"Sweetie, I understand more than you know. Do you think I want to be here?"

Jaycie shrugged, continuing to rest her forehead on

her knees to avoid meeting Cora's eyes. They reminded her too much of Chase's, and thinking about him made her ache and deepened her frustration. Surely he was working to get those doors open and help her escape. Anytime her mind wandered in that direction, she shut it down cold. Not that she didn't trust him to rescue her, but she refused to sit idle. What if something had happened to him? No, she needed to depend on herself and no one else.

Oh, goddess, I'm going to die in here.

"You won't die here."

A low growl escaped Jaycie. She'd forgotten spirits could read minds. "I've asked you not to eavesdrop on my thoughts."

"Sorry." Cora said the word absently, putting its sincerity into question.

Jaycie raised her head but continued to avoid meeting the spirit woman's gaze. Instead, she stared out over the dull landscape. "Maybe I'm tackling this all wrong."

In three directions she saw only dry, dark soil interspersed with rocks. No trees or grasses interrupted the bleakness. In the fourth direction flowed the River Styx, a wide lapis-blue river topped with frothy whitecaps. The violent current made a constant waterfall sound, and mist shrouded the distant shores. According to Cora, that way was barred to Jaycie because she was a mortal. So far, they'd walked parallel to the river because it seemed the safest and most sensible route. What if they left the water? Would that take them closer to the physical plane even if it remained invisible?

"We should stay here," Cora said. She'd made that suggestion more than once since they'd arrived.

Jaycie didn't understand. Why not help themselves? Without a logical reason for staying their course, she ignored the advice, but the words prompted her to stand. She started trudging away from the river without checking if Chase's mother followed.

"What are you doing? Where do you think you're going?" The panic in the woman's voice halted Jaycie's progress and spun her around. Cora now stood with her hands clasped, as though beseeching.

"Away from here. What difference does it make to you in which direction we go? We've seen nothing and no one, and you've done nothing to help me."

"We have to stay near the river."

"Why? You told me the way we were walking held terror. You said the opposite direction held horror. I've found only emptiness and this river. What's over that way?" She waved her hand in the direction she'd started walking.

Cora remained silent, watching. She licked her lips, and Jaycie wondered how a spirit could have dry lips.

"What's over there? If you don't tell me, I'll find out when I get there."

"It's away from home."

"You mean your home. Hades."

Cora shrugged. "You're safer near the river. Chase can locate you here."

Jaycie took a few steps closer to Cora. "If he makes it to this side, he knows how to track me." As she said the words, relief at the truth behind them washed over her. Chase's abilities as a mage eclipsed hers, and if he made it to the spirit plane, he'd have come prepared—unlike Jaycie, who'd been yanked here unexpectedly.

"Follow or don't; I'm going that way." She waved again in the direction she intended to take and resumed walking.

***

Chase stood on the periphery of Hades in his pajamas, bathrobe, and slippers and heaved a sigh. Not appropriate attire for traversing the underworld, but the trip had been … unexpected. At least his footwear had sturdy soles and soft suede that kept his feet warm, and he wasn't naked under the robe. When Jaycie slept with him, he often went to bed nude. Of course, if she'd been there, he'd have no reason to force his way into the spirit realm, so the point was moot.

He drank in the powerful essence of Jaycie's energy. It'd been so long since he'd felt her, touched her, and now he sensed her energy in the spirit plane. The moment the door he'd cracked between the worlds closed behind him, he focused all his efforts on locating her trail. He didn't even care if Risto Fina, master mage and Chase's birth father, followed him from the physical plane. If he did, it would mean access to the spirit realm had opened again, and he needn't fret anymore over helping all trapped beings find their way home; he could concentrate on rescuing Jaycie. Which is what he was doing anyway, but with his conscience hacking away at his emotional equilibrium.

Worry about that later. He pressed his hand to his abdomen, where a slow gnawing threatened to eat its way through his intestines. He could tell himself making Jaycie the priority would help everyone, but his gut begged to differ.

One scan of the dreary landscape and the raging river gave him the incentive he needed to press on after her. The thought of his girlfriend trapped in this depressing place with their unborn child motivated him to follow her trail, the rest of humanity be damned. In due course, he'd get to them. He wasn't forgetting about other people; he was saving his family.

Standing in her energy after days of living without her rejuvenated him and gave him hope. If he helped her, he'd simultaneously help everyone else. A sense of urgency caught up to him then, and he followed her trail, grateful that his mage sensitivities were so acute he tracked her without spellcasting. He strode forward, walking parallel to the raging river he assumed was the River Styx. As he trotted along, he took a moment to appreciate that he'd landed himself in Hades—or at least on the edges of it. None of his fellow students could say the same.

His self-congratulations paused when he detected a large, dark blob in the distance. In the surrounding murk, it appeared as a black mass against the gloomy landscape, the only thing breaking the monotony besides the frothy-white and blue waters of the river. The blob didn't seem human, so he didn't get his hopes up that he'd found Jaycie. Probably just a boulder or scrub brush, but he increased his pace to a jog. He'd seen neither of those things since he'd arrived. Anything not brown-gray dirt would add excitement to the dullness of this place.

When he drew close, the blob took form. It wasn't a rock or bush after all. It was three elderly women hovering over an enormous cauldron. Chase froze. Jaycie's trail led right to the Stygian witches.

CHAPTER 2

Plodding footsteps behind Jaycie signaled that
Cora followed in her wake. The young mage
never turned around and refused to slow the
pace to allow the other woman to catch up. Ever since
their arrival, Cora had triggered nothing but irritation
in Jaycie, and she was determined to figure out why.
After all, whether Cora lived in the spirit world or the
physical plane, she was forever linked to Chase. That
should garner at least some respect.

Chase's mother insisted she'd given him up at birth
to protect him from his father. Yet ever since Chase
had uncovered his birth father's identity as the head of
the Tkaronto Mage Consortium, Master Risto Fina had
been nothing but kind and generous. So far, Jaycie had
found no justification for Cora to have hidden the baby
from Fina. Yes, he was a powerful mage, but isn't that
who you'd want raising your child if the child also had
such powers? And the woman claimed she'd
committed suicide soon after giving away her baby to
take the secret of his whereabouts to the grave.

A grave from which a powerful mage could summon her.

None of what Cora asserted added up. Cap that with the fudged DNA records for Chase's birth mother, and suspicion of her motives increased. Whose identity was she really trying to hide? Chases? Or hers?

Jaycie halted and whirled to face her would-be mother-in-law. Time to do the math.

She waited while the other woman caught up, her long dress and delicate sandals hindering her progress.

"You're not dressed for hiking," Jaycie said for the sake of opening the conversation.

"I never expected to trudge through the outer reaches of Hades."

"You're a spirit. Can't you wear what you want?"

"I am." Cora patted her hair and then smoothed a hand over her gown.

Jaycie glanced back over her shoulder and verified the horizon still held nothing of interest. "Pagans are right. The one God doesn't exist." She hadn't intended to start a religious discussion; the words had just popped out.

Cora laughed. "Think not?"

Jaycie's eyes narrowed. "Think so?"

"I know so." Cora reached Jaycie's side and stared out over the barren lands through which they'd walk. Jaycie followed Cora's gaze with her own.

"Then where is He?" She shook her head. "He's not in Hades. Hades rules Hades. And not alone, either. Multiple gods exist. The pagan gods exist."

"That doesn't mean the One is a myth."

Jaycie shrugged. "Without proof, He is."

Cora took Jaycie's hand. "You have a lot to learn, child."

"Stop talking to me as if you're my guru. Do you believe in God or not?"

Cora grasped Jaycie's arms and stared into her eyes. "Does it matter? The world continues either way."

She pulled free and started walking again, Cora keeping pace this time.

"Yes, because it matters if He exists and lets horrible things happen. He may as well cause them if He can stop them and won't." Before Cora could reply, Jaycie added, "And don't tell me God works in mysterious ways. Not every religion can be right, and we're literally in Hades."

"Yes. *We* are."

When Cora made no further comment, Jaycie let it drop. Arguing would change nothing, and she already regretted raising the subject. Once more, she halted. "This is getting us nowhere."

"As I said."

Jaycie glared but didn't otherwise respond to the jibe. "I'll try a spell again."

Cora sighed. "Honey, magick doesn't work here the way you want."

"I'm not the most talented mage, but I'm competent, and I have to do something." Tears threatened again. "I have to get my baby home." Suddenly bone-weary, Jaycie sank to the ground. "I can't go on like this."

Cora kneeled beside her. "You don't have to. We can return to the river. Chase will find us there."

"Why are you so sure?" At last, she voiced her greatest fear. "What if something happened to him? I'm all my baby has to save her. I can't give up."

"You're not giving up. You're putting faith in the universe that what needs to happen will happen."

Jaycie let out a frustrated snort. "Are you talking about God again?"

Cora put a hand on Jaycie's shoulder. "I'm talking about destiny. Why did you end up here?"

Jaycie gasped, the implications of Cora's words sending shock waves through her. "You think fate brought me here?" She refused to accept that. Cora probably said this to assuage her guilt over dragging Jaycie in here. That had to be it. When Cora was alive, she'd taken charge of her son's fate and hid him from his father.

Yeah, but that didn't work, did it? Fina found him. Aloud, she said, "Fina took action and found Chase. Fina made that happen, not fate."

Cora rose, pulling herself up to her full height and looming over Jaycie. "You want to try magick? Then get up and cast a spell."

Without replying, Jaycie got to her feet, erected a circle, and stood in the center. She closed her eyes, turning inward, gathering strength and energy. She'd learned in school that the best magi, the masters, needed no tools for such work. They needed only energy drawn from the environment and channeled through their own bodies. She tried not to dwell too much on the ones who failed, damaging their bodies and minds in the process.

She only needed to open a door to the physical plane. In her mind's eye, she envisioned an opening, such as the one Chase had created when he'd called his mother through from the spirit world. Strength seeped from the ground below her feet, and she pulled the energy up and through her. She directed it, controlled it. Her breath fell into a focused rhythm, soothing her.

Words formed in her mind, strengthening the image

of the door she visualized. Her mouth opened to speak the spell.

"Stop, girl, before you hurt yourself or your child." The voice didn't belong to Cora.

The power and magick drained out of Jaycie and returned to the ground on an exhale. She opened her eyes to confront the woman who'd spoken.

***

The three women raised their heads simultaneously and stared at Chase—or, rather, appeared to stare at him. Their scarred white eyes saw nothing. The woman in the middle, who held a crystal ball, aimed it in his direction.

"A young one." She licked her lips lasciviously, sending a shudder through Chase.

Had Jaycie met the witches? The trail led right to them, so hopefully, they knew where she'd gone. He'd draw the information out of them—forcefully, if necessary.

They appeared frail and resembled each other closely enough to be triplets. All wore the same white gowns and dark cloaks. He'd imagined the Stygian witches might look more like homeless women, but their luxurious, pristine clothes disabused him of that notion. Still, the woman's suggestive gesture nauseated him and set his guard up.

Might as well get to the point. "I'm searching for someone. Perhaps two someones. Two women."

"I want to see." The witch on the right reached out but missed the crystal ball. Her hands almost hit the cauldron and the boiling black liquid sloshing inside.

Her sister pulled the sphere away. "A moment,

Deino. I'm not done examining our guest. Scrumptious." Her tongue darted out and moistened her lips again, and Chase glanced uneasily at the giant kettle. Perhaps they intended to boil and eat him. With dawning horror, he wondered if they'd harmed Jaycie. Instantly, rage replaced shock. *Then I'll kill them.*

"He wants to hurt us." This came from the third sister. "He thinks we've wronged him."

"Let me see." Deino again. Her skeletal fingers clawed the air, this time closing in on the crystal ball. "Enyo, give me the eye."

Chase stepped closer to the trio but halted at a six-foot distance. The cauldron roiled, and an enormous bubble spurted a gassy stench into the air. It hit his nostrils almost immediately, and he gagged.

Enyo cackled and passed the orb to Deino, who snatched it from her sister's grasp the moment it touched her hands. "Ah, yes, delicious."

Chase gulped but ignored the comment. He had to press on. If they couldn't help him, he needed to keep moving. "Did two women pass through here?"

The third sister, who, by a process of elimination Chase assumed was Pemphredo, replied. "A young one and the queen passed through here, but we saw them not." She bared her lips in a gummy grin that reminded Chase they shared a tooth as well as an eye. He pondered the logistics but only briefly. The desire to catch up to Jaycie remained constant and urgent.

"If they passed through here, at least one of you must've seen them." He ignored the reference to a queen. Perhaps the woman had mistaken Cora for someone else. What mattered was the two women were still together and had passed through here safely.

All three cackled, and Pemphredo spoke again, but

her words continued to be unhelpful. "My turn. Give it. Oh, he does sound yummy."

Chase persisted, forcing kindness into his tone when irritation would've suited him better. "Thank you for your help. Please tell me where they went. Did they seem okay?"

"Afraid, the young one was. The goddess wants her. And the god." This came from Deino, whose blank eyes stared directly at Chase now that she held the crystal ball. "Both goddesses. Don't know why," she added, anticipating one of the many questions forming in his mind.

"Which goddesses? What god?"

"Give us something," Pemphredo said. "We're giving everything. You're providing nothing."

"I have nothing to give." A trickle of sweat dampened his back. What could he have that they'd want? Various gross possibilities occurred to him, and he shuddered.

All three cackled again, and Deino said, "Ah, we'd enjoy what you're thinking, but tasks be our coin."

Relieved, Chase said, "Like what?"

The witches shifted and swayed. One of them, Chase didn't see who, tossed something into the cauldron, raising a splash and another sulfuric stench.

Enyo said, "Don't lie. We know when you lie."

"I'm not lying. What do you want from me?"

"Yet. You're not lying yet," Pemphredo replied. She raised a knife, the blade white and shaped like a canine tooth. She stabbed with it into the cauldron and laughed with delight when she hit her target and drew a glob of meat from the repulsive stew. "Tender. So tender."

"A taste, sister," Deino said, reaching for the

communal utensil.

Pemphredo presented the knife with its dripping jellied package to Deino. "For the eye, the tooth."

They made the exchange, and while Deino gummed the mystery meat, Pemphredo beamed at Chase. "So succulent." She wasn't referring to the meat she'd just passed to Deino.

Chase shuddered again. "What do you want?"

"Persephone. She walks again. Why? It means trouble for us, doesn't it, sisters?"

The others nodded, muttering under their breaths. All Chase caught was the word "danger."

At the mention of the goddess he believed could help him open the doors between the worlds again, Chase's excitement rose. "Did you see her?"

"Before. Not now." Pemphredo held the crystal ball high above her head, but her eyes continued to gaze sightlessly at Chase. "Feel now. She's moved beyond our range. You follow. You'll find out. She wants the unborn child."

Chase sucked in a breath. "My baby?"

All three cackled again in such delight his insides churned.

Deino howled, then said, "Ah, your baby. Yes. The goddess wants it. They all want it. It'll disrupt the world order, you see."

He gulped. "No, I don't."

They howled and laughed again. Deino lifted the orb high above. "We do, young man. Such a menace, that one. The tide will turn at her command but only from the other side." All three turned their vacant gazes on him, and Pemphredo said, "Get her across before you suffer her loss."

Enyo opened her mouth in a silent scream, her face

scrunched with pain and her eyes squeezed shut. Without looking at him, she said, "That's your payment. Get her across."

Message delivered, the three witches faded from his sight as he called after them, "That's why I'm here."

For reassurance, he stuck his hand in his robe pocket to touch the necklace he'd found near the cabin he shared with Risto Fina in Algonquin Forest. The simple gold chain with tiny gold cross belonged to Kelsey Davis, his former employer who'd been like a mother to him before she disappeared one chaotic night months ago.

The trinket was gone.

CHAPTER 3

The newcomer dressed similarly to Cora. She wore a white goddess gown, and a pair of gold strappy sandals adorned her feet. However, where Cora's tresses were unornamented, a thick, gold tiara with an upward-pointing crescent moon nestled in this woman's midnight-black hair.

Jaycie recognized her instantly. "Hecate," she said in a reverent whisper.

Beside the goddess stood a large, skinny black dog and a polecat, and a snake coiled around her neck. In one hand, she held a torch; in the other, a sword. The moment Jaycie named her, the animals and the tools the woman carried vanished.

"I sense your loyalty, child. How may I help?" Without giving Jaycie a chance to respond, Hecate turned to Cora. "Back again so soon?"

Cora waved her hands and made a hushing noise. "I belong here. In spirit."

Hecate raised her brows, but she made no comment and returned her attention to Jaycie. "You're with child, my dear. Come. I'll see you're protected. This is no place for you."

Hope swelled in Jaycie. The goddess could help her return home.

"Can you open the doorway?"

Hecate placed a hand gently on Jaycie's arm. "No. Come along, and I'll care for you."

As the hope drained from her, Jaycie shook her head. "I have to get home. Please. Can't you help me?"

"I can take you somewhere safe."

Jaycie whirled on Cora. "Tell her what happened. I need to go home." All her desire, all her will, bent toward that one goal. If Chase didn't get the doors open again, someone else had to. Surely, a goddess could do it—if she wanted to.

Cora's expression softened into kindness, and she met Jaycie's gaze head-on. "Listen to Hecate. She knows best. We'll follow her, and everything will be okay."

"What about my baby? I have to get her home where she belongs."

Cora and Hecate exchanged glances, giving Jaycie the impression both knew something she didn't.

"What? Is something wrong with my baby?"

Cora took Jaycie's arm. "No, but you shouldn't stay out here any longer. Let Hecate take you to her home. It's a safe place." Her tone was wheedling, insistent.

"Not until I try my spell." At the very least, she needed to try to magick her way home.

Hecate broke in. "You shouldn't."

"Why? I'm quite capable of casting a spell, and I'm already standing in a protective circle."

"Yes, that's how I found you. I'm not the only one attentive to your presence. Come with me." She grew more emphatic with every word. "Time grows short. We must hurry. Someone's coming, and you shouldn't see him. He's a danger to you and the baby."

Jaycie gasped. Who knew where she was? Except Chase and Risto Fina—but neither posed a threat to her or the baby. "Who?"

"A god—and he wants your child. Come with me before it's too late. Give me permission. Allow me to take you to my home. Now."

Fear overtaking reason, Jaycie replied with a shaky breath. "Yes. I'll go."

As Hecate waved her hand and their surroundings faded from view, Jaycie remembered she'd forgotten to remove her circle.

***

An energy circle alerted Chase to the spot where Jaycie's trek had ended. He hit it head-on, as if he'd walked into an electrically charged wall of paste. At first, he didn't break into it. Instead, he paced along the circumference, trying to gauge where she'd exited. What worried him was that Jaycie wouldn't have left up a circle of protection she'd created. If she'd cast one and it still stood, something must've happened to her. Abandoning the energy she'd raised and leaving it to drop on its own was risky and foolish. What had made her do it? When he couldn't pick up her trail anywhere, his anxiety increased. Whatever had happened had snatched her from within the circle.

He forced his way through the thick energy wall and into the center of the circle. Preferably, the mage who erected a circle also took it down, but it was acceptable for another mage to execute the task. That mage would've taken part in the ritual, though, and Chase hadn't assisted with Jaycie's cast. Even so, he did her the favor and prepared to remove it so it wouldn't crash and release random energies into the environment. Doing so also allowed him to consider what he should do next. It didn't take him long to understand Jaycie's trail ended here.

When the circle dropped, Chase assessed the situation. *Few places to go in Hades. You're either in Hades or on the edges of it.* Right now, he stood on the welcome mat. To test his growing suspicions, he relaxed his stance, his knees slightly bent, and closed his eyes. He focused his senses on locating Jaycie, and his body swayed in the River Styx's direction.

No choice now. He'd have to cross the river and visit Hades, a place forbidden to mortals. He only hoped it wasn't too late to get her out.

***

The moment Chase stepped across the veil and slammed the doorway between the worlds in Risto Fina's face, the master mage gave up hope of following his son. He scanned the area to make sure no one else had entered the clearing while he'd been preoccupied, but he saw nothing amiss. As he turned to retrace his steps to the cabin and strategize his next move, moonlight glinting off something on the ground caught his eye. He bent down and scooped it up: a necklace with a gold cross on the end. While its value didn't interest him, the fact Chase must've dropped it did. Fina pocketed the trinket and went home.

CHAPTER 4

Kelsey Davis stood in front of the liquor cabinet and pondered her options. The tequila tempted her, but the extensive booze selection made the choice difficult. Perhaps this was more of a vodka night. She glanced in the kitchen's direction, where the vodka resided in the freezer. Rather than head for it, she faced the bar again. Philip bought good quality booze. Whatever she chose would taste great, but she wasn't as concerned about flavor or bouquet as much as she was about alcohol content.

Three weeks had passed since she'd last wanted to kill Philip Belanger, the vampire who made her life miserable. The homicidal thoughts hadn't eased; rather, more practical ones had replaced them. Killing him would endanger herself and Josh, her son. Philip understood the intricacies of hiding from the authorities and the mob. He'd also know how to handle it if someone discovered their hidey hole in this cabin on the shores of Anstruther Lake in the Kawartha Highlands in Skanadario.

She removed a bottle of tequila from the shelf and a shot glass and plate from the kitchen cupboard. Philip and Josh, as usual at this time of the evening, were out hunting, which left her alone again. Although she hadn't had a drop of alcohol for about the same period of time she hadn't plotted to kill the vampire, she'd developed a sudden craving for tequila shots and butter tarts. She set the bottle and shot glass on the table and retrieved the bakery box of the pastries from the counter. After parking her ass in a chair, she set two pastries on the plate and splashed tequila into the ounce-and-a-half-size glass.

For honesty's sake—and, under the circumstances, honesty was the only option—she admitted the alcohol craving stemmed from a combination of triggers. The first one was the news that Chase Spenser, her former employee at the bookstore café, had vanished. All media outlets covered the disappearance. The mage consortium's head, Risto Fina, assured the public that Chase worked on restoring the balance between the spirit world and the physical plane.

The news triggered déjà vu in Kelsey, and she found Fina's claims difficult to believe. For the first time in her life, she experienced an intuitive tug and hated it. Anything smacking of psychic ability meant the devil's work. If she'd cultivated a sixth sense, she blamed Philip. She held him accountable for everything from dragging her into the search for his daughter to Josh becoming a vampire and everything that followed.

You volunteered to help find Dakota because Josh was missing too, and you permitted him to turn Josh. She flinched at the reminder of the part she'd played. If the truth was supposed to set her free, she still waited for the cage door to open.

Yeah. That's why I need alcohol. She raised the shot glass.

"Cheers." Kelsey tossed back the drink, thunked the glass down on the table, and poured another one. She bit into a butter tart, and it flooded her mouth, overlaying the tequila's salty tang.

Yes, she'd given her permission to make Josh a vampire. Now she had to live with it.

"I didn't know how he'd turn out," she said to the empty kitchen.

Which brought her to trigger number two. Before the pair left to go hunting, she'd tried to hug Josh, and he'd bared his fangs at her. He hadn't bitten her, but that didn't console her. He'd shoved her hard enough to land her on her tailbone, which still smarted hours later.

"Cheers." She downed the second shot. Thunked the glass on the table. Poured another. She scarfed the rest of the butter tart, her teeth grinding into the sweet, gooey pastry.

The third and final trigger? She needed physical contact—craved it like she craved the booze and pastries—and the only option was a vampire she wanted to murder. What made things even worse was that he attracted her physically. If he repulsed her, she could tolerate the situation better. Perhaps this extended isolation with Philip, the only adult male in her life, caused her to ogle him as if he were as tasty a treat as the butter tarts.

"No. Objectively, he's hot." She raised the glass. "Cheers."

She tossed the shot down her throat, slammed the glass onto the table, and bit into another tart. She moaned her appreciation. If she couldn't satisfy the need for touch—and hugs and kisses would do, damn it, she didn't have to get laid—then she'd fill her insides with sugar and alcohol. The two were kind of the same thing, but they filled the void consuming her.

It's eat or be eaten around here. She found that hilarious and laughed long and heartily until it sounded hysterical even to her ears. She remembered little else after that until ...

***

... Kelsey lifted her head up from where it rested on the toilet seat in the en suite bathroom she had all to herself. Awareness of the present moment returned only after she'd prayed to the porcelain god, yacking up everything she'd consumed throughout the night.

Bitterness filled more than her taste buds. No one had stopped her descent into oblivion—not Philip and not Josh. She'd promised herself before they'd fled the Algonquin cabin that she wouldn't do this again, but it sure didn't take long for her to break that vow. Was she an alcoholic? She'd never suffered from a drinking problem before living with the vampire. As always, Philip took the blame for her ills. He was convenient, and he wasn't her. She refused to blame herself.

Tell the truth. Honesty, remember? How she hated owning up to what should rest on her shoulders and not Philip's. *Yes, but how much longer can you avoid it?* She was stubborn and determined—the charade could continue indefinitely. A gnawing in her gut signaled her conscience kicking in, and it churned up enough bile that she ducked toward the bowl and retched.

When the round ended, she flushed and then rested her forehead on the toilet seat to wait for her stomach to calm. When the nausea settled, she eased up from the floor and sidled to the sink. Her reflection in the vanity's mirror stared out, eyes shaded and baggy and damp with tears, skin as pale as a vampire's. Drool clung to her chin and snot dripped from her nose, so Kelsey turned on the taps. Without waiting for a reasonable water temperature, she splashed cold wetness onto her face.

A wave of vertigo had her white-knuckling the sink. When it passed, she painstakingly went through the motions of brushing her teeth. The shower beckoned, but first she needed coffee and perhaps a piece of dry toast. If that soothed her stomach, she'd risk the tub.

She opened the bathroom door and rested a breath against the jamb. What time was it? Had morning arrived? Daylight showed behind the closed curtains in the living room, but the light was weak, grayish. Either the sun hadn't cleared the horizon yet, or the day was another crappy, snowy one. She detected no food cooking, but the aroma of fresh coffee made her knees tremble with desire.

The floor creaked. Philip appeared in the hallway from the bedroom he shared with Josh and blocked her view of the living room.

"Rough night, darling?"

She gritted her teeth, suppressing a snarl. Nothing grated on her nerves more than when he called her that, but she'd given up asking him to stop. She refused to meet his gaze or answer his question. He knew exactly how rough her night had been. She could do without the sarcasm.

"I made coffee. Figured you'd need it."

She appreciated that but didn't tell him. "Where's Josh?"

He exhaled a slow breath, and just as she thought he'd play her game and not reply, he said, "Out."

Her heart seized. "Alone?"

"Not far. He's quite capable of going out by himself."

Kelsey shook her head but instantly regretted it. She lurched into the bathroom, sank down before the toilet, and let 'er rip. When finished, she flushed before the view triggered another round of retching and then washed her face again. When she returned to the hallway, she found Philip waiting for her.

"What if he kills someone?"

"He won't."

Philip's response didn't ease her worry one wit. "Is he hunting?"

"Doubtful. That's how we spent most of the night. If he is, though, he'd limit his prey to animals. Josh knows to avoid anything else."

Tears of frustration streamed down her face. "Why would you allow that? He can't be alone. Why aren't you watching over him?"

Without thinking, she stared into his eyes. The sorrow she found there brought more hitched sobs. She sank to the floor, unable to control her hysteria. Her chest ached, her head throbbed, and if she had access to a gun, she'd turn it on herself.

With a strangled growl, Philip dropped to his knees beside her.

Kelsey fought him as his arms engulfed her, but he was too strong for her. Anyone would've easily overpowered her right now, but his vampire strength guaranteed she couldn't push him away. She struggled to break his hold until exhaustion dropped her against his chest in defeat.

CHAPTER 5

Frustration warred with compassion in Philip. Added to that was fear. The desire to kill herself that he sensed in Kelsey terrified him. He understood it and didn't worry when she thought about killing him. He could handle her and trusted she wasn't capable of carrying out the threat. However, suicidal thoughts were different. The risk of her acting on those was much higher. How long must he stand by and watch this descent into despair and self-harm? Every time she succumbed to the craving to numb her life with alcohol, he died a little inside. Ignoring the irony in that, he waited out first her futile attempts to escape his embrace and then the heart-wrenching sobs that followed her surrender.

What the hell am I supposed to do? He had no one to ask but himself and no answers to give. The previous night, he'd tried to talk to Josh about his mother, and the conversation had gone badly. The boy didn't give a harpy's ass about her. He'd ceased thinking of her as an entrée, which meant progress in his development from baby vampire to something more mature, but he hadn't reached the point where he cared if she lived or died. Josh's solution was to kick her out of the house since Philip insisted they couldn't eat her.

Kelsey relaxed into him, and her sobbing ceased, so he sat with her, savoring the rise and fall of her abdomen as she breathed against him. Hair covered her face, and he swept it aside to study her expression. Her eyes were closed, but she was awake and aware. The emotion radiating from her had turned from suicidal despair to something approaching peace. He rocked her gently, and her head rested on his shoulder. He dipped his head toward hers and almost kissed her forehead but caught himself in time. Afraid to shatter the calm in this moment, he remained silent and refrained from any more gestures of comfort.

The gray light spilling in through the hall window into the corridor slowly brightened and turned golden as the sun rose and the clouds dispersed. Nothing disturbed their peace, but after a while, he knew they couldn't sit like this much longer. Josh would return, and while Philip didn't care if the boy caught them in this position, his arrival would change the dynamic. Kelsey might not want the boy to see her like this, or the sight of him might upset her.

Philip leaned closer to her ear and whispered, "Shall we move to somewhere more comfortable?"

She sighed and opened her eyes. "I can't take this anymore."

He didn't ask for an explanation, and she offered none. His grip tightened on her, and he helped her rise to standing. He lifted her and, cradling her in his arms, carried her to the living room couch. He set her down against the pillow and draped a nearby blanket over her.

"Rest. I'll get your coffee." He started to walk away, but she grabbed his hand.

"Don't leave me."

His eyes widened, but that was the only indication he gave that she'd surprised him. He nudged her deeper into the cushions to make room and sat. For once, she didn't reject him, so he didn't have to retaliate by waving off her troubles with a quip to spare his wounded ego. Something inside him clicked with the revelation of this change in their pattern. *Does she see it? Does she really want me to stay with her?*

He took a chance she'd welcome his attempts to help her and said, "What happened last night?"

She closed her eyes and inhaled a long breath. When she released it, she spoke again, keeping her eyes shut tight. "A few things. Josh ..." Her eyelids fluttered open, and she gave him an agonized look.

"... pushed you away."

She nodded, and her misery tore at him.

He almost told her not to take it personally but stopped himself before the words made their way from brain to mouth. Instead, he said, "He shouldn't have done that. Did he hurt you?"

"I landed on my tailbone."

"Are you still in pain?" He tucked the blanket up around her neck to keep his hands busy.

"No."

"Good, but what I meant was, did your feelings get hurt so much you needed to drown them with tequila?"

She groaned and struggled with the blanket to free her hands and bury her face in them. "Yes, that. Not just that."

"Okay. What else?"

She raised her head; a touch of her typical anger clouded her countenance. Bitterness welled up in her so strongly he almost gagged.

"Shh. Tell me. I'm listening now, all right? I promise." He didn't know why he added that last, but it worked because her frown disappeared and her breathing slowed.

"I don't have anyone to ..." Her breath hitched.

He waited, stroking her hair with one hand. She tilted her head so his palm cupped her cheek.

"I have no one to talk to. To ... touch."

Waves of emotional pain poured out of her, overwhelming him. This time, though, he refused to turn away from it. She was here because she'd helped him. He needed to own that instead of burying it. He also had to admit he, too, craved physical contact, and he desired it most of all with Kelsey.

Damn humans. Years ago, he'd vowed to avoid them, yet the more he tried to keep them out of his life, the more entangled in it they became. He'd never wanted to live with one, but he'd obligated himself to Kelsey the moment he allowed her to help search for his daughter.

Dakota. The thought of her broke his heart, so he pushed her out of his head—easier to do than pushing this human out of his life. The more time he spent with Kelsey Davis, the more he wanted her. She exasperated him, no getting around that, but she also attracted him as no other woman had. Even under such horrible circumstances. Even when she'd flung herself into a downward spiral guaranteed to end in disaster. The worst part was his powerlessness over whatever she did. If she self-destructed, he could do nothing to prevent it.

No, but I can make it difficult for her. He stared at the crazy woman he'd shacked up with. She'd fallen asleep, her chest rising and falling in soft, peaceful breaths. He left her on the couch and strode to the liquor cabinet. Step one: no more enabling the drinking. He should've done this long ago, but he'd assumed she'd control it without any intervention. The previous night demonstrated how misguided that hope was.

One by one, he removed every bottle from the bar and poured the booze down the sink. By the time he finished, the stench of alcohol overwhelmed him. He glanced at Kelsey, surprised the overpowering scent hadn't woken her, but she slept on, oblivious. As the last drop disappeared down the drain, Philip's tortured conscience eased, and he sighed with relief.

The front door banged open.

Josh and a blast of cold air breezed inside. The young man stood pale and rangy, his sandy hair plastered in wet strips to the sides of his face. His jeans and long-sleeved T-shirt also dripped water. He wore a baseball cap, and a bandanna covered his nose and mouth to shut out the sun.

Great. He jumped into the lake again. If Kelsey ever found out her son habitually broke through the ice and swam in the water, she'd blame that on Philip as well. Then she might not let him live to shelter from another sunrise. Speaking of sunrise, Josh hadn't returned home in time. He'd shielded his face well enough, but his hands glistened with blisters.

"Where are your gloves?" Philip tried to keep his voice low and even to disguise his rage. Though Josh was approaching the point where they ought to be able to discuss things, arguing with a baby vamp solved nothing. Right now, Philip simply wanted to let Kelsey sleep.

The boy shrugged and stared down at his mother. In a loud, uncaring voice, he said, "What the hell happened to her?"

Kelsey cried out and opened her eyes.

Philip glared at the boy. "Nice going. You've awakened the beast."

***

Josh strode past his mother without sparing her any more attention. Obviously, she'd spent another night drinking and throwing up. It mattered little to him how she allocated her time—unless she interfered with how he spent his time.

Her shout shattered the quiet.

"Oh, God! He's soaked. What were you doing? Are you okay?"

He snarled but continued walking toward his room. The cold and the water didn't bother him, but he preferred to change into dry clothes anyway. His mind always raced without settling on thoughts of his mother—or not often. Sometimes, something half remembered glimmered inside him, and an uneasiness disrupted his composure. He hated when that happened, and it was happening now.

Kelsey rushed him and gripped his arm; it took all his hard-won self-control, over months of struggle, not to smack her across the room. But Philip—*Father*, he corrected himself, *my maker*—had taught Josh not to wield power in anger. Powerful emotions always simmered beneath Josh's surface, and he'd grown accustomed to living with them. When these heightened urges diminished, he panicked and worked himself into a frenzy of rage, desire, or hunger. Hunger consumed him most often. He lived with a human, which forced him to inhale her savory blood's aroma and hear her beating heart as it pumped food through her body.

Josh whirled on her, his fangs snicking out. His teeth bared, but he kept his hands to himself even though her arteries throbbed with fresh, warm blood. He breathed out a sound like Godzilla blowing fire from his nostrils.

She stepped backward, her face white, her eyes wide as full moons. "Wait ... Stop ..."

Philip swooped in and snatched her up into his arms. In one smooth motion, he set her on the couch again.

"Stay." He pointed at her, and Josh half expected her to protest. *I'm not a dog,* he imagined her saying. It seemed so familiar, so anticipated, that for a moment he thought she *had* said it.

His body vibrated with pent-up frustration, but he remembered his breathing exercises and slowed himself down. While vampires didn't process oxygen the way humans did, they still sucked in air, and they metabolized energy they took in from the environment. Josh's fangs retracted.

The silence stretched and grew unbearable. Kelsey and Philip both stared at Josh. Philip's expression was calm, neutral, as if he waited for the boy to respond. Kelsey wore a stricken look. Josh had hurt her stupid human feelings again. Every time they crossed paths, no matter how briefly, he offended her.

A weird sensation crept over him, and to his amazement, he identified it as ... regret. Since when did causing pain bother him? He remembered the emotion from before his change, but with detachment, as if he watched the past from a distance. Observed but felt nothing from the images that arose. Memories of his mother smiling, hugging him, lovingly preparing food for him, tucking him into bed flashed by, and something in him softened. While he didn't understand her devotion to him, still didn't care if she lived or died, he didn't want to make her cry anymore.

"Mother," he said, because he knew she would like hearing it. "Mom. Is it okay if I call you that?"

Her breath hitched on a sob, and she nodded. Her lips parted, but she remained silent. He sensed a turmoil of emotions from her but couldn't pick them apart. Philip would recognize them, but Josh hadn't learned how to sort them out. Still, he recognized the dominant one: hope.

"I have to change my clothes." He turned his back on his mother and strode from the room.

CHAPTER 6

Disoriented from the flash trip to Hecate's home, Jaycie stumbled when her feet touched ground again. Not that they'd flown to their destination—they'd shifted from one location to the other. Not until after they arrived did it occur to her to worry about how the transition might've affected her baby. She clutched at Hecate, gripping the goddess's arm without considering how disrespectful that was.

"The baby." Jaycie's voice dripped with worry. "Did this harm my baby?"

Hecate needed no explanation, and if she took insult at the physical transgression, she gave no sign. The stern expression she'd worn since they'd met softened. "The baby's fine. I wouldn't do anything to jeopardize the child."

Jaycie exhaled her anxiety and inhaled relief. "Thank you." She didn't know what else to say. Realizing she still gripped Hecate's arm, she released it with a small, self-conscious gasp. "I'm sorry." Her face flamed, and acting on impulse, she dropped to her knees and bowed her head.

"Rise, my dear. You need not fear me." Hecate held out her hand, and Jaycie accepted it. The goddess helped the young mage to stand.

Jaycie surveyed their surroundings.

Hecate had landed them inside a richly furnished living area. The enormous room boasted plush couches and chairs, ornate tables, fancy floor lamps and crystal chandeliers, and finely woven carpeting in rich reds and blues. Paintings decorated the walls, most of them portraits of Hecate, but others were likenesses of what Jaycie assumed were the goddess's fellow deities. A familiar face on one canvas drew her in for a closer look. The model held a pomegranate, her long, brown hair cascading in ringlets over her shoulders. She wore the same gown in the picture that she had on now. Jaycie whirled around to confront Cora.

"Oh, gods." She paled. "You're Persephone."

***

"I request passage across the river." Chase faced Charon, Styx's ferryman, who stood in the middle of a narrow skiff the color of rust. An ankle-length brown robe covered his body; one gnarled hand clasped a pole for guiding the craft while the other held a lantern. The dim yellow light cast a ghoulish glow on his rugged face and reddish beard, making him look jaundiced.

"You're not dead." Charon's voice was a cross between a growl and a moan of despair. It echoed across the river, which had stilled the moment the boat reached the banks where Chase stood. In the water's glassy stillness, he glimpsed faces beneath the surface. Every so often, a hand broke through the water, futilely clutching at the air before once again sinking into the depths, leaving barely a ripple.

Unnerved, he gulped. He attempted to recall who the people were but couldn't. Hopefully, they weren't mortals who'd tried and failed to get passage on Charon's skiff.

"You have no business in Hades." The ferryman said it as though this explained everything and ended the discussion.

"That's where you're wrong," Chase replied. "If that's your criteria for refusing to take me across, then you'll have to let me board. My girlfriend is trapped there."

"Spirits are trapped there." Charon's tone remained reasonable.

"She's not a spirit. She's a mortal."

Charon fell silent, and Chase held his tongue, giving the ferryman time to reason it out.

"You have no coin."

So the objection had changed. Perhaps he'd moved closer to getting across. As if to reinforce his position, Chase took a step toward the skiff. "I need no payment. Only the dead cross forever."

Charon gave a low chuckle, but it was devoid of amusement. "I don't work for free."

But you have in the past. Chase doubted he had the skills to charm the deity—he was a disgraced mage, not a dashing hero—but for Jaycie's sake, he had to try. He strove to recall the previous arguments used. Doing God's work, Virgil had said, and Charon had carried the guide and his follower, Dante, across the river. "I have business with Persephone."

"Have you?" This time, the tone was mocking.

"Yes. The doorway between the worlds is shut."

With what Chase thought was a brilliant stroke of inspiration, he continued, "I closed them. I need her help to force them open. If I don't, nobody will come to you again. You'll be out of a job."

Charon drew himself up to an imposing height. Holding the lantern aloft, he studied the young mage. As Chase tried to think of another argument, the ferryman said, "Climb aboard and sit down. If you fall in during the crossing, I won't pull you out."

***

Unable to articulate what she wanted to ask first, Jaycie gaped at Cora. Chase's mother. If all went as Jaycie hoped, this woman—goddess—would become her mother-in-law. Granted, she'd become Jaycie's deceased mother-in-law, but goddesses traveled between the spirit world and the physical plane as they pleased. She had a sudden vision of future family gatherings and balked.

What do you buy a goddess for Christmas? Immediately, she corrected herself. *Yule. Goddesses don't celebrate Christmas.*

Cora saved her the trouble of speaking. "I didn't want to unsettle you."

"How's that working out?" Jaycie blanched and sucked in a horrified breath. She'd just snapped at a goddess. *Yes, one who lied to her son, to me.*

Had she lied to Risto Fina as well? Was he aware of her true identity? She recalled his words right before the doors between the worlds slammed shut: *Imagine what we could achieve as a family. The power we could hold. The control we could have.* Had he intended that to include Cora? Perhaps that's why he'd impregnated her. But had he done it against her will? Hades had once kidnapped Persephone. Had Risto Fina done the same?

Cora chuckled, bringing Jaycie back to the moment. "Relax. We're almost family."

"Does Risto Fina know?"

When Cora didn't reply, Jaycie suspected she had her answer. "He's unaware you're Persephone?" She extrapolated from that. "You trapped him, not the other way around."

The goddess shrugged. "What if I did? He played with fire."

"What do you mean?"

"He desired to sire a powerful mage. I simply granted his wish."

"And then hid your son from him."

Cora shook her head. "My dear, you know nothing of gods and their whims. I wanted the child, but I didn't want him exposed to, shall we say, jealous acts of revenge."

Jaycie suddenly understood. "You weren't hiding him from Fina. You were hiding him from Hades."

"Yes. And I'm not pleased the boy found me. For his sake."

With dawning horror, Jaycie said, "But Chase will search for me. He might already be here."

"That," Cora replied, "would be unfortunate."

CHAPTER 7

Midnight in early November often brought bone-chilling cold, and this night was no exception. Snow fell in giant flakes, hitting Risto Fina's head, shoulders, and back as he cast a circle in the clearing outside the cabin he shared with Chase. Rather, the cabin he'd share with Chase if the young fool hadn't punched open a door to the spirit world and vanished through it. That he'd also shut it in Fina's face rankled the master mage, but rage warred with pride. His boy had done that. Chase would make a powerful mage after Fina finished with him. The problem was Chase no longer trusted his father and had put himself beyond the master's reach.

But one thing at a time.

Currently, all Fina's energies focused on raising Persephone, goddess of spirits and the springtime, from her winter home in Hades. The original plan was to have Chase summon her. It would've given the boy a tremendous boost in his abilities, but that all went to Hades when Chase behaved so immaturely. What had set him off? Fina couldn't fathom how anything here could've tipped his son to secrets best left buried for a while longer. Not forever, of course. Once the boy proved his loyalty, Risto Fina planned to tell him everything. Almost everything. No need for Chase to know Fina had orchestrated Jaycie's pregnancy. The young woman was as powerful a mage as Chase. That she didn't realize it, that her self-confidence was so far down the crapper that she believed herself untalented, only played into Fina's schemes. He'd set both kids up as his puppets and rule this continent from behind the scenes as a benevolent dictator. Risto Fina didn't want or need fame or money. He wanted power.

He'd cast the circle using a sword. In the center stood his altar, which held everything he needed to execute his spell, including a bronze figure of Persephone. Fina hadn't included a god, not because he wanted the imbalance, but to isolate the goddess to help draw her into the circle. He hoped. Before bringing her forth, he needed to create a door and then punch a hole through it. He'd also have to count on the goddess's desire to come through. Chase had shut tight access between the physical plane and the spiritual plane, but if a goddess wanted egress, she'd get it.

In the book stand before the altar rested Fina's Book of Shadows, or BOS, Chase's research notes tucked inside it. The boy had done well. He'd not only recorded the most relevant data from the flood of information available on the Internet, but he'd also roughed out a decent spell for raising the goddess. If his impatience to recover Jaycie hadn't affected his judgment, he'd have likely succeeded in drawing Persephone out of Hades.

Even though Fina hadn't done the research himself

and didn't personally write the steps to execute the spell, he could still cast it and expect it to work. He tweaked only the incantation. Magick always needed a piece of the mage, and the spell's verse provided the best opportunity to accomplish that.

With the circle cast complete, Fina cleared the space, did the purifications, and called in the elements. Next, he did a quick wine blessing, libating a splash of wine from the chalice into a goblet in honor of Persephone. He then toasted her and took a healthy swig of the drink for himself. Now to create the door, breach it, and summon the goddess.

He closed his eyes and allowed his senses to open. Somewhere, an owl hooted. Mastic from the incense burner wafted up to his nose, and he inhaled the spicy scent with gratitude. It eased any residual tension from his body, and his shoulders relaxed. A breeze rustled the trees, creaking leafless branches and sighing through the evergreens. It stirred his robes and energized him. He opened his eyes and stared out into the darkness, past the soft glow of the candles he'd lit, which stayed that way only with a boost of magick. The breeze wasn't strong enough to constitute a wind, not quite, but it was capable of blowing out altar candles.

To his left stood the cabin, and he viewed it in his periphery. The candlelight and moonlight and starlight made the shadows they cast onto the building behind the covered front porch dance.

Something small scurried through the underbrush outside the clearing, and Fina sensed rather than saw the owl dive and capture it in deadly sharp talons. Fina tossed his head back and roared a challenge to the universe, forcing a door to form from a void he controlled with his powers. The words he spoke rhymed; the energy crackled. He raised a hand that held a wand now instead of his sword, which stood speared into the ground beside him.

Fina always knew a spell had succeeded even before his senses confirmed it, and this time was no exception. His intuition picked up the door forming in front of him before he saw it, before he heard the pop and groan of its formation, before the odor of ozone cleared his nostrils or stung his taste buds. Before the ground vibrated under his feet. All these things happened seconds after he anticipated them, and triumph surged through him. He held his hand, palm out, toward the door and blasted energy at it. Once more, intuition heralded the success ahead of his five senses, and he wished Chase were there to witness such strength and power.

For the next step, he had to refer to his script to refresh his memory. He returned the sheet of paper containing the incantation to the BOS and enunciated each word without hesitation.

"Goddess of the spring, I call upon you now.

"Come to me and slake my need.

"To work in your service, in this I vow.

"Let my voice raise your desire to heed.

"Let no barrier prevent your arrival.

"The way is open, the stage set.

"Your children need you for their survival.

"For your help, I'm in your debt.

"I call to you, beseech you, and beg you to hear.

"Come forth from Hades; let your spirit appear."

He waited, breath held. The tingle that heralded the success of a spell remained dormant. The forest sounds had stilled. Nothing stirred inside or outside the circle. A few flakes of snow spiraled down from the heavens but melted when they touched the ground within the space he'd cast. Time dragged on, though only seconds passed. He felt it with his senses first, and his brain adjusted, explaining away the inconsistency.

The goddess interfered with my intuition. That's all it is.

A white light shone through the hole he'd punched in the door. Fina squeezed his eyes shut against the brilliance. His intuition finally caught up, and his body quivered with anticipation. The door groaned and shuddered, and the scent of roses overwhelmed the air. A flavor of pomegranate made his mouth water, and he swiped his lips with the back of his free hand. He sucked in a breath, and in that moment, the brilliant light vanished, and he opened his eyes.

Initially, he saw only the figure's silhouette. As her features clarified, he recognized her, both as the goddess Persephone and as the woman he'd known.

The shock rendered him momentarily speechless. When he found his voice, he said, "Dear gods. Cora."

He sank to one knee and bent his head to demonstrate his subjugation, his reverence.

"Risto," she said. "Thank you."

He turned his face up to meet her gaze. "I didn't know."

She nodded. "We need to talk."

CHAPTER 8

The goddess he'd slept with and created a child with held out her hand. Fina gripped it, and Cora—Persephone—helped him rise. When she released his hand, he almost clutched after her. Her beauty overpowered him at that moment, as always, but now he understood why. Should he feel angry or proud she'd tricked him? Both, probably, but one didn't chastise a goddess; one simply allowed her to do as she would. He'd still benefit from the relationship despite this—he just needed to tread cautiously. After all, her husband was the god of the underworld. Even if Persephone meant no harm, a relationship with her risked arousing jealous rage in Hades.

"Welcome back."

"A much nicer welcome than the one you gave me when our son summoned me forth."

He winced. "Of necessity. I wanted to hide the truth from the boy."

"You were crueler than you needed to be. Is that how you treat your women?"

He shook his head. "I have no women. Just you. Need I remind you I wasn't the only one spewing invectives that night?"

She smiled, and the way her eyes sparkled in the candlelight told him it was genuine. "We had him fooled. A question, if I may."

Now it was his turn to grin. "Of course, my lady."

She clasped his hands. "Chase called to me—to Persephone. The shut doors prevented me from responding."

He waited for her to continue since she hadn't asked a question yet.

She licked her lips, and his penis responded. He tried to think of anything but ravishing her on the ground right in front of the altar.

Old habits die hard. Yes, his habit was hard all right. Did she still desire him? It would be a bonus.

"Why couldn't I get through? Not one door provided access. All were invisible." She sounded like a petulant child, and his erection vanished.

"Chase slammed them shut. He meant only to close the door he'd summoned you through, but the boy doesn't comprehend how powerful he is." He heard the pride in his voice, but he didn't care. She was the boy's mother. She should share that pride.

"Yes, that makes sense." She frowned, but with concentration rather than displeasure. "Jaycie's still there."

"The banks of the river?"

She shook her head, and a tingle of prescience gave him the answer even as she told him. "She's with Hecate."

"How is she—and the growing babe?" Now it was his turn to frown, but with worry. Nothing good would come of Jaycie in Hades with an underworld queen.

"Fine. Hecate won't allow harm to come to either one."

"Do they know you're the grandmother?" Here, he asked two questions in one: Was Hecate aware Persephone was Jaycie's child's grandmother, and did Jaycie realize Cora was Persephone?

Cora answered both questions. "They both know."

She'd always understood him better than any other woman. If she hadn't vanished with his child as soon as she'd conceived, he'd have happily made a life with her. Now that he knew why she'd disappeared, he no longer craved revenge, and the bitterness eased. Still, if she'd told him the truth, he could've raised the child himself. The idea almost made him laugh out loud. No, she'd done the right thing.

The circle had grown warm from Persephone's presence. Fina was tempted to take it down and invite her inside the cabin for a proper reunion, but her response steered him in a different direction. They'd have to put a pause on their personal relationship and deal with their child's issues first. *Damn the boy.* He'd bunged this up but good.

"You'll have to return then. Jaycie can't stay there."

"Hecate wants her to."

Fina raised his brows, and astonishment laced his voice when he said, "What about what you want? What Jaycie wants? Chase has entered the spirit realm to find her. You must return, if for no other reason than to escort him home."

Her eyes grew wide, and she placed a hand on his arm. "Jaycie expected that. I came the instant you summoned me to verify he hadn't made the crossing."

Alarmed at her reaction, he asked, "Why? What's

the problem?"

"I don't want Hades to learn he exists."

With a sinking sensation in the pit of his stomach, Fina gazed past her at the door. The hole he'd punched in it had allowed the goddess through. She could phase in and out of physicality, but he couldn't. "Go get him."

She stared at him, her expression stony. "You're giving me orders now?"

He remembered his place. Yes, they'd been intimate once—over two decades ago—but she was still a goddess, and he'd better remember that. She might have a milder temperament than most, but she took offense just as easily.

"Not at all. I'm worried about Chase—as you are. He opened a door, dove inside, and slammed it in my face. You can get through and save him."

She remained silent for a moment then said, "I expect he won't leave without the girl. I have a better idea."

When she explained it to him, he agreed the plan was a good one. Before they parted, they sealed the deal with a kiss. After Fina told her he'd wait for her at his mansion in the city, Cora faded into a mist. She drifted through the hole in the door and vanished.

***

Risto Fina performed the motions required to seal the door and drop the circle. The entire process took longer than usual, his mind preoccupied with Chase's safety. Jaycie, in the company of Hecate, was likely protected, though even she'd be at risk if Hades learned of Chase and his child. Gods often took retribution on entire families when they felt betrayed. Trying not to dwell on uncertainties, Fina collected his magick tools and carried them into the cabin.

Once inside, he busied himself with cleaning them and putting everything back into its exact spot. As he puttered about, he turned on the television to the news channel to fill the silence. The not guilty verdict in the Frank Evans trial topped all others. Fina turned up the sound.

A businessman with a reputation for criminal activities, Frank Evans had many important connections. Risto Fina had met with the mob boss multiple times, and they'd helped each other out. They weren't old friends—more like long-term acquaintances and business associates—and Fina had followed Evans's trial with interest. Had the jury returned a guilty verdict, Fina would've done damage control to sever any ties to Evans, but he needn't have worried. The jury declared Evans not guilty.

So far, the cops named no other suspects, which meant the defense didn't get the mob boss off by identifying the real culprit—if another culprit actually existed who hadn't operated under Evans's orders. The man was quite capable of having his own bar torched to collect insurance money, but the execution wouldn't have been so sloppy. No, Fina was certain Evans, for once, was innocent of the crime of which they'd accused him.

He plays the long game, and he's great at it. This gave Fina an idea, and smiling, he finished his tidying up and prepared for a good night's sleep.

CHAPTER 9

"What happened? Where'd she go?" Jaycie spun around in a full circle, scanning the room as though Cora might be hiding somewhere inside it.

Hecate laughed. It sounded merry, which unnerved Jaycie even more.

"Please." She wanted to remain polite and reverential because, well, *goddess*, but she was growing impatient—and frightened. Whatever had yanked Cora from the room, she hadn't left of her own volition.

Hecate corrected the assumption. "She left to attend to an urgent matter." She waved Jaycie to a nearby armchair. "Sit. Relax. I'll order tea and something to eat. You could use it."

Food. The thought brought with it unbearable hunger and then so much fear that her appetite vanished.

"I can't eat here." Then how would she survive? How would her baby survive? But if she ate here, she'd be trapped. Wouldn't she?

Hecate smiled indulgently and shook her head. "Nonsense. You're a mortal who belongs on the physical plane. Nothing you do will trap you here except your death. Then you'd remain here because you'd belong here."

"Hades tricked Persephone into eating the pomegranate seeds, which trapped her here."

"That didn't trap her in the underworld. It tied her to Hades because he offered them to her and she ate them—willingly, by the way.

"Eating such an offering had implications. It was a proposal from Hades, which she accepted, thus binding herself to him. She ate six seeds so she'd only need to remain with him six months out of the year. Clever and calculating is our little Persephone." Hecate's eyes gleamed, and her grin broadened to show perfect teeth. The pride in her voice was unmistakable.

"Now, come." She strode to the couch and halted before a dining cart Jaycie hadn't noticed before. It held a tea service and various covered dishes.

"I don't need food, but you and your baby do. Eat. I'll return in a while to show you to your room."

For a second, Jaycie stayed silent, mostly because she had no idea how to respond to that. In the end, she strolled over to the cart and said, "Thank you." She'd decide what to do about Hecate's offer of a room after she ate.

***

By the time Hecate returned, Jaycie had finished her meal. Her appetite had rebounded, and she'd sampled everything from the cart. When the goddess strode into the room, Jaycie was sitting on the couch, draining the last drops of a hot and comforting tea from a dainty porcelain cup.

"Come, child. I'll show you to your room. No doubt you want to rest after all you've been through." Hecate smiled kindly at her, and Jaycie's heart skipped a beat at the idea that a goddess mothered her.

She's better at it than my real mother. The thought caused an ache in her chest and a lump to form in her throat. Afraid she'd cry, she avoided Hecate's gaze.

Jaycie rose from her seat and hurriedly set the cup on its saucer atop the cart. When the silence grew uncomfortable, she said, "Thank you so much for your kindness."

"I hear you when you honor me."

Startled into meeting the goddess's eyes, Jaycie felt the heat flush her face. Suddenly shy, she said, "I respect you and wanted you near me."

She spoke the truth. While many turned to the gods and goddesses to ask for favors, and Jaycie had certainly made her share of requests, she often called on Hecate to honor and praise her. Something indefinable had drawn her to the underworld goddess, and she'd declared herself a devotee. To learn Hecate heard her gave her mixed feelings. One of the first things they taught at mage school was that attracting a god's or goddess's attention came with associated risks. Sure, benefits existed, but they always came at a cost. What might Hecate ask in exchange for this hospitality? She spoke as though it came without attached strings, but since when did any god or goddess ever provide favors without asking something in return?

Since no alternative existed to taking shelter here, Jaycie allowed Hecate to lead her down the long hallway to a small room in the back of whatever structure they were in. Rather than a brick-and-mortar house, it gave the appearance of having been carved from hardened lava. The room they'd left and the hallway they walked through shimmered with flecks of black sand Jaycie had only seen in pictures from Hawaii.

The rooms they passed all had closed doors, large wooden structures with enormous handles and giant key locks. She stared at them as if trying to see through them, but of course, she couldn't. No sound leaked out either.

At least they're not torturing people here. She hoped.

Hecate had no reputation for torturing spirits in the underworld. The goddess ruled over the souls of the departed, but what that meant exactly, Jaycie didn't know. This could be her chance to find out, but she wasn't sure she wanted to uncover Hecate's secrets. As a follower of the Greek gods, was Jaycie destined to reside here after her own death? Did all mortals come here after death? Were the Greeks right all along, and the Christians had replaced the old gods with a myth that doomed them?

She'd never taken much interest in theology, had simply followed her family's religious beliefs, and preferred to deal with reality. Now she understood she'd neglected the implications of such beliefs. She'd have to think about how she'd live her life when she returned home. It was one thing to pay lip service to a religion; it was another to abide by its tenets.

They climbed a set of stairs to a second-floor hallway and past more closed doors. The odd goddess statue decorated this corridor, all carved from white marble and displayed on waist-high pedestals. Hecate strode quickly, giving Jaycie no time to discern which goddesses stood watch, but she didn't mind. She'd explore later.

Unless she locks me in my room. She froze for a moment, and Hecate immediately paused and faced her guest. *Prisoner?*

"You can leave, child. I won't keep you here against your will. I should warn you, however, that it would be dangerous for you to walk away from my protection."

"To prevent Hades from learning about my child?"

Hecate sighed. "Let's get you settled in your quarters first." She resumed her brisk pace but only for another few feet. She stopped in front of a door identical to all the others.

Jaycie had forgotten to count the number of doors they'd passed. If she left her room, she risked getting lost.

Hecate turned the knob and pushed the door open. She stood aside and waited.

Jaycie hesitated, but if the goddess had meant to harm or imprison her, she'd have done it already. With her head held high and her posture exuding confidence and trust she didn't quite feel, Jaycie strode forward.

She entered a large, lavishly furnished room, complete with king-size bed. A cheerful fire blazed in the enormous fieldstone fireplace, the focal point of a sitting area. A tea service with pastries was laid out on the ornate teak coffee table in front of the love seat. Jaycie envisioned herself curled up there, reading one of the books from the bookcases that lined the room. A door at the opposite end of the room yawned open, providing a glimpse of a modern-looking en suite bathroom. If she stayed here, she'd be comfortable. The entire room spoke of warmth and luxury, from the thick carpeting under her feet to the puffy quilt covering the bed and the soft, warm blanket draped over the love seat.

"It's very nice." She gazed shyly at Hecate.

"I'm glad you like it." The goddess stepped inside and closed the door. "I'm aware you just ate, but I've made refreshments available in case you'd like tea or a snack.

"Thank you." Again she wondered what price she'd have to pay to stay here, but the thought was only fleeting. Her gaze already wandered again to the bookcases and the treasures they held.

"You're an avid reader. I've provided books to occupy you during your stay."

"Thank you." A frisson of fear welled up at how pointedly the goddess demonstrated her hospitality and thoughtfulness.

At what cost? her brain asked again. Jaycie remained where she stood, and even at the risk of raising a goddess's ire started asking questions. "Who even knows about my child?"

"My dear, the gods know. We know all—all we want to know. And Chase's actions weren't exactly discreet when he summoned his mother and sealed the doors to the spirit world. Why does it surprise you that those who see all know all?"

"Who?" She guessed then because, considering who this child's grandmother was on Chase's side, the conclusion was obvious. "Hades?" She said it timidly, wanting with all her heart for Hecate to tell her no but knowing with every part of her that the goddess would confirm it.

For a moment, Hecate said nothing, but then she broke the spell and shattered Jaycie's false hopes for good. "Yes. He knows, and he's displeased."

Tears sprang to Jaycie's eyes, and she swiped at them with a trembling hand. "We've done nothing to him."

"You haven't. The child has, simply by existing."

"But Risto Fina—"

"Stop. Don't mention that name here. Do you want to draw attention to your presence?"

Jaycie shook her head but continued the interrogation. "Does he intend to harm my child?" Because god or not, if anyone tried to hurt her baby, Jaycie would make them pay.

"I like your fire, dear. You have the mother bear in you."

"She's my baby. I'll always protect her."

"Good." Hecate grinned, and Jaycie couldn't determine if it was triumphant or just extremely pleased. The goddess continued. "Stay here. You'll be safe. I'll keep you both hidden and protected."

"With warding?" That would make the most sense.

"Naturally."

"But I want to go home. I have to find Chase." She let the words hang for a moment, but when Hecate didn't respond, she added, "I shouldn't be in the spirit world. I'm a mortal." It made her uncomfortable to have to point that out, but it also heightened her suspicions she could trust no one here.

"And what about Cora? Where'd she go? When will she return?" Jaycie asked.

Consulting with Chase's mother might help. Yes, she too was a goddess, but her love for her child would ensure she'd have the best intentions for her granddaughter as well. Hadn't she given up her own son to protect him? A horrifying sense that she, too, might have to give her baby to strangers to raise overwhelmed Jaycie. Hecate's offer of protection would avoid that, but then, why hadn't Hecate protected Cora and Chase this way?

She licked her lips and cleared her throat. "Okay. I'll stay with you." *For now.*

CHAPTER 10

This is a mistake," Kelsey said for the third time since they'd left the cabin.

She and Philip sat in his car in the parking lot outside a spa resort east of Tkaronto. The gorgeous castle-like stone structure made her almost drool with anticipation, but her cautious side railed against the risk they'd take walking in there. They'd already flirted with capture when getting professional haircuts the day before, though they'd dyed their hair at home before visiting the salon.

Kelsey's hair was now a rich brunette, hanging just above her shoulders in soft layers. Philip's was auburn and weirdly short. He'd also swapped out his cowboy hat for a fedora. Somehow, it worked. He didn't resemble a walking anachronism at all. If he weren't a vampire, she'd consider him classically handsome. Not pretty boy, exactly, but manly without veering into rugged. His face didn't have that chiseled-from-rock appearance but was a mix of noble jawline and even cheekbones on a long face. His most attractive feature was his mouth, which was where her gaze always wandered. She avoided his eyes because they literally hypnotized.

He studied her in turn, and after a moment of silence, he responded to her statement. "Darling, you needed out. One reason for the difficult time you've had is that you never leave the cabin. Aside from stepping outside for fresh air, you go nowhere. At least Josh and I escape on hunting trips, and I visit Tkaronto for supplies."

Kelsey blanched at the mention of the hunting trips, but she forced the reminder of Josh's vampirehood out of her mind. Philip did them all a favor when he went to Tkaronto to purchase supplies. He risked his freedom, though he disguised his identity, and for added anonymity, he shopped in the big city rather than the convenient nearby towns. He was right, too, that she needed to get out. The atmosphere in the cabin was slowly suffocating her. It wasn't his fault she succumbed to the hopelessness and frustration of their situation. She'd spent way too much time wallowing in it and blaming him for everything to avoid blaming herself.

"Ready? The stay starts with a couple's massage and a eucalyptus body wrap."

The absurdity of that statement made her laugh out loud, something she hadn't done in months.

He grinned at her in return, and when he tried to pull his lips into a mock frown, he failed. "What's amusing, darling?"

She noted this second use of the endearment. He called everyone darling, so it never meant she was anything special when he called her that, but this time, it sounded different. Or this time, at least, something fluttered in her chest when it fell from his lips.

"I'm going to a spa for two days with a vampire. You won't even notice the effects." Well, he'd feel the massage, but it wouldn't affect his muscles one bit. He did this all for her. "We're not even a couple."

"Oh, we're a couple all right," he replied, the grin vanishing. "What kind of couple I can't figure out, but we're quite a pair."

She'd agreed to share a room with him, both for safety and to perpetuate the illusion they were lovers on a romantic getaway. She hung her head, unsure what to make of this, and he lifted her chin with a finger so their gazes met.

"That's not an insult. Whether we like it or not, we're together. I hope you don't hate it, but it's time we had some fun. Agreed?"

"I don't disagree." Which wasn't quite the same thing, but he accepted it with a nod.

"One warning before we get inside: keep your eyes to yourself and your mouth shut." When she scowled, he added, "For our protection. You'll see all kinds of hypernaturals in there, and I know they make you skittish. I've got wards set, which'll help. You're carrying the talisman I made you?" He waited, pinning her with his gaze until she nodded. "Where?"

She tapped the front pocket of her jeans.

"Okay, then, let's get checked in."

He moved to open the car door, but she grabbed his arm. "You're sure it's okay to leave Josh alone?"

Naturally, they'd argued about this very subject when he'd told her his plans, but she refused to drop it. Once they were out of the car and starting their mini vacation, she intended to stay for the duration. That didn't mean she wouldn't worry about Josh the entire time.

"He's fine. You'll call him, as we agreed, and he'll talk to you—as he promised."

She squeezed his arm. "He did, didn't he?"

That had almost undone her. Since Philip had turned her son, he'd done nothing to help her or comfort her unless Philip forced the issue. This time, Josh agreed to the terms they'd set for letting him stay home alone. Perhaps it wasn't for her sake. He'd probably wanted time alone, without either authority figure breathing down his neck—not that she had much authority over her son anymore. He was Philip's child now. She jettisoned that line of thinking before it ruined their outing at its start. She loosened her grip on his arm, and Philip opened his door.

"Let's get this party started, darling. Just don't forget to use my alias—and yours, Jackie Kutcher."

He waited and she complied with his silent request. "Of course, Michael Kutcher." Where he'd come up with these names, she couldn't guess, and she didn't ask. All she needed to do was commit them to memory. With a sudden surge of excitement, she joined him at the car's trunk to retrieve their bags. Perhaps this trip was a good idea after all. They'd return home relaxed and refreshed, and maybe Josh would miss her while she was gone.

***

The masseuse worked wonders on Kelsey's muscles. Her body melted into the young mermaid's hands, and Kelsey groaned with pleasure. Embarrassed at the almost orgasmic sound of it, she flushed and sneaked a peek at Philip, who lay on the massage table next to her. A male vampire worked him over, and from all appearances, enough strength poured from those hands onto Philip's back that he, too, looked peaceful.

Both staff members could've passed for human but for the pins on their lapels. Mermaids had legs when on dry land, and vampires only flashed their fangs when emotionally triggered or about to feed. When dressed, Kelsey wore a pin identifying her as human. Philip wore a vampire one. A massage at the hands of a hypernatural had at first made her tense and nervous, but the staff here strove to put her at ease. The incredible massage made her almost forget the young woman working on her wasn't human, and Kelsey concluded she had nothing to fear from mermaids.

She closed her eyes and exhaled, releasing the last of her tension. Her next inhalation drew in another tide of relaxation and lavender.

He was so right. We needed this. And don't start thinking about Josh now. He's fine.

Neither masseuse attempted to make conversation. They treated the pair as a couple. Surreal though the situation was, Kelsey thought she could get used to people believing she and Philip were together. For one thing, since everyone assumed they were here for a romantic getaway, no one tried to converse with them. Any dealings with the staff were all about making them comfortable and ensuring their needs were met with the least disruption of their private bubble.

After the massage, the mermaid led them to a steam room. They hung up their robes and sat, in their bathing suits, on towels spread atop a wooden bench while mint-scented steam wafted throughout the room. Sweat trickled down Kelsey's face and back within moments. She glanced at Philip. Moisture from the air dewed his hair and skin, but he wasn't sweating.

"What does this feel like to you?" she asked. While the heat grew to the point where she had to sip from the bottle of water the hostess had provided, Philip continued to sit cucumber cool beside her.

He winked in response and took her hand. He raised it to his lips and kissed the back of it, fluttering her insides again. "This is about you, not me."

"Thank you. I appreciate everything, but I'm curious. What do vampires experience? I understand cold and heat don't bother you." She hesitated but continued when he remained silent. "So ... what do you perceive? Is it ... nothing? You must sense the steam." She sucked in a breath and coughed from the slight searing in her lungs.

He averted his gaze, which puzzled her. Did it embarrass him that vampires didn't discern extremes in temperature? What if asking about it offended him? Here he'd tried to do something nice for her, at his expense no less, and she repaid him by hurting his feelings.

"I can tell when air pressure changes, and I'm sensitive to touch. I sense the temperature and what it is—warm, cold—but it doesn't affect me. If I'm cut, I'm aware of the cut but not the pain. Unless silver cuts me—then it burns."

When she'd bought her bookstore and café at the crossroads, she'd excitedly anticipated meeting customers of all species. Until that point, she'd led a life sheltered from the city's rich diversity. She'd grown up surrounded by humans, and when she met and married her now ex-husband, Blair Davis, they'd set up house in an exclusively human subdivision. Not that they'd had any prejudices against hypernaturals—or so she'd believed—but they'd never had occasion to interact with them. Blair eventually did, when his professional photography business took off, but as a mother and homemaker, Kelsey had no opportunity. Learning she feared anyone not human had shocked her. She'd discovered that the first time a hypernatural walked into her store and she recoiled at the sight of him. While the gnome browsed the books, Kelsey made an excuse to hide in the back room, grateful Chase, the only hypernatural she knew personally, had no qualms serving any species. Of course, magi were also considered another species, but they at least looked human and didn't unexpectedly sprout fangs or fur.

"What's on your mind, darling?"

She snapped out of her reverie and met Philip's gaze. "Just thinking."

"Oh, don't do that. It'll get you in trouble." He grinned.

How was he always so irrepressibly easygoing and optimistic, even when faced with her negative and fear-filled attitude? Especially under their current circumstances: hiding from the authorities and the mob, forced to give up his only child to the faeries. No, she didn't think he had any reason to be cheerful, yet here he was, smiling and winking at her.

Someone rapped on the door. The mermaid peeked into the room and smiled at them.

"All set for your eucalyptus body wrap?"

"Absolutely!" Philip hopped off the bench and headed for the door. "Lead the way, darling."

Kelsey rose from her seat and followed him.

CHAPTER 11

A night had passed since Jaycie agreed to stay in Hades. She remained tense and unsettled despite the peaceful surroundings Hecate provided. Servants brought breakfast and informed Jaycie she'd also eat lunch there but was expected in the dining room at dinner.

"The goddess eats?" Jaycie asked a pretty golden-haired girl who looked no older than sixteen. Was the girl a human spirit serving out eternity in Hecate's home?

"The goddess can eat," the girl replied matter-of-factly. "She can do whatever she likes."

Yes, Jaycie could agree with that, but the prospect of dining with a goddess freaked her out. What would they discuss?

Chase. We'll talk about Chase. He might be in the spirit world right now, hunting for her and oblivious to the danger he was in. Suddenly, she didn't want to wait all day to talk to Hecate. She started to ask the servant to take her to the goddess immediately, when the door to the bedroom burst open, and Cora strolled in as though she'd never been gone.

With a glance, she sent the servant girl on her way and closed the door after her. "I see Hecate has ensured your every comfort."

"Yes." Jaycie didn't want to insult a goddess, but she couldn't wait for the other woman to volunteer information. Taking a moment to compose her thoughts, she invited Cora to join her. "I just finished breakfast, and there's plenty of tea and pastries left over." Instantly, she wanted to kick herself for sounding like such a sycophant.

Cora ignored the invitation and remained standing beside the door, one hand on the doorknob. "You don't have time for this nonsense. Let's go."

"What do you mean?" Fear leaked into Jaycie's voice. "Did you find Chase? Where is he?"

"Never mind that. We need to get you back to the physical plane. It's not safe for you here."

"Is Hecate—"

"Shh. Don't say her name. It'll alert her."

Jaycie drew closer to Chase's mother and whispered, "To what?"

"To what we must do. She shouldn't find out until we're gone. Follow me." Cora cracked the door open and peered into the breech. In a whisper, she said, "No noise." She opened the door wide and stepped into the hallway. Silently, she strode down the hall toward the staircase.

Feeling trapped, Jaycie pattered after her. *She didn't even tell me why we have to go.*

The whole thing made her uneasy. Was it because Hecate meant to harm them, or was it because Cora had located Chase? Or something else? She deserved answers, but for now, she had to trust Chase's mother wouldn't cause harm to the woman carrying her grandchild.

At the top of the stairs, Cora paused and Jaycie caught up to her. The goddess gripped Jaycie's forearm, and together they crept down the stairs.

"This way." Cora kept her grip on the arm and towed the young woman down the hall, but instead of going to the front entrance, they made their way to a nearby door. Behind the door, a set of stairs led down into darkness.

Jaycie froze.

Cora tugged on the arm she still held. "Come."

Jaycie planted her feet on the stone floor and refused to budge. "Where are you taking me?"

"Out."

"Not until you tell me where we're going." Both women whispered, but as the argument continued, their voices grew louder.

"Trust me. There's no time for explanations."

Jaycie shook her head and wrenched her arm free. "In the time we took arguing about it, you could've just told me."

"I'm hiding you with a friend."

Silence blanketed them for a protracted pause, but when Cora grabbed Jaycie's arm again, the young mage balked.

"I want to find Chase." As she said the words, Jaycie recognized them as true. She had to find her boyfriend, the father of her unborn child—not only because he'd help protect them, but because he too was in danger. "I won't leave without him."

"Listen to me," Cora hissed. "You little fool. You're putting him more at risk with your presence. Come on.

We're out of time. If they're not already searching for you, they will soon, and then what'll happen? I'll get you to safety and then find Chase."

The goddess sounded so certain, so confident, but hadn't Hecate said the same thing? Everyone promised safety, but no one made her feel safe. Still, what could she do? She had to trust someone, and Cora was Chase's mother. Wouldn't she have her son's best interests at heart? Hadn't she given him up to protect him? That had to be a mother's greatest sacrifice. At least Jaycie didn't have to give up her daughter.

"Okay." She held out her hand, and Cora accepted it.

With a wave, the goddess illuminated the stairs before them and guided Jaycie downward, one uneasy step at a time.

CHAPTER 12

The suite Philip had reserved for them contained all the amenities one expected in a luxury hotel: a separate bedroom and living room, a kitchenette, and a bathroom with a Jacuzzi. Philip told Kelsey to take the king-size bed since vampires didn't need sleep. The suite's decor gave off an old-fashioned vibe, more old-world than vintage, with ornate architectural details and large floral-patterned drapes cascading down from the ceiling behind the matching padded headboard. He figured it was everything a woman would want with all the romantic touches to feed her soul. He'd even left a few bodice-ripper romance novels on her nightstand, but so far, she hadn't touched them.

As they settled in, he ensured Kelsey wouldn't encounter even a drop of alcohol. At first, he worried she'd insist on ordering a bottle of wine with their meal when he placed the room-service order for lunch, but she remained silent when he requested spring water and a carafe of coffee to drink. She said nothing even when he specified the coffee should be decaf.

Relieved she was making this easy, he suggested they play cards while they waited for the food to arrive, which he'd scheduled for one o'clock.

She dutifully strolled across the room and sat down at the table. "I assume you have a deck of cards?" Her expression was expectant but devoid of tension. It aroused suspicion in him. By now, she should crave alcohol and snap at him as she suffered withdrawal symptoms.

She hadn't had a drink in three days—not since he'd poured it all down the drain. Either she wasn't an alcoholic or not enough time had passed for her to start detoxing. Granted, he kept her chugging water at regular intervals, he ensured she ate healthy food, and he stayed by her side anytime she wasn't sleeping.

Also a positive, she'd agreed she needed to do this and seemed determined to reclaim her life—such as it was while they continued to hide from everyone who wanted them arrested or dead.

"In my bag." He retrieved the deck he'd packed and joined her at the table. "How are you?" He studied her face.

Her cheeks had a rosy glow; her eyes were clear and bright. She'd stripped to her bra and panties and put on a robe when they'd returned to the room after their body wrap. Without meaning to, she'd aroused desire in him as she so casually removed her blouse and jeans and slipped on the thick terry robe hanging in the closet. While her nonchalance and ease in his presence reassured him, since she typically considered him the closest thing to Satan on the physical plane, he experienced a twinge of regret she now treated him like a brother—or an ex-husband. An image of him hypnotizing her ex, Blair, flashed into his head, and he pushed it away. No sense in traveling down that road. He'd end up ruining their, so far, pleasant time.

"Fine." She yawned and stretched. "I haven't been this relaxed since ..." Her brow furrowed, and her eyes grew sad.

Shit. He hadn't meant to raise the past to her, even though he'd done it to himself a second before. He slipped the cards from the pack and attempted to distract her. "Gin?" As soon as he said it, he wanted to slap himself. *Way to go. Remind someone drying out of what she's missing.* "Go Fish," he amended.

She laughed, and it sounded carefree enough he forgave himself for the slip. "Whatever you like. I've never heard of either game. You'll have to teach me."

He raised his brows. "What card games do you know?"

She met his gaze. "None."

"You are a mystery. Who doesn't know any card games?" He hoped she wasn't hiding childhood trauma.

"I never had the opportunity to learn. When I was growing up, the games were all computerized. I played online solitaire, but everything we did revolved around technology. You played a lot of cards?"

He nodded. "First, the usual—Gin Rummy, Crazy Eights—but then I graduated to poker and betting games. That was well before computers were around." He hoped the reminder he'd lived at least a hundred years longer than she had didn't unhinge her. A soft surge of frustration that she made him second-guess everything he said and did almost made him scowl, but he caught himself in time. If she reacted badly, he'd deal with it. Since when did a vampire care what a human thought?

"I can teach you."

"Sure." She smiled, and he sensed the lightness and peace within her. All too often since they'd met, he sensed only rage or grief or terror. He should've taken her away from it all a long time ago, but she'd have objected. She wouldn't have permitted Josh to go out alone, and that was another reason Philip needed to take her away. He'd allowed the boy freedom to leave their hideout, and for it to go smoothly, Kelsey had to be out of the cabin and distracted. She'd never have approved of the scheme, making life more difficult for them all. It'd been hard enough to get her to agree to leave the baby vamp alone at the cabin. She'd never have agreed to let him risk exposure to check up on Dakota, Philip's half-vampire daughter who lived with the fae.

Philip had almost ordered the boy to stand down when he'd suggested going, but a desire to verify Dakota remained committed to her new relationship with the faerie prince and relief Josh showed an interest in anything besides his own selfish needs made Philip agree to the request. They'd planned out a strategy for Josh to slip into and out of the faerie kingdom without detection, but of course, the endeavor was risky. If Kelsey discovered what her son was up to, she'd turn into Momzilla. No one needed that. So Philip had booked the spa retreat and whisked her away for a relaxing couple of nights. He only hoped when they returned to the cabin Josh would be there waiting for them.

CHAPTER 13

"Honey, I'm home!"

The sound of Chase's voice calling out to her sends a shiver of love and desire through Jaycie, but that's followed by confusion and a touch of fear. She scans her surroundings and discovers she's in a house, in a kitchen, sunny-yellow and spacious. She holds a dish rag pressed to the marble countertop as if she's wiping it down. The stove is on, and two pots, both boiling, rest on burners. The oven is also on, and the smell of roasting chicken makes her mouth water when she catches the scent.

What is this? How'd I get here?

Chase strolls into the room, his grin broad. He's wearing jeans and a T-shirt stretched tight over his muscular chest. Without a pause, he goes to her and draws her into a warm embrace. It sends waves of relief and calm through her whole body. He's solid and strong—her anchor to sanity.

"How was your day?" He grasps her by the upper arms and holds her at arm's length, examining her.

"You look good. The nausea's gone then?"

She stares down at her belly. The bulge is small, almost imperceptible, but she sees it there under the track pants she's wearing. When he releases her, she presses her hands to her belly in a protective gesture she repeats often.

"Yes." She can think of nothing else to say. Should she question him? Would he wonder if she's lost her mind if she tells him she can't remember how she got here? How she found him?

She remembers following Cora down a flight of stairs in Hecate's home. In Hades. Then this house and Chase arriving. Hope has her explaining it all away. Everything is back to normal, and she and Chase have reunited. If that's the case, though, then why aren't they in their apartment? Where did this house come from?

He leans in and kisses Jaycie's cheek.

"Great. Let me wash up, and I'll help you set the table." He sniffs the air and flashes another grin. "Smells amazing."

He heads toward the kitchen's exit, a door-shaped opening through which she can glimpse a darkened hallway with hardwood floors. She doesn't know what's beyond it. What if he walks through and disappears? What if he's a mirage?

"Chase?"

He halts and turns to face her, his brows raised in question. "Yes?"

Timidly, she asks, "How was your day?"

"Same old stuff. You know."

She doesn't, so she says, "Tell me anyway."

"I need to put my tools and robe away and wash up; then I'll help you here. We'll talk while we eat."

She can't bear the thought of him leaving her alone. "I'll go with you."

He glances at the stove. Her gaze follows his. The oven timer reveals they have twenty minutes before the buzzer sounds. To verify, she scurries to the stove and lifts pot lids and cracks open the oven door to check on the chicken. In one pot, broccoli sits in a steamer, the water warming below it, and rice bubbles wetly in another.

"Should be fine. I'll listen for the buzzer."

A fresh salad already sits in a large bowl on the kitchen table. At least the dinner they're having is prepared. Could she have prepped all that food and not remember?

Chase is already in the hallway. She rushes from the kitchen, determined to keep him in her sights at all times. He had his arms around her, his body pressed to hers. If she can touch him, if they can hold each other, it means this is real. Doesn't it?

He leads her into a large master bedroom. Her hope chest stands at the foot of the queen bed, and that gives her another moment of relief. The patchwork quilt covering the bed is also one she recognizes, but it shouldn't be there. Her grandmother made it and promised to give it to Jaycie on her wedding day. How'd it get here? Somehow, she'll have to question Chase without making him conclude she's lost her mind. What if she has? What if she has early-onset Alzheimer's? Could a pregnancy trigger something like this?

She presses her hands to her belly again and whispers soothing sounds to her unborn baby. *Don't worry, baby. I'll protect you.*

Chase opens a gym bag resting on a table in front

of the bay window. Two padded chairs stand on either side. A beam of sunlight streams in through the sheers and lights up the area. She imagines herself sitting at this table, sipping tea, nibbling cookies, and reading a good book. Where is her book collection? If the size of the bedroom is any indication, the house might have a library. She's always wanted one.

The sun. It must be setting if we're preparing to have dinner. She skirts around Chase, who's busy emptying the bag of his magick tools, and peers out the window.

A large fenced-in yard stretches out before her. Snow covers the grass, and she can see the sun is indeed setting. The snow below her sparkles with it. Trees pepper the yard, but they're young. They wouldn't offer much shade in the summer, but they'll grow. She wonders if they've tended the gardens or if this is their first year here. The thought rattles her. How long has she walked like a zombie through her life? She holds her hands in front of her pelvis again. Not long.

We were in the apartment when I got pregnant, and it was fall. But if this is winter, she's lost a couple of months. That's a lot of time.

"So," she says, "how was your day?"

He's moved to the closet, and it's a walk-in. When he replies, his voice is muffled. "Working on a year-end project. It's almost done, so the late nights will end. I'm sure you're happy about that."

The realization she can't see him panics her at first, but relief quickly follows. He's out of her sight, but she can hear him puttering around in the closet and answering her. He hasn't disappeared on her and likely won't.

"Yes, that's wonderful." Should she ask what the project is? Or would he expect her to know that already? She must take care, or he'll suspect something's wrong.

Something is *wrong!* She drops into the nearest chair. "What do you have to do to finish it?"

"Acquire all the ingredients we need. Practice executing it without executing it, if you know what I mean."

She does. They want to verify it'll work without actually casting it. It must be complicated, whatever it is. Simple spells don't need all the rigmarole. This must be for an exam.

Why aren't we doing this together? The only plausible answer is that she quit school. She's afraid to ask why, though she suspects it's because of her pregnancy. Yet she hadn't planned to interrupt her education until much closer to her due date. Why did that change? She wants to scream in frustration. All she has are questions she can't ask. It'll take her days to figure out what's happening.

Then her mouth goes dry with fear as she thinks, *What if I'm under a spell and none of this is real?*

CHAPTER 14

Light filtered into the room, slipping in through the cracks around the heavy drapes covering the hotel suite's large windows. Kelsey sighed and stirred in the king bed she had all to herself. She experienced not a moment of guilt over it. Such an uninterrupted, peaceful sleep had eluded her for months. If it meant forcing Philip to hang out on the couch for two nights, she wouldn't lose any sleep over it. She chuckled to herself, a sense of delight filling her. If her sense of humor had returned, things were looking up. When was the last time she'd joked lightheartedly even to herself? Sure, she'd tossed out sarcasm and gallows humor, but bitterness and despair had motivated it. Had hope returned to her soul?

She strolled across the room and snatched the robe from where she'd tossed it on the chair the night before. As she slipped it on, she mentally ran through the day's schedule. The breakfast they'd ordered the night before should arrive soon, and after that, they'd spend the day enjoying more spa treatments or swimming. How long since her most pressing dilemma was whether to get another massage or sit in a hot tub? *Not even during my marriage.*

Maybe that was part of what had killed the relationship. Always too busy running his business to go away on a vacation, Blair had taken the odd day off to stay home and work around the house. How ironic her relationship with a soulless vampire was better than the one she'd had with her husband.

When Philip had first broached the subject of taking two nights at a luxury retreat, she'd balked at sharing a room. She assumed he wanted to weasel his way into her bed. Of course, if sex was his primary goal, such elaborate lengths to trick her into it weren't necessary. He could've attempted to con his way into sleeping with her at the cabin, but he'd never tried. She wouldn't have allowed it anyway. At least he wasn't the type to force himself on a woman. Sometimes, when her ego pricked, she wondered why he never tried anything with her. Wasn't she attractive enough? Wasn't she desirable? Then she used a mirror to confirm that no, she wasn't. She'd let herself go. No wonder he kept his distance. Yet even after the new haircut and color and the spa treatments that erased ten years from her face, he still hadn't flirted with her.

The night before, he'd acted the perfect gentleman. After dinner, they'd taken a moonlight walk through the gardens then returned to the room to read in companionable silence. Before bed, he'd ordered hot chocolate and pastries, and after they'd shared the decadent snack, he bid her goodnight and ushered her into the bedroom. As the doors closed behind him and she crawled into bed alone, her disappointment surprised her. Now, in the clear light of day, she felt only gratitude and appreciation he wasn't a horny jerk. She even almost liked him.

Kelsey tiptoed to the French doors separating the living area from the sleeping quarters and eased them open. She needn't have worried about waking Philip. He sat on the sofa, watching television. When he spotted her, he waved her over.

"Join me, darling. Breakfast will be here soon."

She stretched like a happy cat and sighed contentedly.

"Sure. I've got nothing else to do." She smiled and padded over to sit next to him. If she enjoyed his presence for once, she wouldn't question it. Time enough for that when they returned home and faced reality again.

***

When Josh entered the library, Dakota Lawson looked up and rested the book she was reading in her lap. She placed her palms on top of the open pages and smiled at him. No recognition flashed in her eyes.

This was Josh's second day among the fae. He'd disguised himself as one of them using a combination of illusory magick and good-ole vampire mesmerization. Thank the gods his illusion held. When his gaze met Dakota's, his concentration wavered, and he almost lost control.

He forced himself to return the engaging smile with a polite nod and continued to push the tea trolley across the carpet and position it next to her chair.

A fire blazed brightly in the enormous stone fireplace. While winter dominated the physical plane, here in the fae's realm, fall held sway. The faerie world never saw snow or cold. At most, the leaves on the trees turned red or orange or golden before dropping to the ground when new, green leaves sprouted and pushed them off. The fall air leaking into the castle, which was as drafty as any medieval building, made the fire helpful but unnecessary until nightfall.

Dakota sighed and stretched. "Thank you so much." She flashed that smile again.

"Will there be anything else, Your Highness?" He was unsure if a servant should address a princess-to-be that way, but since she didn't flinch, he decided he hadn't made a faux pas.

"No, thank you. This is lovely."

She waited, and he realized she expected him to serve her.

She'd sure grown accustomed to getting waited on quickly.

He performed the motions of pouring her tea into a cup and, because she liked sugar and milk in it, he added those as well.

Her eyes brightened, and her smile broadened in delight. "Thank you. How did you know how I like it?"

Shit. Would "my lady" work as well? He'd read plenty of fantasy novels but had never learned how servants talked to nobility. "Oh, I asked before I brought you the tea, my lady." Her eyes widened a little at that, so he decided he'd better stick to "Your Highness."

"Why, how thoughtful. Everyone here is so kind and considerate."

He searched for any trace of sarcasm, condescension, or politeness masking fear and found nothing suspicious. She sounded genuinely pleased, and her tone and posture indicated she was relaxed and comfortable.

Josh uncovered the plate of pastries. "Shall I serve you some biscuits or tarts, Your Highness?"

"Nothing right now, thank you. I'll get it myself in a bit." She accepted the cup and saucer he offered her and sipped.

"Will that be all, then, ma'am?" The ma'am had slipped out, but she didn't blink at it, so his unconscious must've offered it up correctly.

"Yes, thank you. You may carry on."

"Very good, ma'am, thank you."

He started to turn away, but she stopped him. "A moment."

He froze and looked over his shoulder at her. "Yes, ma'am?"

"You're new here? I don't think we've met before."

He swallowed. *Dakota, don't question me. Please.* "Yes, ma'am, I started only days ago."

"How nice. I hope you like it here. What's your name?"

What was a likely name for a male faerie? His mind blanked, so he blurted out the first thing that popped into his head. "Legolas."

"Legolas. Nice to meet you."

He blew out a puff of relief. "Thank you, ma'am." He moved to turn away again and hesitated, unsure whether he still had her permission to leave.

Blast this servant bullshit. Every inch of him wanted to scream at her for thinking she was too good to pour her own tea. Clearly, she'd settled in with this faerie prince as naturally as Josh had taken to his new life as a vampire. He wondered what she'd say if she knew he was no longer human. In fact, he'd outlive her now since she was a dhampir, a half-vampire. Would she love him again then?

But that's not why he'd come, and Philip would thrash him if he veered off book and revealed himself to her, so he cleared his throat politely and said, "Will there be anything else, Your Highness?"

She started to shake her head but paused and sniffed the air, her expression puzzled. "Legolas?"

"Yes, ma'am?"

"Can I ask you a personal question?"

He gulped. "Yes, ma'am?"

"Are you a ... are you half-vampire?"

Drat it all. He'd been able to disguise himself visually, but her dhampir sense of smell wasn't fooled. At least she'd given him the solution within her question. "Yes, ma'am."

The reply seemed to satisfy her. "I see. Were you born here?"

Perhaps she wasn't so content after all. Hope surged. "Yes, ma'am." What else could he say? If he ever returned, he'd better construct a solid backstory.

"Thank you, Legolas. That'll be all." She beamed her beautiful smile at him again, and it touched him somehow. If he'd had a heart, it would've ached for her.

He gave her a neck bow and turned away. He hurried from the room, struggling to maintain the glamour that protected his identity.

***

Night turned to day as Josh Davis stepped from the faerie realm into the physical plane. He paused inside the faerie ring, his ears still attuned to the sounds in the location he'd just left. He heard only birdsong and the breeze rustling the leaves on the trees. No sound of pursuit shattered the calm, and he would've smiled with pride at his success except it was bittersweet. Dakota appeared to have settled into her role as future princess, and then queen, of the fae. It shocked Josh how much it wounded him that she looked so happy and content. He struggled to hold on to the thought that at least the prince she intended to marry treated her well.

Holding his disguise for the week, in faerie time, he'd spent in their realm had cost him, but he'd wanted to ensure the public face Dakota showed her people was the same cheerful face she maintained in private. It was, and his disappointment almost betrayed his presence when he'd served her tea and she'd smiled that captivating smile. That she was more than human attracted him on a visceral level, but seeing her also bubbled up old emotions he barely controlled. The glamour he maintained had slipped a few times, but he didn't think she'd noticed.

The second the portal between the worlds slammed shut, Josh scanned the area to make sure he was alone and dropped the illusion.

He breathed in the crisp, cold air of the physical plane without feeling it and strode away from the mushroom ring, careful not to leave visible tracks in the snow. Stealth was but one more perk vampires enjoyed, as was the speed with which he returned to the cabin.

Kelsey and Philip hadn't yet returned, much to Josh's relief. When he checked the date, he verified one more night alone remained before his mother and vampire father intruded on his solitude. No time had passed on the physical plane while he was away. He entered the home, remembering to remove his boots before he strode across the floor his mother cleaned obsessively now that she'd stopped drinking again.

Reveling in the silence, Josh sauntered to his bedroom and slipped a hairpin from his pocket, putting it under his pillow. He'd stolen it from Dakota when he'd broken into her bedroom while she and her prince strolled in the garden. It was a small trinket, worth nothing. She wouldn't miss it, but when the mood struck, he'd dig out this trophy and remind himself he could sneak in and see her whenever he wanted. The fools had no idea he'd trespassed on their land. Now that he was no longer human, he'd do as he pleased and no one could stop him. Except Philip, of course, but what his maker didn't know wouldn't worry him, and Josh would make sure no one knew when he visited Dakota again.

He strolled from the bedroom, absently giving the speed bag hanging from the ceiling near his bed a swat on his way out. *Better put in some practice later.*

He'd never needed to fight, but his father—his human father, Blair—had made him learn how to box. Blair loved boxing—watching it as a sport, anyway—and had hoped his son exhibited the talent for it Blair lacked. Josh had disappointed his father in that—he fought competently, but he'd never made it to the professional arena. Since he'd become a vampire, though, he needed to fill an eternity of hours added to his life. Practicing his boxing skills not only kept him occupied, but it also helped him release tension.

He walked into the den and sat down at Philip's desk. After booting up the laptop, he logged into his account and opened a browser. Next time he visited Dakota, he'd be better prepared to interact with her.

CHAPTER 15

The skiff bumped against the shore, jarring Chase but not enough to unseat him. He waited for the boat's movement to still before rising to face Charon, who stood in the back of the boat.

"Thank you, sir." Chase winced at the "sir," but it'd been automatic. He was used to saying it to all his professors, to Risto Fina during magick lessons, and to any authority figure who crossed his path.

The shore against which the boat floated was as gray and rocky as the banks they'd left, but on this side, the horizon didn't fade into an endless distance. Here, a range of mountains rose into the clouds, miles away from Chase's location. Flames flickered at the peak, and lava oozed down the sides.

"Hades, I presume?" Chase asked, but his captain remained silent.

With a shrug, Chase hopped from the skiff over ankle-deep water, landing just shy of dry land. His slippers instantly flooded, and he trotted up onto the rocks and sand. He turned back to thank Charon for the lift, but the skiff had already vanished.

Chase squinted at the river, trying to spot the psychopomp, but saw nothing. The river once again roiled and rushed past him. At least he'd made it across. His next challenge would be to get inside those mountains and locate Jaycie.

***

Once again afraid Chase will vanish unless she keeps him in her sights, Jaycie leaps from her chair and rushes into the walk-in closet. He's on his way out, and they collide, Chase gripping her upper arms to steady her.

"Hey, what's up?" His tone is jovial, his grin reassuring.

"I ..." She can't continue. What should she tell him? The truth? *Chase, I think I'm imagining you.* No, he'd either laugh at her or try to reassure her. If he's not real, he won't admit it.

She tackles it from another direction. "How'd I get out of Hades?"

He tilts his head and studies her, his grip still tight on her arms. "What do you mean?" He says it carefully, his tone measured, steady.

"I can't remember coming home."

He draws her in for a hug. "I know, honey. It was a bad time. Do you remember waking up in the hospital?"

A vision of a hospital room with vases filled with flowers, glaring lights, and beeping machines flits through her mind, and she thinks it might be a memory. "But how did I escape from Hades?"

"I carried you."

She pulls away from him even though she'd rather

stay in that embrace forever. "How'd you find me?"

He moves to her side and puts an arm around her. "Come on. Let's not do this in the closet." He guides her back into the bedroom and over to the bed. As one, they sit side by side on the edge, his arm around her shoulders.

"It wasn't easy." He whispers the words. "Hecate had you."

"She was ... she wanted to harm me?" She meets his gaze. If he lies, she'll sense it.

For a moment, she swears fear flashes through his eyes. "Not harm, no. Keep you. Keep the baby." He hugs her again, pressing her head to his shoulder.

To avoid meeting my eyes? Does she trust the love of her life so little she doubts his every word, his every move? *Yes, if he isn't really Chase.* But if this isn't Chase, then who is it? An illusion? She looks around the room again. It's lovely. Exactly what she'd wish for if she could make a home with Chase. Have they set up a nursery yet? She presses her hands to her belly again. *Don't worry, baby, Mama will figure this out.*

"Why would she want to do that?" she asks.

"I don't know. I didn't stop to ask questions. We had to get out of there."

Is that irritation in his voice? Can illusions feel annoyance? Who would be behind this? Hecate? Jaycie doesn't think so. Perhaps Hades found her and put her under his spell. She discards that theory too. The god's methods are more direct. If she fell into his hands, he'd either kill her—turning her into a spirit—or trap her in his prison. Whichever option he chose, she'd know what was happening to her. Hades isn't the type of god to use trickery and illusion. No, this is a long con, whoever is behind it.

The oven timer goes off then, a loud buzzing that cuts into the silence and gives Chase the opportunity to end the conversation. He seizes it and leaps to his feet. "Shall we serve dinner? It smells fabulous."

Unable to argue, she stands and follows him from the room.

***

After what seemed like a four-hour walk, Chase halted and assessed the distance to the mountains. They seemed no closer, and he wondered if they were an illusion. The lava flowing from them certainly looked real. The rumble from within sounded genuine. And the smell of sulfur sure made his eyes water and his throat spasm. He was in Hades, no question, and he headed toward wherever Jaycie was. Since he'd paused his forward movement, he took the opportunity to reassess her location.

Standing with his knees slightly bent and his feet hip-distance apart, he closed his eyes and focused on her energy, allowing his body to sway in the direction that would take him to her. When he opened his eyes, his alignment was still fixed on the mountain in the distance.

I'm coming, baby. No matter how long it takes, I'll find you and get you the hell out of here. Chase started walking again.

CHAPTER 16

Two nights together and not one fight. Kelsey considered that some kind of record. But, she admitted, it was easy to get along when Philip removed all responsibilities from her shoulders and all triggers from her environment. He'd helped her detox in the mildest way possible and kept her distracted with healthy food, plenty of activities, and spa services she didn't even know existed. His presence, too, didn't annoy her, which surprised her. Once, he'd been her biggest trigger, the sight of him alone often causing her to fill with rage.

When did that change? She had no answer to that, but at some point, she'd stopped blaming him for her every problem and labeling him the source of all her grief.

When she opened her eyes on the morning they were to check out of the hotel, she hopped out of bed, excited at the prospect of spending another day with him.

She slipped the robe over her nightgown and opened the French doors. The enthusiastic "Good morning" died on her lips when she didn't see him on the couch. At first, she wasn't concerned. He must've stepped out for a walk or to grab a newspaper. For a vampire, he sure cared a lot about keeping up with current events.

Why wouldn't he? she chided herself. *He might not have a soul, but he lives in this world.*

No matter how hard she tried to eliminate her prejudiced assumptions, they continued to pop into her head. In her defense, how was she supposed to stop thoughts from arising? She couldn't. No one could.

You can if you don't believe them in the first place.

Somehow, she'd have to internalize accepting nonhumans, but how?

Breakfast would arrive soon. Surely, he'd return in time for food and coffee. While he needed neither, he enjoyed sharing meals with her, and in all honesty, she relished his company when they ate together. They both studiously avoided topics that would set her off, which also contributed to the wonderful time they'd spent here.

She searched for a note, but when she didn't find one, she strolled to the window to scan the gardens. Perhaps she'd spot him out there. Snow covered everything, and the maples and other deciduous trees had lost their leaves, giving them a gray, skeletal look. Fountains stood dry and silent. Staff had shoveled the quaint wooden bridge spanning the small brook, which was frozen over. Burlap sacks covered the bushes, and brown stalks poked through the white in the flower beds.

No matter how hard she searched, she caught no sign of him. Everything was gray and dull and lifeless.

Like vampires. Anger bubbled up, and it simmered in his direction. An old habit, but this time, didn't she have the right to be vexed? He'd left her alone in the room without even leaving a note. Where the hell was he?

She returned to her bedroom and retrieved her cell phone from her purse, but when she called his number, she heard the responding ringtone in the living room. Minor annoyance turned to fury when she found his cell phone on the end table beside the couch. He'd not only gone out without informing her where he went, but he'd also left his cell phone behind.

Stupid and dangerous. What if something happens to him?

Panic replaced rage then, and she fought the urge to rush out to search for him in her nightgown. She'd get dressed, and if he still wasn't back, she'd go hunt for him.

Kelsey stripped and grabbed the clean clothes handiest to her: panties, bra, T-shirt, and jeans. She dressed and then washed her face and brushed her teeth, listening for his return the entire time, always expecting to hear the lock click and the door open. She ran a brush through her hair and imagined greeting him calmly, relieved to see him back safe. Without shouting at him, she'd casually ask him where he'd been. He'd give her a reasonable explanation, and she'd laugh it off. Their meal would arrive, and they'd eat together and plan out their day.

Oh, God, please bring him back. I won't take him for granted ever again. I promise. What if he never returned? What if Frank Evans had found them? Why had they so stupidly believed they could visit a spa without getting caught? Philip had assured her it was fine. He'd set up wards around their room; they carried protective and shielding charms on their bodies at all times. No one should be able to locate them, not even the best magician.

A knock at the door announced breakfast's arrival—of course, it was breakfast because Philip wouldn't knock. She choked on a stifled sob.

Kelsey opened the door and waved the young man pushing the breakfast cart into the room. Before he could enter, she spotted Philip strolling down the hall as though he hadn't just tortured her with his inconsiderate absence.

"Good morning, darling. Sleep well?"

She opened her mouth to snap something snarky at him and burst into tears.

***

Swiping tears from her eyes with a brusque backhand, Kelsey stared wide-eyed at Philip for a moment and then vanished into the hotel suite. The server hesitated as the door to the room started to swing shut, but Philip leaped ahead and braced it open.

"Sorry about that," he said, trying to keep his tone light and friendly. "Let me take that for you." He relieved the man of the trolley and signed for the food, leaving a generous tip.

The server, giving him a sympathetic and understanding nod, thanked Philip and sauntered away.

Philip pushed the cart farther into the room and shut the door. Kelsey sat on the couch, her head in her hands. She no longer shook with sobs, but the dejected stoop to her shoulders telegraphed her mood.

"What's going on?" He struggled to keep the

irritation from his voice. Whatever had happened had erased all the effort he'd put into helping her escape her problems and relax. He caught himself on the brink of rolling his eyes at her. She wouldn't have seen it, but expressing the sentiment wouldn't help either of them.

She raised her head and gave him such a despairing look he repented every annoyed thought.

"Tell me. I'll fix it, whatever it is."

Her laugh was so sudden and sounded so carefree he gawked at her. "Oh, Philip."

His name on her lips startled him. She rarely used it. He rushed to her side and sat next to her. Without thinking, he draped an arm around her shoulders and drew her close. "What happened?"

"It's stupid."

"No, it's not." He suspected he understood now what had set her off. "You woke up and found me gone."

Damn it. He'd thought he had enough time to prepare for their departure before she woke up. He'd visited their car in the parking lot to verify the wards and protections kept it undetectable, and he'd walked the grounds, ensuring no one from Evans's team or the police had breached their security. During their stay here, he'd done this regularly, but this was the first time she'd noticed his absence. Just his luck.

She tried to pull away, but he refused to remove his arm from around her shoulders, so when she met his gaze, their faces were mere inches apart. "If you knew I'd get upset, why'd you leave without telling me? You could've left a note." Her eyes, so brilliantly blue it almost hurt him to stare into them, enhanced the accusation in her tone.

"I didn't know. I guessed when I saw your

reaction." He removed his arm from her shoulders and placed his palms on either side of her face. "If I'd known, I'd have left a note. I never want to cause you worry or pain." Yet he constantly did just that.

"I was afraid something had happened to you. You were gone so long." She smiled ruefully. "When you appeared, I was relieved, but I got angry because you made me worry for no reason."

She averted her gaze by looking down, her eyes half lidded, her lips curled again into that rueful smile. "I told you it was stupid."

He suppressed a sudden urge to kiss her.

Knock it off. She's human. They're nothing but trouble. He'd vowed long ago not to get involved with another human, but fate had entangled her in his life.

Not fate. Your own stupidity.

Why had he let her help him hunt for Dakota? He'd asked himself that a hundred times since that night he'd turned Josh into a vampire, but he'd never felt the regret so strongly. Not even when the reality of what he'd done had sunk in and he grasped that, if the authorities caught him, he'd get the death penalty.

Yet no matter how often he relived that night in his mind, he continued to believe he wouldn't do anything differently. The alternative to turning Josh was Kelsey suffering the loss of her son because the pair had helped search for Dakota, and he'd rather die than allow that to happen.

Instead of kissing her, he stroked her hair and then pulled her in for another hug. She'd always allowed him to hug her when she needed it. "It's not stupid, darling." He needed her to understand that.

He opened his mouth to admit how thoughtless he'd acted but paused when she raised her head and gave him that blue-eyed stare again. The words died on his lips.

"Philip." His name floated out of her like a whispered charm.

"What is it?"

She leaned into him and pressed her soft lips to his, sending a jolt of long-suppressed desire through him.

CHAPTER 17

Kelsey hadn't planned on kissing Philip. One moment, they'd been staring into each other's eyes; the next, their lips pressed together, and passion and desire she'd kept tethered for so long broke free. She welcomed it. They'd endured so much pain together, didn't they deserve pleasure too? Couldn't she this once forget every responsibility, every rule she forced herself to follow, and be the bad girl?

Her lips parted. She slipped her tongue out to probe his mouth, and he opened to her. He moaned, making her quiver, and she wrapped her arms around him, sliding one hand up into his hair, that hair so silky and soft her fingers couldn't get enough of it. She'd fought her urges for an eternity, telling herself he was a monster, evil, soulless. He moaned again and, without releasing her lips, spoke into her mouth. "We can't do this."

In response, she pressed her body against his. "I don't care." She didn't. No one else had supported her or protected her as this vampire had. Soulless? If so, soulless didn't mean conscienceless. He'd shown her more compassion than most of the humans who'd crossed her path. Frank Evans might have a soul, but he was more of a monster than Philip. When she'd awoken and found him gone earlier, all that mattered was getting him back safe. She hadn't appreciated how much he truly meant to her until she faced the prospect of a future without him in it.

She deepened the kiss, and his arms crushed her body against his. For a few blissful seconds, she lost herself in the moment, letting desire lead her.

He didn't allow it to continue for long. He pulled his lips from hers, easing his face away so they stared into each other's eyes.

"Kelsey," he whispered, her name so sensuous on his lips it made her weak, "you don't want to do this." His fangs snicked out, and he retracted them, his face contorting as if with pain.

First came confusion. "Why are you stopping me?" Then, anger. "Why do you get to decide?"

He leaned forward and kissed her forehead, her nose. "I'm not stopping you; I'm stopping me."

"What do you mean?"

He stroked her hair and drew her into his lap. Caressing her hair, then stroking her back, he pulled her in tight, and she leaned her head on his shoulder. She couldn't see his expression, but she never felt safer than when she was in the circle of his arms. Her arms tightened around him, and she snuggled in, closing her eyes to savor the moment.

"I'm a vampire."

She nuzzled his shoulder. "I know."

"You hate m—vampires."

He'd almost said "You hate me." She was sure of it. She groaned and shook her head. Tears sprang to her eyes.

"No, no, no." Shifting in his lap, she tilted her head up so their eyes met. The pain in his deepened her shame, but she refused to play the coward and avert her gaze. Would a soulless monster feel such hurt? She'd been the soulless monster. He'd cared for her, cared for her son—hell, he'd risked his life for them. She'd known it, but she'd ignored it, preferring instead to focus on seeing only the vampire and not the human he still held within his core.

"I don't hate vampires. I don't hate you."

"Kelsey." He said nothing more, but the one word held both disappointment and reproach.

"I did once, and I'm sorry for it." She spun around and straddled him, bracing herself with her knees and rising so their faces were level. She placed her palms on either side of his face. "I don't hate you. Not you. Not your species. I fear others of your kind, but I don't fear you. I ... I'm in love with you."

He closed his eyes, and his Adam's apple bobbed as he swallowed. "No." He shook his head for emphasis. "You might think you are, but you aren't."

She frowned. "Are you telling me how I feel?"

His eyelids popped open, and he met her gaze. "No. I'm saying you're misinterpreting your feelings. It's not love, darling. It's probably Stockholm syndrome."

"Don't be ridiculous." She made a move to climb off him, his rejection of her eating a hole in her heart, but he grasped her arms and held her in place.

"No. I won't allow you to pull away. We're going to do this. Now."

"I'm not falling for my captor. You're not my

captor."

"You believe that because you've never tried to leave."

She gasped, a sick sensation growing in the pit of her stomach. In a small voice, she said, "If I tried to leave, you'd stop me?"

He shook his head but not in answer to her question. "Josh keeps you with me. He must stay with me, so he keeps you with me. Tell me the truth. If Josh had died that night, if we'd let him go—"

"No, no."

"Let me finish." His grip on her arm tightened, but when she winced from the pain, he eased up. "I'm sorry. I don't mean to hurt you, which is my point. First, answer my question: if Josh had died, would you have gone with me? Would you have stayed with me?"

She heard no hope or hurt in his voice, only an honest desire for an answer. "I don't know. Back then ..." She shook her head. "It's complicated."

She eased into his lap and put her head on his shoulder. "I'm tired, Philip. So much has happened to us, but we've gotten through it all together. We share a connection because of it. I'm attracted to you, and I care for you." She slid her arms around him and squeezed. "Why question it?"

He sighed. "Because I swore to myself I'd never get involved with another human, and I think I love you."

CHAPTER 18

Silence blankets the house. Chase sleeps, but Jaycie can't shut down her brain. Tired of tossing and turning, she slides out of bed and pads into the kitchen. She checks the time.

Five o'clock. Might as well start the day.

But start the day how? What does she do? Does she have a part-time job? Do volunteer work? Is she simply a homemaker? If so, it's not where she wants to be or how she planned to spend her life.

While she fills the kettle with water, she reflects on all she knows about her situation so far. Everything about where she is and what she's doing feels wrong. Chase appears normal—if he's an impostor, she can't find evidence of it—so she concludes he's a duplicate of the real Chase. Wherever the real Chase might be.

Maybe she's the impostor. What if she's the one who doesn't exist, and Chase is living the illusion?

I think, therefore, I exist. Some philosopher she'd read about at school had said that. The answer pops into her head: Descartes. She agrees with the statement, if only because it reassures her she's still a part of the world. Yes, but which world? Is she in Hades, hallucinating this life with Chase? Or is she on the physical plane in a mental institution, strapped down, drugged, and escaping into a fantasy world? She discards the second option. The last place she recalls is Hades, where Cora led her down a set of stairs. Everything after that remains a blank until the moment she found herself in the kitchen making dinner for Chase.

How domestic. This isn't even her dream life, but it's a dream life forced on centuries of women. Chase wouldn't foist this on her.

The water boils, and she fills the teapot, the little tea bag floating up as she pours. She sets the lid on it and carries it to the table. She splashes milk into a mug and adds a spoonful of sugar. Too agitated to sit and wait, she paces the floor.

What can she do to get answers? She hasn't explored the entire house yet, so when the tea finishes steeping, she carries a mug of it into the hallway. Her first stop is the den, where she and Chase have a home office. A desk dominates the room's center and faces the door. There's no closet, but two file cabinets and a wall of bookcases filled with books compensate for that lack. An armchair, a floor lamp beside it, tells her this is also their library. It's cozy though it doesn't have a fireplace. She wonders how they pay for it all if she's not working. She's not even going to school.

Chase continues his studies, but he's made it clear she's abandoned her studies for the duration of her pregnancy. This irritates her, but she refuses to dwell on it. If her instincts are correct, none of this is real, and trying to change her career path in a false reality would waste time. She must focus on escape. Since it's

Saturday, she assumes Chase will sleep in. She suspects he has a job, but she's not sure where, and she doesn't know the house's location. Are they in Niagara, close to his parents? Are they still in the city? The large backyard would indicate no since that would be much too expensive. Are they renting? Did they buy this place? Why can't she remember any of this?

Frustrated almost to the point of tears, Jaycie begins her search at the desk. The top of the desk is clean and organized. A laptop sits on it, in front of the ergonomic chair. Reference books, propped between a pair of bookends, stand behind the laptop. A two-tier tray sits at the desk's top-right corner. The upper tier is empty; the bottom contains a piece of paper. She examines the paper. A utility bill. They've had this house for at least a month, because the bill is for a full thirty days. How can that be? She presses her hands to her pelvis. In Hades, she was barely three months pregnant. She doesn't look much more than that now. How could they have a house she doesn't remember getting or moving into?

"Jaycie?" Chase stands in the doorway, his brows raised. He's wearing a robe and slippers. "Everything okay? What are you doing?"

"I couldn't sleep." That doesn't quite answer his question, but she doesn't know what else to say. How can she trust him? If he's part of this fake world, would anything she tell him go straight to the world's creator? Or is she in a bubble all her own with this reality self-contained and running on automatic? The prospect she might be in this all alone terrifies her.

My baby. What if I'm asleep somewhere, and my baby's not here with me? She rubs her tummy as if willing the child inside to exist here, but the uneasiness doesn't abate.

"What are you doing here?"

"Nothing." She wants to question him so badly it hurts. If it were the real Chase, she could ask him anything, but she doesn't know who this man actually is.

"I have to get ready for work. Did you want to get breakfast started?"

So she's really the housewife here. She's tempted to toss out sarcasm but holds back. "I assumed you'd want to sleep in."

"Can't take a day off. If I don't meet with the project group on weekends, we'll fall behind."

"Okay." If he leaves, she can snoop to her heart's content. In fact, if he leaves, she can cast a spell, and isn't it about time she used her powers to help herself? She has no one else. If her body lies hidden somewhere, if gods have captured her, she can't sit around and wait for rescue. Even if she lacks Chase's powerful natural abilities and hasn't progressed far in her formal studies, she's still a decent mage. She wasn't first in her program, but she was in the top ten, and she'd worked damn hard to get there.

She beams a smile at Chase. "Bacon and eggs okay?"

He returns the grin, his features flashing relief. "Thanks. I'll jump in the shower." He walks away.

Jaycie sets the utility bill back in the tray and follows him from the room.

***

"Hi, Mom." Jaycie sits at the desk in the den and struggles not to sob into the phone. She hunted for a cell phone and found it on the nightstand next to her side of the bed. Her usual password unlocked it, and even her contact list remains intact. Whoever set up this charade did a great job.

Almost. They haven't quite fooled me. They couldn't give me memories I never formed.

"Oh, hello." Her mother sounds puzzled.

Why? Don't we talk regularly? "How are you?"

There's a pause, and then her mother says, "Is everything all right?"

Jaycie doesn't hesitate. "Of course. Why do you ask?"

"We talked yesterday."

No, we didn't. She doesn't say it aloud. If her mother believes it happened, she'll accept that, in some sense, it did.

"I'd like to have lunch together. Tomorrow."

"It's a little last minute, don't you think?"

"We could meet ... Where would you want to meet for lunch? My treat." As she says this, she doesn't know how she'll pay for it or how she'll get to the restaurant. Does she have a car? She at least knows now where she is. The address on the utility bill named the city as North Tkaronto. Not the city core, but not the boonies. She assumes they rent the house. They'd have to have millions to buy a home here, but if this is all a dream, she needn't worry about it. She has no idea where her parents live in this world, though.

"All right." Her mother heaves a weary sigh.

"Thank you." This isn't a surprise to Jaycie. Her relationship with her mother was always strained, especially since Jaycie left home for mage school. Her mother doesn't approve of magick. She's human. Jaycie's father is the born mage, and he changed careers and gave up magick for the sake of his marriage. Jaycie never understood that—which is why she refuses to accept she's given up her career for Chase and Chase demanded it. He always supported her career. They met at school, where she took mage training seriously. Never once did he suggest she give it up.

She grits her teeth against the fury arising from how trapped she feels in this situation.

Her mother names a restaurant Jaycie recognizes, and with relief, she sets the lunch date in the calendar on her phone. She'll get answers from her mother tomorrow and figure out how to escape this nightmare.

CHAPTER 19

"You think you're falling in love with me?" Kelsey asked, her voice breathless, hopeful.

"Against all that I believe, all that I want, yes."

"What could it hurt?" *A lot*, but she didn't want to accept that. He'd have to talk them both out of this folly, because she wanted to drop headlong into the abyss.

"We're doomed. The relationship's doomed."

She leaned back and met his gaze. "Why would you say that? I'm the negative one. I'm the one who thinks life sucks and then you die." If he held no hope for them, what chance did they have?

"Because it's the truth. Why didn't you want Josh involved with Dakota?"

"Oh, God. Because he'd die and she'd live lifetimes after."

His hand stroked her hair, and she shivered. Her body wanted his, and she had to face the reality that it would never happen. He wouldn't allow it.

"Exactly. He loved her, and she loved him—as much as teenagers are capable of love."

Kelsey hung her head. She'd fallen in love with Blair when they were in school. They were young, but they'd stayed together, married, and had Josh. She'd tried to force her own son to give up the girl he loved for practical reasons. Love wasn't practical. She never should've interfered. She looked up again when Philip spoke.

"I'll outlive you because I'll never turn you. I love you too much."

"You turned Josh."

"It was a mistake that'll always come between us."

Tears slid down her face. "It doesn't have to. The mistake was mine, not yours. I made you do it."

He shook his head. "I gave you the choice. I could've let him die, and you'd have hated me for it, but you hated me for turning him anyway." He tilted his head up and rested the back of it on the top of the couch, his gaze fixed on the ceiling.

"We'll get past this. I understand so much more about myself now. About you. Please. I don't want to live without you."

He closed his eyes. When he opened them again, he eased her onto the couch next to him and rose to his feet. The sudden loss of his physical presence created a chasm between them she wanted to leap, but if she clung to him, she'd make everything worse. If they were to have any chance at all, she'd have to be strong, not needy.

"If this relationship gets physical, we'll be trapped in it. We'll both want me to turn you. You don't understand what that would cost us."

The truth of what he said hit her. If he turned her

without going through proper channels, they'd both face legal ramifications beyond what they already faced for creating an undead Josh. If he didn't turn her, she'd die and he'd live forever with a hole in his heart. She lowered her head in defeat.

"You're right." Circumstances forced them to live together, but they'd never be together. "I love you, Philip."

When he didn't respond, she raised her head and met his gaze. The moment she did, he said, "I love you, too, Kelsey."

***

"Josh, we're home." Kelsey stepped from a misty-gray day into the cabin and searched for any sign of her son. Only silence greeted her.

Philip, carrying their bags, followed her inside and set them down in the foyer. "I'll find him."

The anxiety she'd released during their two nights at the spa returned full force. She swallowed, tamping down the rising panic. Just because Josh wasn't inside the cabin didn't mean something terrible had happened to him.

She forced calm into her voice. "Sure. I'll unpack while you do that."

He vanished into the mist, and she shut and locked the door behind him. She picked up her bag and carried it to her bedroom. The room was just as she'd left it: neat, clean, comfortable. She set the suitcase on the floor and popped it open. Not in the mood to unpack, she did it anyway to fill the time between now and whenever Philip returned with Josh. If she didn't keep busy, she'd stress about where her son was and how he'd spent the last few days.

After she finished her unpacking, they still weren't home. She strode out into the living room. Now what could she do? Her gaze scanned the room and landed on Philip's suitcase, still sitting on the foyer floor.

The least I can do is carry it into his room for him.

Holding the handle with two hands, she heaved the bag up and dragged it into the bedroom he shared with Josh. She set it upright just inside the door with a thud so loud she had to verify she hadn't dented the floor.

"What's he got in here, rocks?" she joked to the empty room. The only reply was silence. Even Kelsey didn't laugh.

She seized the opportunity to snoop despite how much her conscience niggled her while she did it. The furnishings in here were simple but comfortable. Twin beds stuck out into the center of the room, their headboards resting against the wall on either side of the window. Each bed had a nightstand beside it, and Josh and Philip shared a highboy at the other end of the room. There was no mirror but not because vampires couldn't see their reflections. It was a guy thing. Vampires didn't grow whiskers if they didn't have them when they turned, so they didn't need a mirror to shave. Both Philip and Josh had been clean-shaven at their time of death.

Not death. When they became vampires. She refused to acknowledge that to become a vampire they had to cross through an instant of death: no heartbeat, no brain activity. She'd read articles so she'd know what Josh had endured at that moment, but she avoided thinking about it. Otherwise, wondering if what Philip had revived was indeed Josh and not some demon inhabiting his body would drive her mad.

Everything appeared undisturbed. The beds were both neatly made. No clothes lay strewn about the floor. Josh had become much tidier and more organized as a vampire. She missed his teenage sloppiness and their fights over her necessity to pick up after him. She'd resented his bad habits then, but she'd have given her life to have him throw his towel on the floor one more time.

What a ridiculous thing to pine for, but it wasn't his inconsiderateness she missed. She missed his humanness, his normal teenage-boy behavior. That had all vanished, fangs and bloodlust replacing them. She buried her head in her hands and prayed Philip would find her son.

***

The mist grew thicker the closer Philip got to the lake. The temperature had risen, moistening the air. Hard-packed snow and ice crunched under his boots as he made his way down to the rocky shore. They'd moved the floating dock away from the spot in the lake directly in front of the cabin. It spent the winter in a small inlet, where it rested on the shore, protected from the damaging ice coating the lake. Josh had punched a hole where the dock floated in the milder seasons, and Philip found the young man's boots, hat, bandanna, and gloves a few feet away.

Uncertain how long before Josh returned from his underwater excursion, Philip sat in the snow to wait. He stared out across the lake and sent out psychic feelers to check on the boy. Nothing seemed amiss when they'd discovered the cabin empty, so Philip wasn't worried, but he hated how upset Kelsey got whenever Josh went to the lake. No matter how much Philip tried to tell her neither cold nor water would hurt a vampire, she continued to fret about it.

The wait lasted another twenty minutes.

Water splashed up from the hole in the ice, and Josh's head poked out. He hauled himself up and met Philip's gaze without a hint of surprise.

"She send you?"

"You mean your mom?" Philip frowned, annoyed at the boy's tone. He tried to recall if he'd been this obnoxious as a baby vamp but couldn't. It probably didn't matter. Philip had been in his forties when he'd turned; Josh, a teenager. Likely, some of the kid's angst was a symptom of his human age at the time he became a vampire.

"Whatever."

Yup. A teenager and a baby vamp. Through gritted teeth, Philip said, "Not 'whatever.' She loves you."

"We've discussed this before. Nothing's changed."

"Something has. You're not the same asshole you were in the beginning."

Josh belly crawled over to Philip's side. He sat up and slipped on his boots and other items. "Do you want to hear about Dakota?"

Philip nodded and dropped the argument about Kelsey. "You got in and out okay, I assume, since you're here and in one piece."

"Yeah. No problem."

"You saw her?" If Philip would've had a breath to hold, he'd have held it.

"Yeah. She didn't recognize me. I made sure the glamour held. It was tough, but I pulled it off." The kid's voice held unmistakable pride, so Philip validated it.

"Good job. I know how difficult that can be, the effort it takes."

Josh beamed. If Kelsey could see him now, it would break her heart.

"How'd she look? Is that faerie muckety-muck treating her well?"

Josh stared out over the frozen lake. "Looks that way. She seemed ... content, if not happy." The way he said that put Philip on alert.

"So what, then? Anything wrong?"

The boy shrugged. "She shouldn't be there."

"I won't dispute that, but it's where she chooses to be." Where was he going with this?

"Yes, but I don't like it."

"We never liked it. The decision was hers. You're not planning to mess with the fae, are you?"

Josh snapped his gaze away from the lake and stared into Philip's eyes. "Not at all."

"Because the last time we tangled with the fae, we brought the wrath of Frank Evans's criminal organization down on us and you ended up a vampire."

"I won't mess with the fae."

Again, uneasiness jabbed at Philip. Josh sounded as if he meant it, but his phrasing seemed awfully precise. "You don't mess with Dakota, either."

"Like you said, she made her choice."

"Exactly."

Philip opened his mouth to suggest they get back to the cabin when Josh interrupted him. "I've had memories return."

"What memories?"

Josh gazed out over the lake. "About before. With my mother."

"Do they frighten you?" Is that why the boy had

treated Kelsey so rudely?

"No. Confusing, more like."

"What did you remember?"

"The bookstore. Living at my mom's." His expression turned anxious.

A wave of relief flowed through Philip. For the first time since Josh had turned, he wanted to talk about his previous life with his mother. It was a good sign. The kid just needed some reassurance, so Philip offered it. "You're fine. You're evolving—getting back some of your past. It's normal."

The worry left the boy's eyes and he nodded. "All right. She home now?"

"Yes."

"I'm ready to see her again."

Philip rose and offered the boy a hand up, and the pair strolled back to the cabin.

**

Kelsey didn't realize she was crying until she heard the cabin's front door bang open and an icy breeze hit her wet face. She swiped at her cheeks and strolled from the guys' bedroom, plastering a neutral expression onto her face.

"What were you doing in our room?" Josh's brusque tone stabbed at her heart.

Every time he spoke to her, it felt as if he shoved a stake into her chest. She'd thought things had improved before she and Philip left for the spa, but now she wondered if she'd dreamed it.

"I put Philip's bag into the room for him." She refused to act offended and chide him for his suspicions. Maybe if she placated him, he'd recover some of what they'd shared just three short days ago even though it wasn't much compared to what they'd had before he became a vampire. And it was difficult to get indignant when she had, in fact, snooped through the room. That she'd found nothing helpful escalated her guilt over it.

Philip closed and locked the door. "It's fine, Josh."

Both vampires removed hats, gloves, and bandannas and dropped them into the basket beside the door.

Kelsey's gaze met Philip's. She raised her brows and silently asked where he'd found her son.

Philip shook his head in response, warning her to keep quiet.

Water dripped from Josh's clothes and hair. He'd been in the lake.

She bit her lip to keep from shouting at him.

He didn't feel the cold, he'd never feel the cold, and he couldn't drown. Why did he flee to the water so often? He refused to explain himself, and she'd have to accept that.

She strolled across the room, passing Josh without touching him though every fiber of her being wanted to hug him and kiss his face. To avoid further conversation, she walked into her room.

She contemplated picking up a book to read when her gaze shifted to the window. The mist had dispersed, and a weak sun filtered through the gray-tinged clouds.

"You okay, darling?" Philip sauntered into the room, closing the door behind him. "I know you don't want him near the lake, but he's safe."

She turned to meet his gaze. "I understand. It's just that he left without ..." Her eyes widened.

He nodded his understanding, and his expression grew sympathetic. "Without even leaving a note," he finished for her. "He's a grown man even if he's still a baby vamp. You can't control him."

"No, but I can expect a little common courtesy. We're in hiding. What if something had happened to him? How would we know?"

"For one, Josh and I have a psychic connection. I'm his maker. If he were in danger, I'd know it."

She scowled at him. "You're just telling me this now?"

He ran a hand through his hair. "I guess. It never occurred to me to mention it before."

"But you see me upset about his comings and goings. Why didn't you try to ease my worry?"

"I'm sorry. I should've told you. It was just one more vampire trait I assumed would upset you."

Her tone hopeful, she asked, "Can he sense you, too? If you're in danger, would Josh know?"

She wasn't sure if her son would tell her if something happened to Philip. She hoped so, but he never kept her in the loop on anything. Still, if Philip was away from home and didn't return, she could at least ask Josh. Surely, he'd tell her if she asked.

"Yes."

She blew out a relieved breath. "Okay then."

She eyed the dirty clothes overflowing the laundry basket from when she'd unpacked her suitcase. A glance at the time told her it was getting late. No sense starting that chore now.

"I'll get dinner going." She headed for the door, but as she passed Philip, he put a hand on her shoulder, stopping her.

"He's fine. I spoke to him. All's well." He kept his

voice low, conspiratorial.

She studied him a moment before she replied.

He appeared calm, unconcerned. Either he was a great actor or she had nothing to worry about.

"All right," she said.

He released her, and she left the room.

CHAPTER 20

"**S**ir, your guest has arrived." The butler stepped aside and ushered Frank Evans into the den of Risto Fina's palatial Tkaronto home. The moment Evans entered the room, the butler bowed to Fina and left, closing the ornately carved dark wood door after him. Evans strode forward, his head turning this way and that, his one functioning eye taking in the opulent room.

The circular room stood two stories high and comprised two levels. Open railings provided views of the bookcases, floor-to-ceiling windows, wall sconces, and artwork that mirrored the decor on the first floor.

The master mage set down the book he'd been reading on a nearby table and rose from his chair. "Welcome, please, sit." Fina swept his arm around to indicate the rich leather sofa. Before it stood a coffee table laden with trays of pastries with coffee and tea service.

"Thank you." Evans held out his hand, and the two men shook before the mob boss took a seat in the designated spot.

Fina, who already had a cup filled with coffee on the table beside him, picked it up and sipped. "I've told the servants to give us privacy, so it's self-serve today. Help yourself."

Evans nodded and went through the motions of pouring coffee and doctoring it with milk.

"How's the family?" Fina asked though he didn't care.

Evans sipped from his cup and then settled back in his seat. "Fine, fine. I appreciate you seeing me so quickly."

"Anything for an old friend." They weren't friends, more acquaintances, but Fina had his own reasons for wanting to deepen the relationship right now. Evans didn't need to know he had resources Fina wanted, but it wouldn't hurt to make the mob boss believe the two had a stronger bond than they did.

"Thank you. I'm hoping you can help me with a serious problem."

"Tell me and we'll see."

"My men discovered a security breach at one of the fae portals." Evans set his cup and saucer on the table. Picking up a dessert plate, he daintily set an oatmeal cookie on it. "A young man entered their realm. I had my boys install hunting cameras to monitor comings and goings. The lad entered disguised as one of the fae, but when he left, he dropped the glamour and revealed himself." Evans bit into the cookie and chewed.

Fina waited.

Evans swallowed the morsel and continued. "Turns out he's someone I'd thought was dead. Someone I need to find urgently."

Fina understood now why the mob boss had

contacted him. "You want me to track him."

"Him and, hopefully, his mother and the vampire they're with."

"Haven't you tried using magick to track them already?"

Fina deduced Evans wanted Philip Belanger and the woman who disappeared the same night as the vampire. News reports identified her as a potential witness to at least one murder in her bookstore café. They'd identified the killer—had him cold—but her family and the authorities were also concerned for her safety. Fina doubted Evans worried Kelsey Davis was a kidnap victim in danger. If anything, the danger would come from Evans if he ever caught up to her.

"I did, but they failed."

Obviously, or you wouldn't be here. Evans's bad luck was Fina's good fortune. "And you assume I can succeed where the top magi didn't? You flatter me."

"Master Fina, you have levels of power few, if any, can rival. If you help me with this, I'd be eternally grateful."

Fina smiled. "Happy to help."

Evans returned the grin. "Wonderful. When can we get started?"

***

Each of Kerberos's three dog heads trained its gaze on Chase. Drool dripped from each open mouth, the fangs glinting in the lava-orange light outside the cave opening that led to Hades. Snakes grew from each death-dog head, and the creature pawed at the ground with lion claws. The serpent tail on his hindquarters whipped back and forth in a potentially killing blow.

All the heads growled in unison.

"Good doggie." Chase's hands shook as he raised his arm to show the hell beast the three juicy steaks he'd conjured as a bribe. If this didn't work, he'd perish here, and then Kerberos would let him in without the bribe—but not out again. Nevertheless, Chase refused to back down. He wouldn't be the first mortal to slip past the beast, but he had to hurry.

When he'd first arrived, he'd expected to toss one steak to the animal and, as it munched, slide past, but when he saw the size of the creature, he'd backed off and conjured two more. He'd have a better chance of keeping it distracted with food if a separate treat occupied each head.

He crept closer to the slavering beast. It leaped forward, but the chain tethering him to the cave's entrance snapped taut and jerked him back. The heads yelped, and Chase used that moment to set the steaks near the hound's farthest reach. Forcing the creature to work for his meal added precious seconds to Chase's opportunity to race past it.

The second the steaks hit the ground, the dog lunged at them, and Chase barreled forward. He ran headlong, barely watching where he stepped, his sole aim to get beyond the reach of the dog's snapping jaws.

The bathrobe he wore wasn't conducive to racing past a hellhound. It tangled around his legs, and he pitched forward, executing a roll that impressed him even as he feared breaking his neck. He slid, hoping against hope he'd land out of biting distance. By the time he stopped and turned to make sure he'd cleared the gate, the steaks were gone and the hound snapped its jaws once more in Chase's direction—from at least a ten-foot distance.

"Sorry, pup. Had to do it, but you at least got steaks out of it."

Kerberos only snarled in response, so Chase backed away and then continued his journey down the tunnel.

He didn't get far when Cora appeared before him.

***

"Come quickly. You can't stay here." Cora hooked her arm through Chase's and started pulling him along—back in the direction from which he'd come.

He dug his heels into the dirt floor and yanked her back. "Not a chance. Not without Jaycie."

She snarled at him, her eyes flashing fire. "You little fool. You shouldn't be here at all. Don't you realize the risk you're taking?"

He took a sharp breath in and instantly regretted it as he sucked in an odor of rotten egg. *Sulfur.* Reek from the volcano. Or demons?

"If you know something I don't, tell me. Otherwise, help me get Jaycie out of here." Panic rose in him when he remembered the two had vanished together. Why wasn't Jaycie with Cora? He clutched at his birth mother with both hands and gripped the skirt of the goddess gown she wore.

"Where is she? What happened to her?" His heart thudded painfully in his chest. What if he'd lost her forever, lost their baby?

"Shh." It came out as an angry hiss rather than a gentle soothing. "She's safe. Now let's go before we're discovered."

He fisted his hands on his hips and thrust out his chin. "Not without Jaycie. Where is she?"

"In a safe place. Don't argue with me. We'll get her

before she gives birth." She grabbed his arm and tugged, but he didn't budge.

"Damn it, Cora, she's the love of my life. She's carrying my child. I'm not leaving her in Hades." He tried to keep his voice low but only half succeeded. The last part he almost shouted.

She shook her head and gave an exasperated huff. "She's asleep. Safe. In Hecate's basement."

Something in her tone tweaked his intuition. He dropped his hands to his sides and frowned. "What do you mean 'asleep'?"

A look of pride flashed across Cora's face. "Clever lad. Hypnos and Morpheus have given me aid to contain her. One has put her to sleep, and the other has given her dreams. Don't worry. She's dreaming her perfect life, and she'll continue to do so happily until we return to wake her."

Chase's jaw dropped, and his horror grew more profound as his brain processed what that all meant. "You've put her under a spell from which she can't wake? What's wrong with you? I'm not leaving her like that."

A frown of worry crossed her face. "You don't understand."

"I completely understand. You've got her living some fake twilight life she can't escape."

"Better that than Hades getting his hands on her, and he will if you don't cut it out and come with me."

He continued to resist, and his strength and stubbornness held him in place. "What would Hades want with Jaycie?"

"Not now. Come on, please. You're putting her in danger the longer you stay here." The urgency in her voice put enough doubt in his head that he hesitated.

Even so, the thought of leaving Jaycie in a strange place—Hades, no less—in what amounted to a coma overruled his doubt.

"If I take her home, I'll keep her safe. You only need explain to me what's going on." He spun on his heel and stalked away from Cora. After a few feet, he paused and looked back. "I could use your help." Asking for help had always been difficult for him, but he'd learned recently that things worked out much better when he admitted he needed a hand.

She stared at him, looking as if she contemplated leaving him there, but after a moment, she strode to his side. "You'll regret this. We'll both regret this, but if you insist, then I'll help you." She put a hand on his shoulder. "Hades will want you, too. You must be careful we're not discovered. He'll know you're my son, and he might kill you, kill Jaycie for carrying your child."

Chase gulped. "Why? Why would the god of the underworld care about me, my girlfriend, or my baby?"

She met his gaze, and when she spoke, her words seared through him. "My real name is Persephone. Hades is my husband."

CHAPTER 21

L ocator spells didn't work. Spells drawing on the laws of correspondence didn't work. Conjuring spells didn't work—not that he'd expected them to. Fina had never used them to locate a person before, but he'd grown desperate. All the usual methods of a missing person search using magick failed him.

Fina took down the circle he'd cast in his basement room and put away his tools. He'd avoided entering this room ever since Chase vanished into the spirit world. It reminded him too much of the work they'd done together, and it also reminded him that time slipped away and Cora wasn't back with the boy.

Nothing he worked on lately succeeded, and it grated on his nerves and scorched his ego. Unfortunately, the more infuriated he got over it, the worse the outcome of everything he attempted. He couldn't afford to let emotion cloud his judgment and interfere with his abilities, and he didn't understand this surge of emotion. He'd spent years erecting a shield of detachment around himself.

Frank Evans had called that morning, probably to ask for a progress report, and Fina let voicemail answer it. He refused to admit to Evans that he'd failed in the task like every other mage. A solution existed—he just needed more time to find it.

From his altar, he picked up the three photos he'd used in this latest spell, intending to put them away. He paused to examine each one.

The first was a photo of Josh Davis. Fina focused his search on the boy because that's who Evans's men had caught on their security cameras outside the faerie ring.

Every spell he'd used to track the boy's energy had failed. He couldn't explain it. It was as if the kid had vanished into another dimension.

Maybe he did.

The master mage huffed out a frustrated breath. He'd even visited the faerie ring to track the boy from his last known location but had found no trace of human energy spoor anywhere. Somehow, the kid had scrubbed any trace of his presence.

The photo Fina examined was a still from the trail camera set up outside the faerie portal. The figure in the image was a bit blurry, as if he'd been snapped in motion, but it was unmistakably Josh Davis. Other, clearer, photos of the boy existed, but Fina used this fuzzy one because it was the last known photo of the boy and placed him alive and well on the physical plane. A great clue, a perfect item for a locater spell, and it'd failed utterly.

Fina picked up the next photo, this one of Philip Belanger. It came from a surveillance camera inside Frank Evans's home.

Belanger and the two Davises had visited Evans

shortly before they disappeared, and cameras recorded them entering through the front door.

Belanger's image, too, was slightly blurred, but that was because he was a vampire. Either Belanger didn't know about the cameras or didn't care if they photographed him. He hadn't used vampire tricks to disguise himself or make himself invisible to the camera. Carelessness? Stupidity?

I don't think so.

Belanger and Evans were friends once. Business associates.

The vampire trusted Evans. That's the only thing that made sense.

Fina held the two images next to each other. The blurriness on Josh Davis looked identical to the blur across Philip Belanger.

"My gods," Fina said aloud. "The kid is a vampire." That was why he'd left no human energy traces. *Belanger turned him.*

He dropped the two photos onto the table and picked up the one of Kelsey Davis. This, too, came from the security cameras at Frank Evans's home. No vampire blur on this one, but he didn't expect to see it.

Other images from the same visit captured Josh as well, without the blur, which confirmed both Davises were human when they visited Evans. Too bad no photos of Kelsey Davis existed from after the trio's disappearance.

If Belanger had turned mother and son into vampires, it made sense they'd gone into hiding. Belanger could've destroyed Frank Evans to get him off his tail, but if he'd broken the law as well, a law that came with a death penalty, then the vanishing act made a lot more sense.

Fina scooped up the other two photos and moved to set all three into the box in which he stored them when a locket Kelsey wore around her neck caught his eye.

He'd seen that necklace before, and it remained in his possession. Chase had dropped it when he'd crossed into Hades.

Fina's hand trembled, and in his excitement, he almost dropped the photo. The necklace belonged to Kelsey Davis, and somehow, Chase ended up with it, whether by accident or design.

Finally, a solution to my tracking problem. I'll locate all three fugitives with one more spell and call Frank Evans with the good news.

***

The basement holds the key to her escape. Jaycie heads downstairs after Chase falls asleep for the night. She examined the rest of the house earlier and suspects the basement holds all the magick tools and equipment. Her guess is correct.

She steps into a finished rec room with area carpets over ceramic-tile floors and pale-yellow walls lined with storage units. All their magick tools, herbs, incense—everything required to cast a spell—line the shelves. A water cooler in the corner and a bar fridge next to a sink make getting water and storing perishable ingredients convenient.

Out of habit, she places her hands under her belly button, lacing her fingers together. She takes comfort from her growing baby's presence, and the thought of her little girl firms her resolve to return to the physical world.

It has crossed her mind that if she doesn't her body will go into labor one day and deliver her child to whatever god trapped her here. In this world, she'll believe she has her baby and is raising her—unless once her sleeping self gives birth, she ceases to be useful. They might let her die then.

She swallows past a lump in her throat and is tempted to execute a spell immediately, but the risk of discovery is too great. She'll wait until she returns from meeting with her mother while Chase is still at work.

With luck, this will be her final night in dreamland.

CHAPTER 22

A Christmas tree filled the living room window. Kelsey draped strings of popcorn across it. She laughed at the horrible job she was doing, but their preparations for Christmas had buoyed her spirits more than expected. She hadn't even planned to celebrate Christmas. Why bother? The vampires didn't care about it, and she'd lost faith in religion and God and the birth of baby Jesus. Then Philip had dragged the pine tree into the house when he and Josh returned from one of their hunting trips, and she found herself making popcorn and creating decorations for it. She even contemplated what she would buy the two men in her life. She planned to shop online and have Philip pick up the packages at the nearby town's post office where they had a PO Box.

"What's funny?" Philip asked. He sat on the couch, watching her and sipping hot mulled cider. He refused to buy alcohol even though she insisted she was done with drinking her troubles away.

"This." She waved a hand at the tree. "Such a mess,

but I'm having a wonderful time."

He smiled and sipped his drink. "I'll help you in a moment, but I'm enjoying just watching you."

Her heart still ached when they shared intimate moments. Such a domestic scene, but they couldn't do what came naturally or enjoy what everyone else in the world had. It wasn't fair—and if she dwelled on it, she'd break down in front of him, maybe even beg him for alcohol. She refused to drop to such depths again.

Life isn't fair, cupcake; suck it up. Somehow, when she was firm with herself, it eased her angst. *Just live in the moment.* She'd never understood what that meant, but now she realized it meant she should accept her circumstances and focus on the right now. Things were good—not perfect but good—and she appreciated that.

It'd be much better if Josh didn't insist on swimming under the ice. She worried he'd get trapped down there, but he dismissed her concerns, and she accepted she couldn't control him. The less she thought of him as her son, the better he treated her, she noticed. They now managed an uneasy camaraderie, which enhanced her Christmassy mood.

Philip set his empty mug on the coffee table and rose, still beaming the smile at her. "You've done a great job of—"

The front door crashed open and banged into the wall. Josh sped into the house. He slammed the door closed and locked it. If Kelsey didn't know better, she'd think he was out of breath. Water dripped from him, and his expression betrayed panic. He spun around to face Kelsey and Philip.

"They've found us."

***

Josh had barely finished speaking when Philip sprang into action.

"Turn off the lights," he ordered Kelsey. He flew to each window, closing the interior shutters as he did. With his vampire speed, it took only seconds. He verified the back door was locked and raced to his bedroom closet. From the top shelf, he took down a lockbox and used a key from the keyring in his pocket to open it. He lifted out the gun and its bullets, armed the weapon, and returned to the living room.

Kelsey was just stepping from the kitchen, feeling her way in the fresh darkness. She smelled of fear and panic.

"I'm here." He whispered so he wouldn't scare her when he touched her, and then he took her hand. "Come. They can't hurt me and Josh, but they can kill you."

"They can hurt you. Or are you pretending silver and wooden stakes don't exist?"

"If they're cops, they'll want us alive. If it's Evans's men, they're only human. I'm not afraid of them." He led her to the couch and sat her on it. "Stay there. Stay low."

She gasped, clutching after him when he released her hand and tried to step away. "No, don't leave me. I won't let you go out there."

"I'm not going anywhere. When we leave, we'll leave together—and we have to leave now that they know our location." Venom laced his voice.

How the hell did they find us? He was so careful about putting up wards and protections, sealing them into their little cocoon of invulnerability.

Not quite invulnerable, or they wouldn't have found us. He squelched a frustrated scream, and a surge of hate and violence made him want to run out into the night and snap all their necks. He forced calm down his throat and focused on what mattered instead.

"Josh!" He didn't search for the boy—Philip sensed him in the back of the house.

"Father." He appeared in the hallway.

"What happened? Did they follow you here?"

Josh frowned mockingly. "Of course not. I spotted them; they didn't spot me. Two men and a vampire."

Shit. Which vampire? It made sense that if Philip and his former business partner and fellow fugitive, Dwayne, no longer worked with Evans he'd find a replacement. Hopefully, just the one, or they were really screwed. Outpacing another vamp would be much more difficult.

"Where were they?" He had to decide what to do: stay or risk leaving the relative safety of the cabin to escape into the forest.

"Close. They're heading this way. Not fast. They're hiking in. Parked about a mile away."

"You saw the car?"

"That's how I spotted them. I was hunting. I heard the vehicle and checked it out. When they stopped, I saw all three of them. I recognized the two humans as Evans's men. Then I sensed the vampire. I came here immediately."

"They'll be here soon, then. We can assume they know we're in this cabin." *But how?* He'd worry about that later. He made his decision. "We're leaving. Don't bother to pack. Grab your cash and identification and let's go." He waved to Josh, indicating he should hurry, and rushed to Kelsey's side.

Even in the dark he could see she was wide-eyed with terror.

"Philip." She said only that, but it speared his heart.

"It'll be okay. I promise." The vow held good intentions, but he didn't know if he could honor it with a vampire on their tail. Philip feared no man, but he didn't want to tangle with another vampire. It would be a fight to the death, and he didn't want to risk Kelsey's and Josh's lives. He didn't want to lose his own life either, not now. Kelsey and her son needed him alive. If he was gone, who'd protect them? Evans would have them at his mercy.

That spurred him on.

"Come on." He took her arm and helped her stand. "Grab what you need and let's go. Nothing more than you can carry in your pockets. Josh and I need your help."

Her fear eased, and he sensed determination replace panic. She raced into her bedroom. A moment later, she reappeared. Her eyes had adjusted by now to the darkness, and she walked more confidently.

When Josh returned from the bedroom, Philip motioned for them to follow him. He had nothing in the bedroom he needed. He always kept his wallet, credit cards, and other identification on him. Their fake passports and anything too bulky to carry he'd stowed in a safe-deposit box at the bank. He'd made sure they could move out in seconds if the need arose, but he hadn't expected it to.

When he peered through the back door, he didn't see anyone, so he cracked it open. He listened, Kelsey and Josh standing patiently behind him.

Trees rustled in the breeze. An animal raced through the underbrush. When Philip spotted the hawk in the sky, he understood why the smaller creature, a snowshoe hare, exuded such panic. For a second, panic of his own overlapped that of the hare, and he commiserated with it telepathically. Giving it a push, he helped it race into its burrow. The hawk gave an angry squawk and flew away.

Philip stepped outside and moved aside to let Kelsey, who now wore a parka and winter boots, and Josh walk past him. The pair waited on the back deck while Philip locked up. Evans's posse would have to break into the cottage to learn their quarry had already escaped. It would buy the fugitives time but not much. The vampire would pick up their trail quickly.

With a nod, Philip took the lead and headed into the forest.

CHAPTER 23

"Well, dear, to what do I owe the pleasure?" Donna Nevil asks when Jaycie arrives at the table where her mother sits.

The restaurant where they agreed to meet is neither posh nor cheap. The establishment boasts a bright and cheery ambience with tables not too tightly packed and offering seating for at least seventy patrons. Each table seats four and can be pushed together should a larger party require it. Shouts and laughter in the bar area punctuate a low buzz of conversation in the dining room. Aromas of garlic, freshly baked bread, and roasting meat waft through the air, and Jaycie's mouth waters. As soon as she sits, she helps herself to a fresh roll from the basket and a butter curl from the dish beside it.

Donna, as always, looks neat, trim, elegant. She wears her chestnut hair in a casual upsweep that must've taken ages to perfect. The cream suit she has on sets off her tanned skin, and her makeup is understated, enhancing her natural beauty rather than coating her face. Jaycie's mother, who detests magick, uses some to boost her appearance without recognizing the hypocrisy.

This feminine style is a sharp contrast to her daughter's casual one. Jaycie's shoulder-length, medium-brown hair, as usual, is tied into a ponytail. She wears jeans and a T-shirt—her good jeans and good T-shirt, but her mother disapproves anyway. Donna's mouth turns down and her eyes squinch as she speaks, making Jaycie self-conscious. When Jaycie hooks a backpack over the back of the seat, Mom frowns and shakes her head but doesn't comment.

Jaycie's tomboy fashion sense always annoys her mother. Once, the budding mage would've accommodated Donna and worn a dress, but those days are well past. Years ago, when Jaycie accepted her mother would never think her enough, would never praise her, she metaphorically threw up her hands and vowed to do as she pleased. Donna's frown of disapproval sends a flash of smugness through Jaycie. How could this be a dream if such details are so accurate?

The information must come from my brain. It must.

Can she use this to her advantage? Make her mother approve of her for once? It's possible, but only if Jaycie can sell herself on the idea of a mother who loves her unconditionally, and that'll never happen. She's stuck with the mother she's always had.

Look who's not loving unconditionally now.

"I'm worried about Chase." Jaycie automatically takes the napkin from the place setting before her, opens it, and drapes it across her lap. Donna's gaze follows each motion, and her frown smooths out a little, the closest to approval Jaycie gets.

"What's wrong?" The worry in Donna's voice sounds genuine, but Jaycie doesn't trust it. In the real world, she never introduced her mother to her boyfriend. She doesn't believe her mother would accept him—especially after his so very public disgrace.

"He's working a lot. It's too much for him to carry everything alone. I should get a job." She's taking a risk veering into this territory, but if it triggers her mother, she might get careless enough to spill useful information. A suggestion to work outside the home ought to do it.

Donna smiles—fake, sympathetic—and reaches a hand across the table to pat Jaycie's arm.

The server appears and flashes the pair a smile— genuine, eager. Jaycie returns it. Her mother retracts her arm and beams at the young man.

"Afternoon, ladies. I'm Rick, your server for today. Would you like drinks to start?" He glances at the menus sitting unopened on the table.

"I'll have the white house wine, please, and my daughter will have a sparkling water."

Jaycie flashes annoyance at her mother and corrects her even though sparkling water is what she wants to order. "Make mine a cranberry juice with sparkling water, please."

"Of course. Would you like a few minutes to decide on your food order?"

Donna responds briskly before Jaycie can open her mouth. "Yes, thank you."

Jaycie nods to participate in the decision.

The server leaves, and Jaycie picks up the menu. She flips to the sandwiches and zeroes in on the turkey club. It comes with salad or fries. Her mother would want her to have the salad. Jaycie chooses the fries. She snaps the menu closed at the same time as her mother closes hers. Jaycie regrets they didn't figure out what to eat before the server showed up. That will extend the time she spends with Mom.

"You know, dear, he's working hard to support you and that baby you're carrying." She says "that baby" as though it's a parasite invading Jaycie's body. Technically, that's true, since it would die without sustenance from its host, but tears spring to Jaycie's eyes. Fake or real, this world has replicated her mother exactly. Jaycie spent her entire life feeling like a parasite sucking her mother dry.

"He doesn't have to. We're partners. I should do my share of earning money."

"With what? You didn't finish mage school, and I, for one, am happy you quit."

Okay, so that explains school. "Maybe I should go back. I had potential."

"Honey, there's no need. He's managing. It's unseemly for girls to work magick."

"How can you say that? How can you think that?" Jaycie grits her teeth. Her mother's beliefs hearken back to a time before the species war. Species World War I though, so far, SWWII doesn't seem likely. She hopes they've all learned their lessons from the devastating first war. She assumes those in charge labeled it as the first war to distinguish it from the human world wars, or they'd have labeled it WWIII.

When the world unmasqued and the hypernatural species revealed themselves on the physical plane, conflict ensued. The vampires sought control, and it took an alliance between magi, shifters, and humans to quell the uprising. Most hypernaturals came with antiquated ideals, and some humans eagerly embrace those beliefs. Jaycie agrees with the majority of people that females are entitled to equality. Her mother follows the old views.

Donna gazes over Jaycie's shoulder and shakes her head. "Not now. Shh."

The server steps up to the table. "Ready to order?"

Jaycie jumps in ahead of her mother. "Yes, I'll have the turkey club with fries, please." She smiles sweetly at her mother's sour expression.

***

Silence blankets the house when Jaycie enters, still unsettled from the visit with her mother. A driverless cab brought her home, similar to the one that had transported her to the restaurant. She doesn't own a car in this reality either, and Chase takes his to work. She learned the night before he works at the municipal offices. Somehow, he's landed a government job, and he speaks of running for mayor. Of Tkaronto. Jaycie thinks that's absurd. Chase wouldn't aspire to mayor, but he talks about it enthusiastically enough and credits his birth father with putting him on that path. The thought of it makes her head spin. Could Risto Fina have put her in this dream world?

Whoever did it holds her here with magick, she's certain of it. The only escape would also be through magick, and she'll have to cast the spell herself. She's not sure what effect working magick can have if she's doing it in a dream world, but she's heard of active dreaming and thinks its principles might help her here. In active, or lucid, dreaming, the dreamer is aware they're asleep and can often take control of what happens in the dream. In typical dreams, the realization you're in one can wake you up. If Jaycie is correct, and this is a spell-induced dream, she needs more than awareness of the situation to escape from it; otherwise, she'd already be awake.

She checks the time and is relieved she has at least three hours before Chase arrives. Part of her—a tiny part—wants to keep the dream going. She loves living with Chase, but the core of who she is refuses to accept domesticity and focusing on her husband's career at the expense of her own. Whoever put her under doesn't know her so well, or she'd have a career here. That means they couldn't pull all information from her mind. She sends gratitude out for this small favor that her sleep prison isn't so perfect it lulls her into staying.

She goes to the master bedroom and, after removing the glass bottle of water from her backpack, she drops the bag in the closet. It doesn't contain much: her wallet, a book, her cell phone, some makeup she never uses, and a packet of tissues. The wallet holds her identification, her credit and debit cards, and cash Chase gave her. She examined everything in the bag the night before when Chase handed her the money, solicitously stating he wanted to make sure she had enough. It grates. More than anything, she cherishes her independence. It gives her the impetus she needs to execute a release spell and get the hell out of here.

The bookshelves in the home office hold the spell books she needs to get started. She zeroes in on the one she wants and removes it from the shelf. Opening it, she locates the relevant information and heads into the basement.

CHAPTER 24

"Why aren't we taking the car?" Kelsey panted from the exertion of wading through foot-deep snow.

"We're done with that car," Philip replied. "And we'll visit the safe-deposit box for new IDs." His voice held irritation, not concern. "It'll be fine. I expected we wouldn't stay off the radar forever. I just didn't expect to have to run again so soon."

"Why are we walking? Why don't you carry me?" She tried to keep the whine out of her voice and thought she'd succeeded. He didn't comment, so she assumed she'd done all right.

"I have to figure out where to go first."

"If you expected this, didn't you plan an escape route?"

He tossed a glance at her, but he was smiling, so she hadn't pissed him off. "You're full of questions tonight, aren't you?"

"Of course. We're fleeing for our lives. Again." This time, her angst leaked through.

He slowed so they walked side by side. "We'll get past it and hunker down somewhere else. Start fresh."

The prospect of doing this over and over again until they were caught or she died of old age brought tears of despair to her eyes. She lowered her gaze so he wouldn't see, but he sensed it.

"We'll manage. It's not as hopeless as you think." He clasped her hand, which reassured her enough to stifle the tears and the fears.

Josh padded along behind them, but he suddenly growled and spun around. "Behind us."

Kelsey's breath whooshed out as Philip snatched her into his arms and raced through the trees. She sucked in air in shallow breaths until she feared she'd hyperventilate. Scenery sped past in a blur, and she grew even more lost and disoriented. Josh's face floated behind Philip's shoulder, and she closed her eyes as vertigo set in and threatened to make her lose her lunch.

A shot rang out, and then she was sailing, thrown from Philip's embrace in a headlong plunge. Her mouth opened in a scream, but the breath slammed out of her when she slammed into a hard surface, powdered snow not providing much cushion for her landing. Her vision faded for a second, and when she shook it off, she wondered if she'd passed out for a moment. Body aching, she struggled to orient herself.

Icy wind sliced at her face. She'd left her scarf at home, something that wouldn't matter if Evans's men and that vampire caught her.

Where's Philip? Josh? She eased into a sitting position and scanned the surroundings.

To her horror, she realized she was out on the ice-covered lake. She spotted Philip on the shore, wrestling with a dark figure. *Evans's vampire.* The humans were nowhere in sight. Josh, too, sat on the ice. He oriented toward the battle on the shore but turned his head as though searching.

When his gaze landed on her, he frowned. "Don't stand. You'll fall right through. We've had too many mild days. Don't trust that ice."

Her heart thudded. Under the sounds of the fight, under the sound of Josh's voice, came distinct creaks and groans from the ice. Her mouth went dry, and sweat bloomed under her winter layers.

"Crawl." He said only that one word and then followed his own advice, belly crawling toward Philip, who appeared to be losing the battle.

With a flash of terror, Kelsey realized why. Blood spattered from a wound on his shoulder. The other vampire had shot Philip, probably with a silver bullet. His energy flagged, and his efforts to fend off the attack weakened with each blow that landed. He barely held the other vampire off.

Kelsey shifted to lie on her belly and started crawling after Josh. What she planned to do if she reached the vampires, she didn't know. If the only option was to find a rock and smash the vampire's head as a distraction, she'd do it.

The sound of ice cracking accompanied her every move, and her panic rose with each painful inch forward. The cold penetrated her coat, and her legs grew numb. She wasn't dressed for a night on the lake, hadn't prepared for this. The painful slowness of her progress gave her plenty of time to berate herself.

They'd grown complacent, accustomed to their peaceful nest in the woods. Since no one had found them, she'd put the monster searching for them out of her mind. Sure, every once in a while, the thought that the cops or Evans would discover them intruded into her days—or nights, mostly—but she'd pushed away the fears. She'd trusted Philip hid them well, and all indications had shown that to be the case.

Too late to wish they'd done things differently now.

Josh reached the struggling pair, offering Kelsey a moment of relief. Her son would save Philip. Surely the attacker couldn't fight off two vampires, one of them unwounded and a vicious baby vamp.

To her dismay, two other figures burst from the trees right then. Josh spotted them and veered away from Philip.

Kelsey growled in frustration and redoubled her efforts to reach the shore, her gaze alternating from one fight to the other as she moved.

Josh handily dispatched both humans, knocking their heads together and discarding them, out cold, on the snow-covered rocks along the shoreline. But the moment of distraction had been enough. Philip fell, the attacker pinning him with a silver chain.

Kelsey screamed, and the attacker's head snapped up. He stared her in the eyes, and a triumphant grin crept across his face. In a flash, he grabbed a nearby boulder and heaved it at her. It landed on the ice before her, smashing through. She managed one quick suck of air and sank into the icy black depths.

Water saturated her coat, her clothes. It trickled into her boots, which, though tied tight at her calf, couldn't keep out a lake. Her arms reached upward, but she had nothing to grab, and her heavy gear dragged her down. With a depth here of only fifteen feet, in summer, in a bathing suit, she'd have shot right back to the surface. When her feet hit the soft bottom, she forced her racing mind to think and tried to push off and up again. She might've moved a foot off the bottom but quickly hit ground again.

Her world reduced to a desperate quest for air. She struggled out of her coat and pushed off again. The boots dragged her back, and with the situation getting dire, she tried to force her now frozen fingers to untie the drawstring. The cold penetrated her body, and she slowly lost the battle.

Suddenly, she viewed everything playing out as though from above.

Josh struggled with Evans's vampire while Philip lay unmoving on the shore. She couldn't see her own body and knew it'd lost the fight to escape the killing water.

Am I dead?

Philip had said the veil between the worlds was closed. Would she now be stuck as a spirit on the earth plane? What about God? Why didn't he help her?

She prayed, mostly out of curiosity. She felt no particular attachment to the Lord's Prayer she recited now, only a desire to test its effects. As she prayed, she kept her gaze on the battle below.

*****

When Kelsey dropped through the ice, Josh started toward her but stopped when Evans's vampire defeated Philip and chained him to the ground with silver. Josh's decision to attack the vampire didn't demonstrate a preference for his sire over his mother. He had to be practical. If he tried to save Kelsey, Stranger Vamp would catch them both, and they'd all lose their lives.

Hoping the fight with Philip had weakened his

opponent, Josh leaped at Stranger Vamp. As the pair slammed together with an echoing crash, Josh steered the fight in Philip's direction. Immediately, Stranger Vamp shifted positions, directing them away from the shoreline.

No good. Josh punched out at his opponent's face and landed a solid blow. The years of boxing lessons and competitions hadn't been a complete waste. *Who'd have thought those stupid lessons would pay off after I died?*

He fended off a counterpunch and retaliated with a blow to Stranger Vamp's jaw, followed by a rapid fist to the creature's gut. The blows threw Evans's vampire off his feet and onto his back, and Josh launched himself after. The fight had taken them close to the tree line, much to Josh's relief. He zeroed in on a two-inch-thick branch on the nearest leafless tree and wrenched it off.

Stranger Vamp leaped to his feet and hurled his body at Josh, but the baby vamp was ready. Just as the two would've crashed together, Josh pulled back and raised his stick, aiming at the other vampire's chest. With all Josh's strength behind it, the branch rammed through Stranger Vamp's rib cage and into his heart. He roared and thrashed, his fists flailing. Josh leaped backward and grabbed the chain of silver off Philip's body. He ignored the burning in his hands and wrapped the chains around Stranger Vamp, but the extra effort and the burns to Josh's flesh hadn't been necessary. The makeshift stake had done its job.

Turning away from his now dead opponent, Josh examined Philip. His father still lived. The bullet had passed through him. He'd heal on his own now that the chains no longer burned him. Josh raced to the water and hurled himself in.

CHAPTER 25

Fire burns in the gas fireplace in the basement's corner, the blower pushing heat into every part of the room. Jaycie stands before an altar in the center of the circle she cast. When she recites the words to the spell she wrote, she says them with confidence. Power surges through her. It doesn't come easily, but after more than a few false starts, she's sure it'll work.

"I collect the world into my fist

"And release it to take me beyond the mist;

"Help me step through the door

"Let me wake and sleep no more."

Her voice fills the room along with the warmth blowing from the stove. Even with her eyes closed, she can feel the air waver and shift.

Nothing can keep her here. She's a mage and can work magick like few other magi at her level of experience can.

I'm more powerful than Chase.

Everyone made her believe she's weak, especially

her mother. When this revelation hits her, she drops the emotional and mental restraints, and her abilities surge.

She seizes control, control she never expected to have. Control that escaped her even when she believed it was in her grasp. She's tall and competent, and there's nothing she can't do.

Something pops.

Jaycie opened her eyes and sat up.

***

"We need to get Jaycie out of here." Chase planted his feet on the ground and fisted his hands on his hips. He'd barely recovered from the devastating news that his birth mother was Persephone, but for Jaycie's sake, and their baby's sake, he had to act fast. His thoughts snapped to the tarot card he'd pulled before entering the spirit plane: "The High Priestess."

Persephone's card.

He'd interpreted it literally except where the woman on the card represented the goddess in maiden form. That pointed to metaphorical translations: inner knowing and intuition, feminine influences, and lunar magick. What else would that card represent to him other than the effects of Persephone on his life, both past and present? Now that she'd revealed herself to him, she'd affect his future, too.

My mother is a goddess. He'd need time to process that.

The high priestess also represented the perfect woman, which to him was Jaycie. Didn't she always play the priestess to his priest when they cast spells?

With a headshake, he returned his focus to the current problem. "Where is she?"

"Safe. You're not."

His expression softened. "Mother, why not? I'm with you."

Her lips twitched as if she battled against a spontaneous grin. "Indeed."

She studied him. "Yes, this might be the solution after all." She gripped his arm and tugged him in the direction he'd wanted to head. "Come on."

They traveled down a long corridor, which then forked into three. Cora sped down the center one without hesitating. They hadn't gone far when a woman blocked their path.

"Persephone. I can't believe you're still here. What happened to the girl?"

Cora halted. "In a safe place. Chase has come to take her home again."

Hecate raised her brows. "You mean retrieve her from Hypnos and Morpheus?"

Cora gasped. "Yes." She whispered it in a trembling voice. "Tell me she's still there."

Hecate shook her head. "You should've left her with me. She needed only my protection."

Unable to stay silent any longer, Chase cut in, but he forced himself to speak calmly and respectfully. "Goddess, I'm honored to be in your presence. I'm seeking my girlfriend and am grateful you've kept her safe. Please, will you help me find her and take her home?"

Hecate studied him. "Polite. I like that." She turned to Cora. "Hypnos couldn't hold her."

Cora swallowed. "Is she still here?"

Hecate nodded. "For now. She's free and Hades is on the prowl. He's aware mortal intruders have penetrated his realm. Either we find her, or he will."

***

The bed on which Jaycie had lain was large and cushioned with the best mattress topper and comforter. Pillows surrounded her, and if getting out of there hadn't been her most pressing need, they'd have tempted her to sink back into sleep. Which was, of course, the point.

She scanned her surroundings.

The sumptuousness and comfort stopped at the ends of the bed. The rest of the room was bare, cave-like. Whoever had left her here to sleep for eternity hadn't needed to worry about her comfort when awake.

Throwing back the covers, she stepped from the bed.

Her bare feet landed on a cold stone floor. She shivered in her flimsy nightgown.

Someone had folded her clothes and placed them on the end of the bed. Her shoes rested on the floor, tucked out of the way.

Fury flooded through her and gave her the impetus she needed to dress quickly and try the door.

Naturally, she found it locked.

She held her hand to the lock. "*Aperta*."

The power she'd unleashed in the dream world flowed through her. The lock clicked and the door popped open. Jaycie stepped into the hallway and gazed first left, then right.

The left-hand side led to darkness. The right ended in a sliver of light in which she spotted wooden stairs leading up. She recognized them. Cora had led her down them before ... whatever had happened.

"Tsk. You're awake." The voice was male, strong.

She faced the speaker. Before her stood a god she couldn't identify but who looked familiar. With relief, she concluded he wasn't Hades—she'd seen too many statues and pictures of Hades not to recognize the king of the spirit realm. This god was shorter, had no facial hair, and seemed gentler than she imagined Hades would be, especially if he knew who she was.

"Are you the one who put me to sleep?"

"At Persephone's request, yes." His voice held regret. "Morpheus provided the dreams. I hope they were to your liking."

She nodded, not wanting to offend him. He was, after all, a god, and they had a reputation for getting testy. "The dreams were pleasant."

"Why did you leave?" He sounded genuinely interested, as if wanting to know for future reference.

She gave him the truth. For some reason, she thought he deserved it. "I want to live my real life, not a dream life. Please understand that it wasn't perfect. In the dream, I lost my career. In the dream, the love of my life was my husband, but he didn't support my ambitions. It helped me realize it was all an illusion."

"Morpheus must do better."

"You'd trap someone in a dream world again?"

"Sometimes the need arises."

Something compelled her to step forward and clasp his hands. "The need arose in my case? You'd have let me sleep my life away? My baby's life?" She released him and placed her hands over her belly.

He hesitated. "Persephone said the need existed."

She averted her gaze but couldn't keep silent, so she looked him in the eyes once more. "Did you question her at all?"

His expression turned to one of surprise. "Of course, child. I don't do this lightly."

"Then why?" Her voice broke and she fell silent.

"She said she wanted to protect you. We saved your life, you see." He looked up and down the hallway and then whispered, "Hades wants you dead."

"Then I'd better hurry," she said.

CHAPTER 26

Josh had jumped into the water to save her. The sight of it warmed Kelsey's incorporeal heart, but it saddened her to know he was too late. Would he grieve? She had nowhere to go now that the doors between the worlds were sealed shut. She'd be able to watch him, to watch Philip.

This was what Philip had dreaded—losing her if they became involved—but she didn't want to leave him either. It was bad enough she was dead, but it was so much worse that they'd never permitted themselves to love each other while she lived. Why hadn't they? His reasons didn't seem valid now that his worst fears were realized. They'd all die sometime. Kelsey had a friend whose husband had died in a car accident while the couple was on their honeymoon. So what if vampires outlived humans? Couples who stayed together until death parted them rarely died in each other's arms.

Josh dragged her body through the water to the shore. Philip lay nearby, and his moans reached her ears. His pain hurt her, and she desired his nearness. No sooner did she have that thought than she was there, hovering beside him.

His eyelids fluttered. He opened his eyes, but they didn't focus, and he continued to writhe and moan.

Josh hauled Kelsey's body out of the water and dragged it onto more solid ice at the shoreline. He started chest compressions, and her spirit smiled to watch his attempt to revive her.

"Mom. Wake up." He persisted, pressing so hard on her chest a rib snapped with an audible crack.

"Let me go, baby," she said. "I love you. I should've told you more often." That would be her biggest regret—that and all the time she and Philip lost avoiding a romantic relationship.

Josh stopped pounding on her chest, and for a second, she thought he'd heard her. Then, with a snick, his fangs came out. He tilted her head back and bit into her neck. Behind them, Philip roared in protest and struggled to rise.

Kelsey's world tilted and whirled around her, and a thud jarred her. Her whole body screamed with pain as the virus from his bite spread through her body. Her lungs deflated. She couldn't breathe, but the nuzzling at her neck comforted her. Her eyes opened, heavy lidded and glazed over. The pain and cold drained from her. The orgasmic pleasure of the blood pouring from her into the vampire stimulated her. She wanted him to take it, to slake his thirst and hunger with it. She craved for him to drain her. When he stopped, she cried out, a howl of despair, but then something warm and delicious dripped past her lips and onto her tongue.

She mewled and sucked, and when he pressed to

her lips firm flesh torn open to allow the nourishment to flow, she sucked eagerly, loudly.

Philip's panicked shouts registered as background noise. When the life-giving wrist suddenly ripped away from her mouth, she screamed in fury. Her arms stretched out, hands grasping at air. Her eyes, still half blind, sought the fountain of life: her son—her new father. Hunger crippled her. Her empty stomach squashed flat as a patty. Her mouth stretched open, and fangs slid from their gummy sheaths. She scented blood, fresh, pumping, and turned toward the source.

***

Philip wrenched Josh away from Kelsey, but the turning had already started. When her fangs sprouted, the transition completed. Kelsey was now a baby vampire with all the needs and desires that went with it. Ignoring Josh for the moment, Philip focused on the woman he loved.

She leaped onto the nearest human and bit ferociously into his neck.

Philip positioned himself behind her, one of his hands on each of her shoulders.

"Easy, darling," he said tenderly. "You don't want to kill him." Part of him wanted to let her murder both sons of bitches. They'd have killed them all or dragged them to torture and death at Evans's hands, but Philip didn't want Kelsey's vampire journey to begin with murder. He knew from personal experience that would be difficult to return from.

She slurped and suckled, and when he saw she risked taking the man's life, Philip eased her away. She fought him, as he expected her to, and he firmly guided her to the other man. This one revived as they approached. He screamed when he spotted the two vampires—one with fangs out and blood coating her mouth. Philip gazed into their victim's eyes and subdued him. He'd have to teach her so much now that she was one of them. Correction: Josh would have to teach her so much. He was her maker. Her sire.

A surge of resentment and fury almost made him forget to monitor Kelsey, but he controlled the urge to fight it out with Josh. He stroked Kelsey's hair as she fed and watched her closely.

"You're doing well. Just a little more and we'll stop."

Footsteps approached, and Josh appeared in Philip's periphery.

"I had to. She almost died."

Philip met Josh's gaze. "You shouldn't have. She was already dead." The cold had preserved her, slowed the decaying process, which was why the boy could revive her, but that didn't matter. "You should've let her go."

The boy's expression changed from shock to fury. "You'd let my mother die?"

"It was the right thing to do."

"I don't understand. She saved me, so I had to save her." Josh dropped to his knees beside Philip and reached a hand out. He hovered it over Kelsey's head for a moment and then gently stroked her hair as Philip had done. "She's one of us now. She'll understand me."

Philip's head drooped, and he felt worn, tired. "Josh. My son. You don't know what you've done. To us and to her." He sighed and looked up. Josh stared wide-eyed at Philip.

"It's okay," Philip said. "We'll figure it out."

With firm hands, he gripped Kelsey's shoulders and drew her away from her victim. When she struggled and fought, Philip pulled her to him and held her close. "Shh. That's enough for now."

"I'm hungry." Her tone was whiny, petulant.

He kissed the top of her head, her cheek. "Don't worry. You'll have more." He stared over her head and met Josh's gaze. "We'll teach you how."

CHAPTER 27

Voices made Jaycie freeze, and she turned a frightened gaze in Hypnos's direction. He straightened to his full height and shifted to stand in front of her. His willingness to protect her, a stranger, gave her the courage she needed to step out and stand beside him. The ground and the walls shook, and a brawny, bearded figure strode into view.

Hades.

Jaycie gasped, and without thinking, she clasped Hypnos's hand. When she realized what she'd done, she released him but felt gratitude when he patted her arm.

"My lord." Hypnos bowed.

Trembling, Jaycie bobbed her head and curtsied.

"I know who you are," Hades said.

"Hypnos," the god of sleep replied.

Jaycie couldn't decide whether that was a brave move or a crazy one.

Hades scowled. "The girl. She carries Persephone's grandchild."

Jaycie drew herself up and faced him head-on. "We'd like to go home—where we belong."

Before he could reply, Cora's voice broke into the discussion. "The girl is under my protection."

Hades froze, his expression morphing from surprise to relief. He spun on his heel and strode to meet her. "Where were you?" His voice held a touch of irritation.

"I had to attend to some things."

He chuckled. "What sorts of things might require your attention?"

She hooked her arm through his and leaned in conspiratorially. "I met my son. We're going to be grandparents, Hades."

Jaycie tried to keep the shock from her face and barely succeeded. Then she saw movement behind Cora, and Chase strolled into view. She gave a small cry and took a step toward him, but Hypnos placed a restraining hand on her shoulder. She met his gaze, her brows rising in question. He shook his head. She stepped closer to his reassuring presence and turned back to watch Cora—Persephone—handle her husband.

"We? These children are not of me. You've been unfaithful." Rage and hatred had crept into his voice, and Jaycie flinched.

"I never betrayed you." She gave him a shrewd, appraising stare. "As you've never betrayed me. Isn't that right?"

Jaycie held her breath and, without thinking, gripped Hypnos's arm. When he patted her hand, she realized the insolence of what she'd done. Wide-eyed, she stared at him, but the gaze he returned to her was kindly rather than insulted. She released a slow, relieved breath.

Cora continued. "My life on the physical plane has nothing to do with my life here. That's our deal. I live in Hades for six months of the mortal year and return to the surface for the other six months."

His eyes crinkled and his lips twitched, the amusement in his expression startling Jaycie. "You are clever, as always, my love."

"You also. You seek the surface during my time above more often than you let on."

He laughed now, a hearty roar, and whirled on Chase, whose pale face grew paler still.

"Well, boy, it would seem she expects me to spare you. What say you? You've disrupted the underworld. Spirits have ceased entering my realm."

Chase might have been terrified, but he stood firm and drew himself up tall. "It was an accident I intend to fix." He glanced at Cora. "With help from my mother. Her power added to mine will open the doors once more."

"This boy's life is a blight on my reputation." Hades said it in a low, pondering tone, as if he conversed with himself.

Even so, Chase responded. "If you will, my lord, I would dedicate my life to honor you as a father to all souls, including mine."

The giant man stooped so their eyes were level, and he studied Chase. "You have your mother's eyes. I always loved her eyes. She's a beauty." He straightened. "Very well. I give you leave to repair what you've damaged." He whirled around and strode to confront Jaycie and Hypnos.

She sucked in a breath. Hypnos gave her hand a reassuring squeeze, but when Hades reached them, he addressed Hypnos first. "You kept this a secret from me, my friend. I'm aggrieved."

"Nay, I knew not the truth, my lord. I simply obeyed the queen of Hades when asked for a favor."

The intimidating god contemplated for a moment and turned to Jaycie. "I could stop his line and kill the child you carry."

Her heart thudded. Chase gave a cry, but Cora hissed at him and held him back. He glared at his mother, but she whispered something to him, and he remained in place.

"You could," Jaycie said. "But she's innocent."

"She's more than that, so I hear."

"I don't understand."

Instead of explaining, he said, "I see her. She's in spirit and stays close to you." Hades lifted his head and peered over Jaycie's shoulder. She angled her body in the direction of his gaze but saw nothing.

"Despite my will, or my desires, fate has a hand here, but I must warn you: if you don't have a care, she'll bring the world to its knees." He turned his back on Jaycie and strode away. As he passed Cora and Chase, he said, "Fix the doors. I need fresh souls."

***

The moment Hades vanished from sight, Chase shrugged off Cora's hand and raced to Jaycie. They threw themselves into each other's arms. She sobbed and gripped him tight while his hands roved over her body as if verifying nothing was broken.

"Gods," he said. "I thought I'd lost you forever."

Her breath hitched and she tilted her head up. He covered her face with kisses and finished by covering her mouth with his. He never wanted to let her go.

Cora broke into the moment. "Save the passionate reunion for when you're on the other side."

Chase pulled away from Jaycie but held her at arm's length, reluctant to release her. He gazed into her eyes. "Mother's right. We have to go, but first, is the baby okay? Are you okay?"

She nodded and, in a breathy voice, said, "We're fine." She remained silent but looked as if she wanted to say more.

Chase stroked a finger down her cheek. "I'd have searched for you forever."

"I know." Her gaze examined him from top to toe, and she grinned. "Nice duds. Did we get you out of bed?"

He chuckled. "Something like that." Reassured, Chase dropped his hands to his sides and turned to Cora. "Thank you for helping me. It wouldn't have gone well otherwise."

She shrugged. "You're my son. Hades is brutal in his punishments and has a jealous streak, but he's fair. He doesn't damn the innocent."

Jaycie frowned. "Then why did you have Hypnos put me to sleep? Why didn't we speak to Hades first?"

"It's easier to avoid a lion than to beard it in its den. Now, if you're both done chattering, we must go."

They parted from Hypnos, and Cora led them from the underworld. They sidled past Kerberos, who watched them with wary eyes but allowed them to pass. Charon, too, came at Cora's request and carried them back across Styx.

Once on the shore, Cora led them to the spot where she and Jaycie had first entered the realm. "We'll cast the spell here."

CHAPTER 28

Kelsey glimpsed spirits in the surrounding trees and even on the lake, and then Josh's efforts yanked her back into her body. After that, she knew only hunger and cravings. An all-consuming need enveloped her, and if she didn't get blood, it would devour her from within. First Josh fed from her, and she'd never known such sheer joy in giving before. Then he fed her, and she knew the pleasure of taking. When he stopped, she thought she'd go mad from the loss. Then the hearts of the two humans nearby pumped in her ears, thumping and throbbing as they pulsed sustenance through their bodies. She smelled it too, a thick metallic scent with distinct notes: one spicy, the other sweet. She gorged on each one, and their blood tasted as delicious as she'd expected.

Philip pulled her away from her feast. Initially, she raged and fought him, but he showed her such tenderness she calmed and now sat cradled in his arms. When they'd first met, she'd disliked him, feared him, but that had gradually mutated into a grudging respect and then affection. Finally, she'd had to admit she loved him, but now she desired him in a different way. With every fiber of her being, she wanted him to bite her. She wanted to bite him back. To let themselves explore each other in every possible way. Before it all, though, she wanted to drink blood again from a living human.

"Hungry." She stared into his eyes and bared her fangs.

"I know, darling." The term soothed her. "We'll eat." He glanced away from her to Josh, and a frown replaced the tenderness in his expression, but when he met her eyes again, the compassion resurfaced.

He rose, keeping her cuddled against him. "Follow me." He tossed the command over his shoulder at Josh and raced away.

In the past, when he'd raced with her like this, their surroundings became a blur and their speed took her breath away. Now, it felt as though they flew forward in slow motion. Everything around them grew more clear and distinct. She could see in all directions without losing track of where they traveled. They'd never trip and fall—something she'd always worried about before because she didn't understand what vampires saw when they traveled this way. It explained why the one chasing them followed no matter how quickly Philip had moved. Stranger Vamp not only kept up with them physically, but he'd also tracked their scent.

Aromas from the environment assaulted her nostrils. Flora, fauna. Dirt. Snow. She considered it a miracle she distinguished one from another. Why didn't they blend into a cacophony of smells?

She had time to wonder where they headed before

he set her on her feet. She clutched at him, wanting him to stay close.

Josh landed next to them, and she grasped at him, too. He put an arm around her, and the three of them huddled together.

"You made me," she said.

"Mom." With his mouth beside her ear, it was as if he roared the word at her.

"I'm hungry." She could focus on only that one thing. "Feed me." The petulance in her tone resembled Josh's tone ever since Philip had turned him. She understood it now and forgave him for it.

"We need to get her hunting, Father," Josh said.

"First we need to find shelter."

"Feed me." Didn't they understand how urgently she needed food?

Worry furrowed Josh's brow. "Let her eat. We can find her an animal. I smell rabbits nearby."

Philip's eyes narrowed and he growled in frustration before he responded. "No, we must leave here. We'll get her bottled blood after we settle our shelter for the night."

Tears sprang to Kelsey's eyes, and she swiped at them. Her hand came away tinged with red. "My eyes are bleeding."

"Vampire tears. You're not bleeding." He blotted her face with a handkerchief. "Most vampires carry these for such occasions." He sighed as if the universe weighed on his shoulders.

Her intestines gnawed at her. "Please, I'm so hungry."

Philip snatched her up. He raced again, Kelsey in his arms, the wad of cloth pressed to her eyes.

***

Philip took them to a hotel in downtown Tkaronto. It might be a mistake, but for now, it was safer than holing up in a motel in a small town or along a highway. Evans and his lackeys would find them more easily in an isolated place. The noise and bustle of the city, along with the extra protections Philip put up around them and the use of an alternate ID, would hide them and provide a night's respite.

Leaving Kelsey in the room with Josh, Philip walked to a nearby variety store for supplies. Included in his purchases were bags of donated and synthetic blood from the store's refrigerators. He glamoured his face and body, making himself appear older and shorter. If the surveillance cameras picked up anything, it would show a stocky, balding man in his late sixties. By the time he returned to the room, his energy flagged from maintaining the disguise, and Kelsey was crying again, sopping up the bloody tears with the handkerchief. Josh's arm draped around her shoulders.

The pair sat on the couch, the television playing across from them. Josh had set it to the news channel, but he'd muted the sound.

Philip dropped the bags onto the round table in the suite. "Hold her," he said.

As Josh held Kelsey tight against his body, Philip unpacked the bag with the bottles of blood. He opened one containing donated blood. The moment the cap came off, Kelsey's fangs slid out. She snarled and her arms flailed as she struggled to break Josh's hold.

"You won't get one drop until you control yourself." Philip sauntered over to stand before her, out of reach. "Retract your fangs."

He hated to treat her like a dog or a toddler, but she needed discipline. Vampires had to learn how to blend in with humans. If she let her inner monster loose in public, she'd attract attention from the authorities or Evans's crew, or, even worse, hurt someone.

She snarled and growled, behaving little better than a feral animal. "Gimme."

Philip refused to give in. The sooner she accepted he was in charge, that he was the authority here, the sooner she'd become civilized enough to appear in public. Their lives depended on it, so he couldn't compromise. Even though he hadn't sired her, he'd take charge of her training. Josh hadn't yet learned enough or experienced enough to provide her with the leadership she needed to develop into a responsible vampire. He still struggled with his own evolution.

He never should've turned her. The situation tore Philip in two. On the one hand, turning her meant she wasn't dead; on the other, it ruined her life. Philip had made the same decision for Josh, but it'd been at Kelsey's behest. Had Josh turned her to get revenge for the part she'd played in making him a vampire? It made Philip sick to think so.

"Retract your fangs," he said.

"Mom, you can do it. Calm down and they'll pull in on their own." Josh nuzzled his face against hers in a gesture meant to help settle her.

In Kelsey's case, it only angered her further. "Don't tell me what to do."

Son of a bitch! She's more stubborn as a vampire than she was as a human. How is that possible? Philip gave a heavy sigh. This woman did nothing easily. "This'll go a lot faster if you settle down and pull in your fangs." He kept his voice gentle, even. He hoped the neighbors didn't hear the animal-like snarls and grunts Kelsey emitted.

It would be just my luck if they reported us for having an animal in the room and sent security to investigate. He almost laughed aloud at the thought.

"Father, maybe a sip would calm her."

Philip frowned and shook his head vigorously. "Absolutely not. And never contradict me. I'm in charge. Understood?"

Josh nodded his head.

"Don't nod. Tell me." Kelsey needed to witness her sire relinquish control to Philip. If she thought she could get around Philip through Josh, disaster would come of it. The lad wasn't strong enough to resist his child's pleas.

"You're in charge, Father. I'll do everything you ask." Josh's white face hung like a moon over Kelsey's shoulders. The boy was terrified, but why? Was he afraid of what he'd done to his mother? The daunting responsibility associated with creating a new vampire life? Or did Philip frighten him? He didn't want either of them to follow orders out of fear. They should follow orders because it was the right thing to do—the smart, practical thing to do.

Kelsey kicked out but Philip dodged the blow.

"Damn it," he said. "Pull in your fangs, or I'll pour it down the drain."

She tilted her head back and opened her mouth, but before she cried out, Josh tugged her onto her back on the couch and jammed a forearm against her throat.

Philip froze, watching the scene play out, ready to pounce if it got out of hand.

Josh held his mother pinned, but she didn't react as if he hurt her, which meant he wasn't using enough force to crush her windpipe. Even if he had, it wouldn't kill her—vampires could only be killed in specific ways—but it would cause pain. She struggled to buck him off, but he held firm.

He pressed his face to hers. "Stop. Philip's our master whether or not you like it. He's our teacher. You'll accept it or you'll die." He eased back on her throat, and she emitted a mewling cry.

"I'm hungry. So hungry."

"You'll get fed if you do as you're told." His voice grew gentle. "I know what you're going through. I experienced it too. Listen to me. Calm yourself. Pull in your fangs. We'll feed you."

Kelsey's thrashing stilled. She closed her eyes and sucked in a deep breath. Her cheeks and temples bore red-streaked tearstains. Her lips relaxed, and her fangs retracted with a soft snick.

"Okay," she said. "I'll do what you want."

Philip's heart swelled with pride.

CHAPTER 29

Chase led the spell—he'd closed the doors, so they needed his powers to open them. Jaycie cast the circle and supported the spell's execution with her power and skill. Cora added her energetic strength to help him succeed. They worked together, each contributing everything they could.

As she worked, Jaycie stole glances in Cora's direction. Could she have helped open the doors when they'd first crossed? Had the goddess wanted Jaycie trapped on this side of the veil? Cora had denied dragging the young woman across on purpose, and she'd believed the claim, but doubts arose once more. Whenever she'd attempted to use magick, the goddess discouraged it.

Jaycie set aside her questions to focus on the spell, but she wouldn't forget them.

The spell they'd created looked deceptively simple, considering what they sought to accomplish. None of them carried tools, and since a goddess helped them, they needed none. Chase explained he'd arrived in the underworld without using his magick gear and could duplicate the result as long as he drew on their energies.

The trio stood at three different points in the circle, forming a triangle within the energy sphere Jaycie had erected around them. Without an altar in the center, without a wand or sword or Book of Shadows, Chase improvised. Jaycie had used her arm and index finger in place of a sword or wand to draw the circle. Next, Chase used his right index finger to draw a pentagram in the air above him. He chanted the prepared verse twice, all three participants raising their hands to the sky and drawing power from above. From below, they pulled power from the earth beneath their feet, and he chanted the verse a final time:

"I draw on my power and use the energy of three

"To open the doors and set spirits free

"From earth plane to underworld, part the veil

"Let souls cross and the entrance prevail."

When he fell silent, they dropped their arms and waited, gazes directed to where the doorway should form.

The ground trembled, and Jaycie spread her feet farther apart to steady herself. She raised her arms for balance. A glance in Chase's direction showed he did the same. Cora stood unfazed. However much the ground trembled, it affected her not at all.

A speck of light appeared. It grew, stretched, and formed a rectangle seven feet tall and three feet wide. As they watched, it shimmered opaque and then cleared. On the other side, Kelsey Davis's garden, bathed in moonlight, materialized.

"Go," Chase hollered, and he rushed to push Jaycie through.

She shook her head. "We have to take down the

circle."

"I'll do it. Hurry."

"Not without you."

He gripped her arm and stepped toward the doorway, but she stayed put. "I'm taking down the circle. The door will remain open until we step through and close it. Or don't you trust the magick?"

Surprise crossed his face, and he released her. "Be quick. I trust the spell, but I don't trust everyone in Hades wants to let us go—especially you and the baby."

Her instinct was to question that, but instead, she hurried to the northeast point of the circle and raised her arms. She held her right arm high and imagined dropping the circle. She faced the west and walked the circle's circumference three times. When she arrived in the northeast again, all the energy they'd raised was gone.

"The circle is down. This rite has ended." She stamped her foot and dropped her arms to her side. She strode to the still-open doorway. "Let's get out of here."

Confident that Chase and Cora followed, she stepped through the doorway and into Kesley's backyard.

***

Cora followed Jaycie, and the pair turned to watch Chase step through, but he remained standing in place on the underworld side. A mist formed, separating them from him.

Worry twisted a knot in Jaycie's abdomen. "What's he doing?"

His mother squinted and then frowned. "Hecate."

Terrified the goddess wanted to capture Chase, Jaycie stepped toward the doorway, ready to leap back to the spirit plane. Cora placed a restraining hand on the young woman's shoulder. "No. She wants you to cross. He'll deal with her."

She tried to shrug the hand away, but Cora held fast.

"Let me go. I won't let her kidnap him." Jaycie visualized herself punching Cora to get free, but common sense made her reign in her temper.

On the other side, Chase argued with Hecate. The roar of the River Styx behind them drowned out their words.

The goddess displayed no emotion and seemed calm, rational. Chase, however, appeared agitated, which almost made Jaycie attempt another leap through the doorway.

A sudden whoosh had her spinning around. She ducked, dropping to the ground as incorporeal shapes flew headlong toward the doorway. Soon they obliterated her view of Chase, Hecate, and the river.

Cora had stepped aside and watched from inside the gazebo.

It seemed like forever before the flood of spirits returning to where they belonged abated, and the view of the underworld returned. Chase now stood alone, and no sooner had the last spirit crossed than he stepped through the doorway.

Jaycie jumped to her feet and rushed him, throwing her arms around him. "I thought she'd keep you there."

"It's fine."

When she received no further explanation, she said, "What did she want?"

He shook his head and glanced pointedly in Cora's direction. "Not now. I have to close the door." He had to shut the door without sealing it against souls who needed to cross when they died.

"I'll cast the circle." She called Cora over to help them and then raised energy for a circle, walking clockwise around the garden and capturing the doorway within it.

Chase once more cast a spell, this time of closing, but took care not to make the same mistake as before. They'd carefully planned out a script, and when the spell was done, the door became invisible to humans. Cora assured them it still existed and that all the doors were available to migrating souls.

Jaycie closed her eyes and sighed with relief. "I can't believe it's over."

When only silence greeted her, she opened her eyes and met Chase's gaze. He held it for a while and then looked at the store.

"Someone might call the police if they heard any of this ruckus. We'd better leave."

What he said was true enough, but his body language and the fact he hadn't told her what Hecate wanted made her uneasy. Perhaps it wasn't over after all.

CHAPTER 30

The butler once again ushered Frank Evans into Risto Fina's mansion, this time to a room used as a home office. Fina sat at a room-dominating desk, tapping on a laptop's keyboard. He stopped working and closed the screen when his guest entered. Tilting backward in his chair, he waved Evans to a seat facing the desk.

Fina got right to the point. "I take it things didn't go as planned?" He righted his chair, propped an elbow on each armrest, and tented his fingers in front of his chest.

"You could say that." Evans settled into one of the two available chairs.

"What happened?"

"They killed my vampire tracker and fed off the two human soldiers."

"But the trackers found your fugitives?"

Evans wasn't sure how to interpret the question. Did Fina consider the job done? Evans didn't want to split hairs with a master mage, especially one that had done him a favor, but the point was to capture Belanger and the two Davises, not simply locate them. To make matters worse, the trackers had lost their quarry after a violent confrontation. The locating portion of the job hadn't lasted long. Evans considered that a swing and a miss, not a promise fulfilled.

"They did, but they lost them again."

"You asked me to locate them. I did. Are you complaining about the results?"

Yes, that's exactly what I'm doing, you pompous ass. "Not at all." He shifted in his seat, crossing his legs so he angled away from Risto Fina.

"Then to what do I owe the pleasure? Couldn't we have discussed this over the phone?"

No, you muttonhead. I don't want phone records showing we talked. Evans forced his expression to remain calm and neutral, and he evened his tone. "I wanted this conversation off the record." As he said it, he realized Fina knew that. So what was the mage's endgame? What did he want for repeating the locater spell?

The conversation halted at a tap on the door, which opened after a breath's pause. The butler entered, pushing a tea cart loaded with coffee and tea service and a platter of pastries. All the same as before. The mage had a sweet tooth.

As ever, Risto Fina was the gracious host. The butler poured coffee for Evans and tea for the master mage. He handed each man a plate while offering selections from the pastries with a pair of tongs. With his duty done, he gave a slight bow and left the room, closing the door behind him.

Did this hospitality mean Fina would grant Evans's request? Or was this a prelude to a bargaining session the crime boss would regret? Somehow, he needed to capture Belanger and the two Davises. Evans's soldiers had confirmed that Josh Davis still lived, and he lived as a vampire. Where Belanger's former partner, Dwayne Rathburn, had vanished to, Evans didn't care. He'd only wanted to confirm the identities of Philip Belanger's associates.

At first he'd assumed the former friends and business partners had reconciled when he'd learned two vampires hid out in that cabin in the woods. He'd decided that if the other vampire was Rathburn, he'd punish the creature for aiding Belanger and the Davis woman. Now that he knew the boy they'd believed dead was the other vampire, his objectives changed. He imagined Belanger getting the death penalty and smiled.

Fina noticed immediately. "Something amusing?"

Evans set his cup and saucer down on the desk. His plate of pastries rested on his lap. "Contemplating probable outcomes. You see, I'm hoping to assist the authorities in their quest to locate Philip Belanger. Now that he's created a ... new vampire, I can alert investigators he's broken the law."

"I assumed you'd want to avoid more legal entanglements." Fina sat up straight and set his cup and saucer next to his empty plate on the desk.

"I'm not concerned about what Belanger might tell them."

Fina's eyes widened. "Is that so? Weren't you linked to his disappearance? You've taken over his bar, correct?" He leaned back in his seat.

"Yes, I own and am rebuilding Blood Shots, but I'm not connected at all to his disappearance. A former associate of mine is—was—but what happened the night Belanger and the two humans vanished had nothing to do with me. The boy becoming a vampire explains why they disappeared rather than called the authorities and reported the crimes."

"Why haven't you taken your information to the police? Why come to me?" He frowned as though troubled. "What are your intentions here?"

Evans hesitated. He just wanted Fina to execute the locater spell again and find the fugitives. Instead of involving his own personnel, he'd alert the cops to the location—he had a few in his pocket he might send. They'd not only arrest the vampire, but they'd also take the Davises into custody. From there, Evans could do whatever he wanted to them without direct involvement.

"I would like you to repeat the tracking spell. Find Belanger and the Davises again. I'll make it worth your while. This is a lot to ask, so I'll pay you whatever you want."

Risto Fina tapped his fingers on the arm of his chair as he considered. At last, he said, "Perhaps we can work something out. If I do this—and it's not a small ask, you understand—but if I do it, I'll expect more than money from you."

Evans rubbed the back of his neck and then crossed his arms over his chest. When he realized his body language telegraphed his anxiety, he uncrossed his arms and busied himself with setting his plate on the desk beside his cup and saucer. His gaze focused on the half-eaten muffin still sitting on the plate. "What would you need?"

"Loyalty." Fina said it as though it should be obvious. "I have plans to run for office in the next state election. Having you and your organization in my corner would make an enormous difference to my campaign."

Evans exhaled a slow, relieved breath. Was that all? He had no problem backing Fina in an election bid. It would benefit him to have a powerful mage as an ally in office. The only question was why Fina considered a crime boss's alliance as a positive.

"I'd be more than happy to offer my support. I assume you don't mean that to become public knowledge?"

Fina nodded. "Correct. I might have need of certain services you provide, but we'd keep that between us. You have important contacts. Wide influence."

It startled Evans how much Fina seemed to know about his personal affiliations, but he could shrug it off as long as the mage located Belanger. Evans stood and offered Risto Fina his right hand. "Deal."

CHAPTER 31

Blood trickled from Kelsey's lips. She reveled in the thick, wet slickness of it and let it drip for a moment longer. Then, with a sudden flick and swish of the tongue, she licked around her lips and cleaned it off. She crouched in the snow. A rabbit, drained of its blood, hung limp in her hands.

They'd left the hotel behind after Philip found new living accommodations. The new place wasn't as luxurious or comfortable as the others they'd stayed in. She blamed Frank Evans for that, and her thoughts frequently turned to revenge for the ruination of their lives.

"Bag it," Philip said behind her.

She gazed down at the burlap sack he tossed at her feet. He made them stow the animal carcasses and take them home. The remains always disappeared that night. If he sold them or donated them, he never revealed, and she never cared enough to ask. Her human self would've demanded answers, but he'd told her nothing about these hunting expeditions. Human

Kelsey had questioned him, but he'd refused to reveal anything. Now she understood why and didn't hold it against him. Human Kelsey would've raged at him; baby vampire Kelsey didn't give a shit.

She stuffed the rabbit into the sack and tugged the drawstring tight, sealing it inside. A measure of pride filled her when she reflected on how well her first kill had gone, but she preferred the flavor of human blood to that of animals. The hunt had exhilarated her, though, and she looked forward to doing it again soon.

"Can we go back now? Have some of that synthetic blood?" She'd have preferred donated, but in their current circumstances, they had no way to store real human blood.

His brow furrowed. "You still hungry?"

"Not ravenous. I want human blood." What would it feel like to hunt down and bleed human prey? The thought of it made her body tingle with anticipation, but irritation quickly followed the excitement. Philip would never allow such a hunt. Humans, unless they offered their bodies willingly, were off the menu. Even then, she wouldn't be allowed to drain them, to feel their life force fade away under her bite. There were laws against it. Stupid government, controlling them, squashing their freedoms. Even the Vampire Consortium insisted on these laws. They'd sold out to the humans; Kelsey understood it now she was a vampire. Her mind wandered to her bookstore's employee. Where was Chase now? How did mage blood taste?

A rustling in the bushes made her whirl around to face the newcomer, but she smelled his identity before her gaze found him. *Josh.* He'd run off to hunt on his own and now returned to their meeting place. He showed no traces of blood on him, but he bore the satiated look of a vamp who'd fed well. His hands were empty. Had he disobeyed the keep-the-carcass rule?

Philip and Josh exchanged knowing looks, and Philip said, "Leave it for the wolves. We can't haul a deer out right now." He sounded regretful. Deer carcasses would be more valuable than rabbits if he was selling the leftovers.

They went into vampire-travel mode and sped across the snow and through the brush, leaving little trace of their passing. Kelsey followed close behind Philip, and Josh brought up the rear. She had no trouble keeping up, especially after the recent refreshment, but she looked forward to getting to their cabin and drinking some of that blood.

The shack they rented contained one bedroom and had no electricity and no running water. If Kelsey were still human, she'd have detested it. Even as a vampire, she hated it, and Josh echoed her sentiments. Though Philip didn't comment, she knew he hated it, too, but he'd decided they needed to stay so far off the grid even they could barely figure out where they were.

When they arrived, Philip insisted on walking the perimeter. He inspected all the doors and windows to verify no intruders had entered.

"Who's going to find us?" Kelsey grumbled to Josh.

He blinked at her for a moment before answering. "Who found us last time? Evans's men."

She hissed at him. He was right. She'd complained reflexively. Was this a holdover from her human traits, or was it baby-vamp bitchiness? All she knew was that whenever she wasn't fangs-deep in food, she wanted to lash out at everything and everyone around her.

The cabin's front door opened, and Philip's upper

body leaned outside. He waved them in and disappeared.

"Guess it's okay." Her tone suggested he'd wasted their time even checking.

Josh ignored her and strolled into the house. She followed at a slower pace, taking in her surroundings as she approached the cabin.

The cloudless sky teemed with thousands of stars. The thin sickle moon hung over the nearby lake—this one frozen over and snow covered. She stared at it, remembering what it was like to sink into the water and drown. She'd stopped breathing, and though Josh had brought her back to some kind of life, it was one that no longer involved breathing.

The cabin's door stood open a crack, so she pushed it wider and stepped inside.

Philip hadn't rented this one. They'd broken in, which was another reason for the added paranoia. Chances were slim the owners would show up during the winter, but the odds weren't zero. However, the advantages outweighed the risks. Philip hadn't needed to step out of hiding to acquire it. They'd simply scouted the area until they found a rustic shack without surveillance equipment guarding it, not even battery-operated trail cameras.

Philip had also taught Kelsey to create her own protective charms. Casting spells and dabbling in magick didn't bother her anymore. If becoming a vampire damned her in God's eyes, it no longer concerned her. She couldn't recall why it'd mattered to her when she was a human.

Since the cabin was so tiny, she had few options for where to settle. Vampires needed little sleep, so she stayed in the living room and dropped onto one end of the shabby couch in front of the fireplace. They didn't need a fire for warmth either, but Philip had sparked one anyway for the ambience. Josh sat at the other end, and mother and son stared impassively at one another, waiting—for what, she couldn't say.

Their master stalked the cabin as though on sentry duty, and after making a few rounds, he paused before them. "I have to go out."

Both baby vamps stared at him, unblinking and silent.

"I'll return before sunrise."

"Yes, Father," Josh said.

"Both of you stay inside. No hunting. That's why I took you out." He handed Kelsey a bottle of blood, and she muttered her thanks with no sincerity behind the words.

She cracked the bottle open and took a long draft. He'd taken it from the cooler on the back porch—no electricity meant they stored everything in coolers, under a tarp, on the screened-in back porch.

Philip kept his eyes on Kelsey but spoke to Josh. "Protect your mother. Stay close and keep an eye out for intruders."

"Yes, Father."

Kelsey scrunched up her face in a sneer. "I don't need a babysitter." She hadn't planned to go out, but she resented Philip thought she needed her own son to sit on guard duty when he left them alone.

"I'm afraid you do, darling, and it's nonnegotiable." He headed for the door.

The sack with their leftovers leaned against the wall in the foyer. He picked it up and slung it across his shoulder. With a whoosh and a slam of the door, he vanished.

Kelsey peered at Josh, who sat staring into the fire. "Why do you do everything he says?"

"You know why. He's our master even if I'm the one who made you."

She brushed that aside and picked up the thread of something she'd wanted to discuss with him ever since he'd created her. "Why'd you turn me?"

He glanced at her and then returned his gaze to the fire. His expression grew contemplative, and he remained silent for a while. Just as she opened her mouth to press him on it, he said, "He loved you."

Shock silenced her, and she waited for him to continue.

When he did, his voice carried a measure of regret. "I thought he wanted it but was too afraid to do it himself."

She found that absurd and laughed. "Philip fears no one and nothing. He does whatever he wants."

Josh shook his head and met her gaze. "Is that how you see him? After everything he's done for you?"

"He ruined our lives."

"I thought so too, once."

"You don't anymore?" She drained the rest of the blood from the bottle she still held.

"No." He stared into her eyes. "I blame you."

CHAPTER 32

Based on the crescent moon's position, it was after midnight on the physical plane. Jaycie and Chase made plans to return to the apartment.

"You have to call your parents," Chase said. "They've been insane with worry."

Jaycie recalled her interactions with her mother when she was in the dream world and gave a sigh heavy with weariness. "I will."

Her mother would be relieved to have Jaycie home again, but they needed to address a lot of issues. She didn't look forward to it.

"I'm leaving you here and returning to the underworld," Cora said.

Jaycie wanted to question her but remained silent, waiting for Chase to do it.

"What will you do next?" He stepped close to his mother, uncertainty in his expression and his body language.

She smiled. "Spend some time with Hades. Make sure he's not planning anything unpleasant for any of you."

He threw a worried glance in Jaycie's direction. "Do you think he might?"

Cora shook her head. "I'll make sure. If I'm with him, he won't even consider it."

"Thank you for helping us." He stepped forward and hugged her.

Her mouth dropped open, and she stared wide-eyed over his shoulder, but she reciprocated. "You're welcome, my son. I'm happy we met." She released him and turned to Jaycie. "Take care of my granddaughter. We need to keep her safe."

"I will." *Safe from what?*

Chase vocalized what Jaycie was thinking. "Is she in danger?"

Cora shook her head. "Not imminent. Watch over her. She's ... special."

"What do you mean?" Jaycie's hands drifted to her pelvic area and laced protectively together over her small baby bump.

"She's the granddaughter of a goddess and a master mage. She's the daughter of two powerful magi."

Jaycie's brows raised at that last bit, but she didn't comment. She'd felt her power strengthen when she was in the underworld, but she'd thought she'd hid it well from everyone else. If Cora knew, who else did?

"Some might want to exploit her." Cora's gaze moved from Jaycie to Chase. "Watch over them both."

"I promise," he replied.

Cora hesitated as she turned to face the now invisible doorway. She gazed back at Jaycie.

Am I supposed to hug her goodbye? She took two steps in Cora's direction, halting an arm's length from the goddess. "Thank you," she whispered. *Why am I thanking Cora?* After all, the goddess had handed her over to Morpheus and Hypnos. *She did it to keep me and the baby safe. Probably.*

Cora smiled indulgently in response. "Yes, of course. Keep in mind, everything I do has our best interests at heart. Farewell. For now." She stepped through the doorway and vanished.

Jaycie and Chase stared in silence at the spot where the doorway should stand but saw only the back of the yard.

Jaycie checked her phone. "How will we get home? My phone's dead."

Chase took her hand. "We'll walk to the nearest variety store and call one of my roommates. Someone will come get us."

"You're wearing your robe and pajamas."

"You go in, then. I'll wait outside."

"Okay."

Hands clasped, they left the yard to return to their lives.

***

Rustling from the hallway alerted Risto Fina to an intruder. It wasn't part of his dream because he hadn't been sleeping. Lately, he tossed and turned throughout the night, falling asleep in the early morning hours to grab an hour or two of precious rest. He still hadn't located Philip Belanger and the Davises for Frank Evans, but more than that, he'd heard nothing from Cora or Chase. Shouldn't she have brought him back by now? What if he'd refused to return with her? Every time Fina tried to peer into the veil, he saw only murk and darkness. The way remained closed—at least, it'd been shut when he'd tried at ten o'clock the night before.

He glanced at the clock on his nightstand. Three o'clock. He stared into the darkness. If someone had broken in, why hadn't his security triggered? The house should be alive and reacting. He protected his home with both electronic surveillance and magick. Anyone breaking in wouldn't get two steps inside without paying for it in pain and immobility.

A feminine voice broke into his thoughts, answering his questions. "Did I wake you, Risto?"

Cora. That explains how she got past all my security. The gods and goddesses didn't adhere to natural laws, even the natural laws of magick.

He sat up and, though it was dark, waved her over. She sashayed to his side, her gown making the rustling sound that had attracted his attention.

He opened with what was uppermost in his mind. "Where's Chase?"

"Don't worry." She perched on the edge of his bed, near his hips. The height of the bed had forced her to jump up, taking away a bit of her dignity, but once she settled herself, she recovered her decorum. "He's home, and so is the girl."

"She's fine?"

"Yes, and the child as well."

He breathed out a sigh of relief. For the first time in his life, someone else mattered to him. His primary motives remained selfish, but underneath that lay a genuine concern for the boy, the girl, and the baby. It bothered him, but what could he do? The boy had grown on him while they'd lived and worked together, and by default, the girl and the child now concerned him as well. He hadn't realized just how much until

Chase vanished into the spirit world. Now his relief at hearing they'd returned safely was so great it nauseated him. Even so, until he saw them for himself, he remained uneasy.

"Why didn't you bring them here?" He leaned across the bed and clicked on the lamp to better see her face. Still lovely. Still compelling. Her hair flowed over her shoulders in waves so soft he almost reached out to touch them. He controlled the urge.

"I didn't want them to know we're working together. Not yet. I also had to return to Hades before I came here." She frowned. "I don't have to explain to the likes of you."

He reached out hesitantly, and when she didn't pull away, he put a hand on her arm. "I'm not grilling you, nor am I demanding you make an account of your decisions and actions to me."

She met his gaze, and he saw surprise and wariness in her eyes. He dropped his hand, and it rested on the coverlet as if awaiting further instructions.

"I'm only interested in learning what happened and why. Information only, for the sake of communication. If we work together, we must be honest and open with each other." He never thought he'd utter those words with any sincerity, but here he was telling her the gods' honest truth. He had no intention of lying to her or betraying her. If anything, he risked her betrayal. Goddesses, like gods, changed loyalties when it suited them. He could trust her now, but how long would that last?

"I like the girl," Cora said. "She's a fitting match for our son, and she's more powerful than she let on."

"She didn't know before, and neither did he. Does she now? Does he?" Something must've happened for

Cora to learn of Jaycie's true powers. He'd once told Chase she had average abilities, but he'd lied. He didn't want anyone to learn what a formidable team Chase and Jaycie made. Almost as formidable as Risto Fina and Cora—even before he'd discovered she was really Persephone.

That's just the cherry on the sundae. A ridiculous expression—he hated maraschino cherries—but the metaphor fit.

"Oh, yes, she knows. We'll have to manage her if we want them to join us. He still doesn't realize."

Fina rubbed his chin as he contemplated the news. "Chase and I didn't part on good terms. He hates me." It smarted. All he wanted was the best for himself and his family. Wasn't it better to have wealth and power than not? Let the masses scrabble for the crumbs the elite let fall. Far better to be not only one of the elite but also the one who dictated where and to whom the crumbs fell.

"How's your relationship with them?" he asked.

"Fine. Jaycie believed I'd betrayed her." Cora explained how she'd handed Jaycie over to Hypnos and Morpheus. "I had to. Hecate invited her to dinner. I needed to keep Jaycie from revealing too much about herself and Chase." She squinted at Risto Fina. "You tampered with their birth control herbs. They resent you for it."

"I had to. Without this child ..."

She patted his hand. "Yes, we need the child. She's the perfect combination and will carry on our legacy. If we're fortunate, she'll be easier to handle. We'll teach her from the moment she's able to speak." She shifted to face him.

"What's in it for you, Cora?" *What does a goddess want*

with human politics?

"It's simple. I want humans to dominate. That includes magi, naturally. Those who worship the gods should rule the earth. It's why we created you. These godless beings, these vampires and creatures that believe in nothing, diminish us." Her use of "us" included only gods and goddesses, and that's why he couldn't fully trust her. Her loyalties lay with divine beings, not mortals or magi.

"Gods didn't create them?" It hadn't occurred to him that not all life forms had divine origins.

"Some creatures evolved. We didn't intend for them to exist."

"But if you created the beings they evolved from, doesn't that make them your creations?"

She shook her head. "It makes them accidents." She shuffled closer to him and stroked his face. "You're still a beautiful man, Risto. You always were."

All thoughts of species and their origins vanished from his mind, and he put his arms around her and pulled her in close. Her lips were as soft and sweet as he remembered, and he hardened from the anticipation of what they would do next.

She gave a sexy sigh and climbed on top of him, and after that, nothing mattered to him for a long while except the goddess in his bed.

CHAPTER 33

No part of Kelsey reacted with despair when Josh told her he blamed her for ruining their lives. Human Kelsey would've sobbed her heart out. Baby vampire Kelsey no longer had a heart to break—but she had nerves he could grate on. She snarled, her fangs sliding out, and glowered at her son.

"I could say the same for you. You shouldn't have gotten involved with Dakota."

"Pull your fangs in. Who cares whose fault all this is? We're vampires now. We can do anything we want."

Pointedly, she let her gaze rove over their shabby surroundings. "Clearly, we can't. Why didn't you let me die? You say it's because Philip loves me? Philip told me he'd never turn me. I saw him try to stop you. You broke the law. You should've let me die." She rose from the couch and paced around the tiny room, forcing herself to take small, slow steps. The activity eased her nerves a little, and she kept her attention on Josh.

"All right. You want the truth?" His eyes flashed

fury.

She strode to the couch and stood in front of him, her hands fisted on her hips. "Yes."

"You made Philip create me." He stood and shoved his face into hers. "To live with pain. Torment. Hunger." He gripped her chin in his hand. She tried to slap it away, but it remained firm. "You tried to control me when I was a human. To control every part of my life—and then my death. You interfered in that, too. Now I'm your father. How's it feel? I get to control you now. Give you orders. Tell you when to eat. What to eat. When to stay or go." He released her chin but grabbed each of her upper arms in a tight grip.

Vaguely, she noted an absence of physical pain, but she resented him touching her.

Through gritted teeth, he said, "How does it feel, Mother?"

From somewhere deep within her, a laugh bubbled up. Why had she wasted so much time despairing and mooning over this boy? He'd cared nothing for her. "Thanks for the lesson. You'll be relieved to learn I don't care what you do now."

Hurt flashed across his face. He dropped his hands and spun away from her. "Perfect. Then we're equals now." He looked over his shoulder at her. "Go to your room and stay there."

She stormed into the bedroom, but after she slammed shut the door and locked it, she didn't stay there.

***

Cold had a smell. It filled Philip's nostrils, but he'd grown so accustomed to it he no longer noticed it. He noticed only its absence, so when it disappeared, he froze, trying to identify the scent replacing it.

He stood at the edge of a clearing, mere yards from the cabin, and opened all his senses. Wind rustled the trees. Above him, beyond the tree canopy, the stars sparkled around the thin crescent moon. An owl swooped past, but it didn't dip down. Philip heard no sound of animals scurrying through the underbrush. His nostrils caught the odor of death and decay with the aroma of pine underneath it. Then he identified Josh's familiar scent of spice, wood smoke, and clean lake water. He was out here, but the whiff of the boy's presence gradually faded, showing he moved away from Philip's location.

He listened, but he'd taught the boy to move stealthily, and he'd learned the lesson well. Where was Kelsey? Philip couldn't detect her, which meant Josh had either left her alone in the cabin or she'd escaped him. Either way, the boy would answer to Philip—as soon as he corralled the pair and dragged them back to the hideout.

Philip was returning from an underground market where he'd sold the carcasses of the animals they'd hunted that evening. The money didn't amount to much, but it helped him avoid a trip to the bank. At a bank, he risked exposure to cameras or recognition from civilians who'd consider turning him in to the authorities. Even with glamour, an exhausting effort, he risked exposing himself when out in public. One slip was all it took, as they'd recently learned.

How did we get on Frank Evans's radar? he asked himself, as he'd done repeatedly since it'd happened. No doubt they'd screwed up and exposed themselves enough to allow Evans's men to find them. *But how?*

He traipsed through the trees, heading in the direction in which he sensed Josh, his mind obsessed with fear for Kelsey. Ever since Josh had turned her, she caused him worry—as all baby vamps did. But Philip wasn't her maker, which caused problems. He had no physical hold over her. Now she'd lost her humanity, he had no emotional hold over her either. She'd said she loved him when she was a human, but the moment she turned, she lost all emotional attachments.

The irony of their situation frustrated him. When she was human, they couldn't get involved romantically for many obvious reasons. Now that she was a vampire, an intimate relationship was possible, but she'd lost the desire for one. If this wasn't the worst example of "be careful what you wish for—"

A soft crunch of snow up ahead alerted him to the boy's proximity. That, and he caught the lad's scent now. Philip slowed his pace.

The cabin Philip had found for them was in the heart of the former Killbear Provincial Park. The government had ceded control of all provincial parks to indigenous species after the big war. Humans took over Killbear. Most of them used their cabins for recreation rather than to escape society the way other species did in other parks. The decision to hide in Killbear brought substantial risk. The cabin they'd commandeered reeked of human, but it gave them shelter—and isolation since no neighbors lived nearby.

Philip assessed his surroundings.

Josh had made significant progress away from their hiding place, almost reaching Blind Bay Road. That he headed for Highway 559 Philip didn't doubt. He quickened his pace but remained silent and stealthy. He followed Josh's trail for another mile, deliberately hanging back. The boy kept up an even, rapid pace but never reached vampire velocity.

He's tracking Kelsey or else he'd move faster.

Philip sniffed the air and caught Kelsey's personal scent: lavender, citrus, cinnamon.

Something caused Kelsey to bolt, and Josh chased after her. That thought gave Philip the impetus he needed, and he increased his speed until he overtook Josh.

"Where's Kelsey?" He kept his voice even, his tone calm and patient, but he struggled to do so.

Josh startled and spun around to face his father. He'd been so absorbed in tracking his quarry he'd neglected to listen for pursuit. Philip made a mental note to teach the boy to do both, but for now, all that mattered was learning why they'd disobeyed his directive to stay home.

Fear showed in Josh's eyes, and he took a step backward. "I'm sorry."

The boy sensed his father's rage and worry. Philip cursed under his breath. He hadn't intended to scare the kid.

"Tell me what happened—fast. Then we'll catch up to her."

Josh's mouth opened and his gaze registered surprise. "You know she left?"

"You're following her spoor. Now tell me what the hell happened. We don't have much time. All of us are now outside the protections I put up. Why do you think I told you to stay put?" His anger and frustration leaked through this time, and he shook his head, negating what he'd said. "Tell me and we'll fix it."

Hesitantly at first, Josh relayed the discussion he'd had with Kelsey and how it ended with him sending her to the bedroom. The more he talked, the more agitated he became. His voice rose and he talked faster. By the time he finished, he was frantic with worry.

"She made me mad, and I wanted to punish her. I shouldn't have, but I couldn't help myself."

"Forget about that for now. We'll work it out when we catch her. Why'd she leave?"

Josh shrugged. "I went to check on her, to fix it— you know, how you always fixed things with me after we fought. She's my daughter, no matter what she was before I turned her. I'm responsible for her."

It relieved Philip to hear the boy say that. He never should've turned Kelsey. He was just a baby vamp himself and unready for the responsibility of creating a new life. That he at least acknowledged his role as her father boded well for the relationship. The important thing now, though, was catching up to her.

Philip had a sudden, terrifying realization he knew exactly where she headed.

CHAPTER 34

Kelsey smelled the cold as well, but her quarry's scent buried it so far down the olfactory layers she didn't acknowledge it. Months of living with vampires had helped her adapt after Josh turned her, and she'd developed an arsenal of vampire skills. This enabled her to slip onto the grounds of Frank Evans's home without triggering security. Now, she rested atop the roof of the sprawling story-and-a-half bungalow and contemplated breaking in through an upper-floor dormer window. Indecision over what to do after prevented her from taking the step.

While she sat there, she watched for any activity on the grounds. No one manned the gates—they were electronic, entry gained through a button push and an intercom system. Nothing moved, but she didn't expect activity yet. The time was closer to dawn than midnight, though, and that made her position more precarious as the minutes ticked by. While she was certain she could hide on the roof indefinitely, once the day began for the crime boss, more of his personnel would appear or he'd leave. Neither of those options helped her. She needed to act, but she also had to decide whether she'd take her wrath out on Frank or his entire family.

Revenge was unfamiliar to her, and she didn't want to do anything regrettable. Even a baby vampire understood consequences. Her plans would enrage Philip, but the force of that rage depended on the amount of devastation she wrought.

Decision made, she crept to the window. She'd already peered inside the curtainless room and verified they used it for storage. The locking mechanism wouldn't cause her any problems, but the entire house was wired. She had to first disable the security system. While human Kelsey would've balked at that, baby vampire Kelsey considered it a minor inconvenience. If she hurried, she could shut it down at the box before the time limit expired and the police appeared. The entire household would wake up from the racket unless it was a silent alarm, but all she needed was one of them in her grip, and the rest should fall in line.

She rose and smashed the window in with her foot. No sound but the tinkling of glass. The alarm was silent. She cleared the glass and slipped inside. The last time she'd visited the home, terror had prevented her from noticing the alarm panel, but she remembered her way to the front door. As with most alarm systems, the control panel was mounted on the wall next to it. She ripped it open and tore out the wires and the batteries. With vampire speed, she began her search for Frank Evans.

***

Philip had guessed correctly: Kelsey's trail ended at Frank Evans's home. He and Josh stood outside the view of the cameras and surveyed the house.

"There." Philip put a hand on Josh's shoulder and pointed at the house's roof. "That window." The words had barely left his mouth when their quarry kicked in the glass and slipped inside.

"*Tabarnak*," Philip cursed. "Let's go. Move fast to blur the cameras in case she hasn't already disabled them." He rushed to the roof and followed Kelsey through the window.

Inside, he scanned the storage room. She'd already left it, so he rushed down the stairs to the front hallway. When he followed her trail, he discovered she'd hit the security panel and then backtracked down the hall to the bedrooms. With Josh on his heels, Philip raced for the master bedroom, where he expected to find Kelsey. Muffled voices told him he wasn't too late—he distinguished both Frank Evans's gruff voice and Kelsey's light, feminine one.

He wheeled around a corner and raced through the door to capture her in his arms. "Make sure Evans and his wife don't move from the bed," he told Josh. The last thing they needed was for Evans to grab a gun while Philip struggled to contain Kelsey—and struggle they did.

"Let me go." She kicked at him and fought to escape his arms, but he overpowered her easily, not only because he was physically stronger but also because she was still just a baby.

"What the hell do you think you're doing?" he said in her ear. He allowed his rage to leak through in his tone. "I won't let you kill a human."

"Belanger, control your dog." Evans sat in the king-size bed, his wife cradled in his arms. His tone turned soothing. "We'll be fine, Noleen."

Philip saw no sign of Evans's two kids and hoped Kelsey hadn't already harmed them.

"He's responsible for Josh. For me. He killed us." Kelsey stopped struggling, but Philip kept his arms tight around her. Josh stood next to the bed, Evans splitting wary glances between the trio invading his room.

"She's not wrong," Philip said, staring into the crime boss's eyes.

"What's happening? Why are these people in our home?" Noleen's eyes widened. "The children." She made a move to leap from the bed, but Josh held her down with a hand to her shoulder.

"Stay," he said.

"My babies. I want to see my babies." Her voice held terror and desperation.

"Where are the kids?" Philip asked Kelsey.

With her gaze leveled on Frank Evans, she said, "Indisposed."

Noleen cried out and struggled to get free.

Kelsey's gaze shifted to Evans's wife. "They're alive—which is more than I can say for how your husband's goons left my son. One of them shot him in cold blood."

Tears streamed down Noleen's face. "Please, I didn't know."

Kelsey hissed. "Because you didn't care to know. As long as you can live in luxury, you don't give a damn how many innocent lives your sociopath husband destroys."

"That's not true. He's a businessman, not a criminal."

Kelsey shook her head. "Don't lie to me. If you don't lie to me, perhaps I'll let you live."

Philip tugged on her arms, and she squirmed against him. "You're not killing anyone."

"You turned them both," Evans said. "Whether or not you kill us, you'll pay for that. If you let her kill us, she'll pay with her life as well."

Philip allowed the crime boss to assume he'd turned both humans, but Josh corrected him. "I turned my mother."

Shooting his son a dirty look, Philip said, "I'll do the talking here."

Chastened, the boy hung his head and said, "Yes, Father."

Evans pounced on the admission. "Then you'll both get the death penalty." He rubbed his chin as though contemplating a brilliant idea. "Maybe ..."

Philip recognized that look. Evans intended to make an offer that would tie Philip to the crime boss, the way he'd done thirty years before.

"Tell you what, Philip. May I call you Philip?"

The vampire snarled. "Say your piece."

He considered taking Kelsey and Josh and going on the run again, but if he did, Evans would report them to whichever cops he had on his payroll. Some of them were high-ranking, and then it was only a matter of time before they tracked down and arrested the fugitives. Evans had tracked them down once; he could do it again, and the whole nightmare would start over.

Alternatively, they could kill all the humans in the house, leaving no witnesses, but Philip refused the idea of murder as an option, especially the murder of children. And turning them all into vamps? The thought flitted through his mind with barely an acknowledgment.

If the crime boss offered a solution to end their running, Philip would consider it.

Frank Evans patted his wife's shoulder and released her. He sat up straight and met Philip's gaze with no hint of fear or concern. "Very well. Here's what I propose."

CHAPTER 35

Sunshine streamed into Jaycie's bedroom when she threw open the curtains just after eight in the morning, three days after their return from Hades. Chase was already awake and in his room, getting dressed. They alternated their nights between the two beds. She wanted to suggest buying a queen bed and moving into his room, which was larger, but so far, she hadn't broached the subject. The exact cause of her hesitation eluded her. Maybe it was because his explanation of how he'd settled the argument with Hecate seemed thin and made Jaycie suspicious. He claimed the goddess tried to talk him into returning Jaycie and her baby to Hades, and he'd talked her out of it, but he refused to elaborate on how.

What convinced the goddess of the underworld to relent and walk away from something she considered important? Hecate and Chase had argued passionately before the goddess relented.

What did he promise her?

He insisted he'd only given the goddess assurances

he'd protect mother and baby—which was where the doubts came from. Would Hecate put all her trust in Chase after a simple assurance of protection? Jaycie loved him, but she doubted he could guarantee her safety even if she'd grown in power since she'd entered Hades and was able to protect herself.

She didn't press the point with Chase, but she also didn't believe he'd told her everything, and that added a measure of distrust to the relationship.

The door opened and Chase stuck his head in. "Going out to pick up the food now."

Jaycie sucked in a breath and released it slowly. "All right. Are Daniel and Martin leaving?"

"Already gone."

"I don't have a problem with them meeting my parents; I prefer it happened some other time."

Jaycie had phoned her parents as soon as she and Chase arrived home and reassured them she was safe. Now she needed to tell them she was pregnant, and she wanted to do that in person—without an audience. That scene with her mother in the dream world's restaurant remained fresh in her mind. Unwilling to risk a public meeting, she'd invited them to Saturday brunch. The roommates had cleared out, and she vowed to make it up to them.

Chase stepped into the room. "They're happy to help. Besides, it gives them an excuse to go out with their girlfriends, so your conscience is clear."

She gave him a shy smile. "Think Mom will mind if I don't make the food myself?"

His expression turned serious, and he rushed to her side. "It doesn't matter what *we* serve."

She appreciated the reminder they'd face her demanding and judgmental mother and stoic and judgmental father together.

Stress on the "mental." She didn't find her little joke funny, just sad.

Jaycie waved him off and spent the time during his absence cleaning the apartment she'd already cleaned the day before. When her phone rang, she was in the middle of giving the kitchen floor a final cleaning. She checked the call display and didn't recognize the number, and the name showed as an unkown caller.

She almost didn't answer it, but when her uneasiness increased the longer she ignored the ringing, she propped her mop against the kitchen counter and accepted the call.

"Hello?"

"Jaycie Nevil?" a man with a powerful voice asked.

"Can I help you?" She hoped it wasn't some scammer wasting her time. She considered hanging up on him, but she couldn't do it without learning who called and what he wanted.

"It's Master Risto Fina." He said nothing more.

At first, she was too stunned to respond. The silence grew awkward and unbearable, so she broke it. "Hello, sir."

Her face flushed with embarrassment, and she scurried into the living room. Dropping onto the couch, she pulled her knees to her chest. Again, the silence grew, and she realized he was deliberately making her uncomfortable. This time, she determined to wait him out.

He called me. He can damn well tell me what he wants. And why isn't he calling Chase? Maybe he had, and Chase refused to answer. He'd told Jaycie everything that had happened since she'd vanished into Hades. She'd never trusted Risto Fina before the disastrous summoning of

Cora, and she trusted him even less now.

"I see my son has told you about our issues."

"He told me you tampered with our birth control and tried to prevent him from rescuing me." She swallowed around a lump of fear and added, "I was trapped in Hades, and you left me there."

"Not forever. I wanted him to summon Persephone and open the doors first."

"You mean, for the good of the many, you abandoned me in Hades." She sat up straight, letting her feet drop to the floor.

"Yes. One person's needs are important, but he needed to handle the priority situation he created."

She had no reply to that. How could she argue against it? The needs of the many did outweigh her needs. Spirits had been trapped on the physical plane. Helping them would've given her a way to leave the spirit plane also—if she hadn't been under a god's spell at the time.

In a calmer voice, she said, "How can I help you today, sir?" She flushed again. *I sound like a customer service rep*. On the heels of that thought came another. *How does he know we're back if Chase never called him?*

They'd dealt with the easier parents first: Jaycie's parents and Chase's adoptive parents. All were relieved and delighted at Jaycie's return, and Chase's parents already knew about her pregnancy and had promised to provide all the help they needed. Chase planned to tackle Risto Fina later that day, but the master mage had beaten them to it. They should've expected this.

Of course, he knows we're back. She frowned. Where had Cora really gone when she'd left them three days ago?

"I'm inviting you both for dinner at my place

tonight. We have a lot to discuss."

She waited so long to reply, he said, "I'm calling you because you can make Chase listen to reason. He's angry with me. He loves you and wanted to make you the priority despite broader obligations. I want to talk. Explain."

When her silence continued, he did, too. "Jaycie, you're carrying my grandchild. I want to be involved."

I bet you do. You got me pregnant. She said, "What time should we come over?" *As long as I can convince Chase to go.*

CHAPTER 36

Donna Nevil shifted in her seat and held her coffee mug out to Jaycie. "Top me up, would you, dear?" She dabbed her mouth with the napkin she'd set in her lap at the start of the meal and then placed it on her plate.

As always, Donna had overdressed for such a casual event. This time, she wore a green chenille jumpsuit with gauzy, cuffed sleeves. Her light-gold pumps, covered in gold rhinestones, sported four-inch heels with a green chenille stripe down the back of the heel. She'd left her light-gold handbag, also rhinestone studded, on the living room couch.

Jaycie wore her typical T-shirt and jeans. As in the dream world, she'd done it to make a statement, but unlike in the dream world, her mother hadn't frowned with distaste over it. Jaycie appreciated that and wondered how much of the blame for the volatile relationship fell on her own shoulders. Had her dream mother been a construct of Jaycie's psyche rather than an accurate reflection of the real woman? If so, Jaycie needed to revise her assumptions and consider how much of the judgment she felt from her parents resulted from projection.

Jaycie rose from her seat at the dining room table where she sat with Chase, her mother, and her father.

Sandor, her father, grunted and held his mug out as well. "Make mine a double." He laughed at his own joke, and Jaycie and Chase chuckled. Donna gave him a tolerant but affectionate smile. Sandor wasn't as dressed up as his wife, but he wore black dress pants and a collared shirt with a jacket. Chase wore jeans and a shirt and jacket, a compromise between Jaycie and her parents. She hadn't coached him to dress that way—he'd intuited the need and acted accordingly.

The introductions had gone smoothly enough when Jaycie's parents arrived. Donna and Sandor both greeted Chase with enthusiasm. They probably still celebrated Jaycie's rescue from what they believed was a kidnapping. They'd heard the news reports about Chase and his role in closing the doors between the worlds. When they'd learned he'd trapped their daughter on the other side, their fury made them resent him. Now that she was back and he'd fixed the problem, they forgave him. Jaycie expected their attitude would change when they learned Chase had also gotten their daughter pregnant.

So far, no one had broached either subject. She'd asked Chase to avoid both topics until they finished eating. Perhaps a full belly would soften her mother's wrath though her mother ate sparingly, always watching her weight. At the very least, the nibbles of eggs Benedict and sips of coffee should reduce the chances low blood sugar would cause her to lash out.

"Shall we take the coffee into the living room? We

can eat dessert there." Jaycie filled each mug with coffee from the coffeemaker's stainless-steel pot and carried it to the coffee table.

Chase pushed his chair back and stood up. "A great idea. I'll get the pastries and take them out. Would you like me to carry your coffee for you, Donna?"

To Jaycie's surprise, her mother had suggested Chase call her Donna rather than Mrs. Nevil, and Sandor had followed suit. That they were all on a first-name basis now boded well, but how long would the affability last once they divulged their pregnancy news?

Once everyone settled in the living room, Jaycie placed her mug on the coffee table and motioned with a tilt of her head for Chase to follow suit. When he did, she took his hand and moved her gaze to her mother and then her father. Her throat tightened, and she cleared it with a rumble.

Both parents looked up, and her mother frowned as if she recognized something she wouldn't like was coming.

Jaycie kept her gaze on Donna, who she suddenly saw with fresh eyes. Her mother, after all, had carried Jaycie for nine months, gave birth to her, cared for her all her life. Not that her father hadn't cared for her, but this was different. Perhaps the baby would provide the opportunity they needed to draw closer.

"We have news." Jaycie glanced at Chase, and his warm presence next to her made her smile. She faced her parents again and barreled ahead. "I'm pregnant. Chase and I are having a baby girl."

Chase released her hand and placed his arm around her shoulders.

Sandor shook his head and stared at Jaycie. "Well, I'll be. I thought you were going to mage school.

You're going to be a wife instead?"

Before Jaycie could respond, Chase said, "Not at all."

She was grateful to him because her initial reaction had been to lash out. Her father hadn't even acknowledged he was about to become a grandfather. This was his unsubtle way of telling her his preferred course of action.

"Jaycie will finish her education. It'll just take longer," Chase said.

"When?"

They all turned to look at Donna.

"Well, after the baby's born. I can finish this semester and next semester though it'll be close," Jaycie said.

Donna shook her head. "When's the baby due?"

"Mid-July," Jaycie replied. "Close to your birthday."

Her mother sat up straight on the edge of her seat, her legs crossed at the ankles and canted in a ladylike posture. Her mug hovered near her face as though she'd forgotten she wanted to sip from it. She gazed down her nose at it and tilted forward to place it on the coffee table. She once more held her head high and folded her delicate hands in her lap. Her gold and diamond wedding rings glinted in the sunlight coming in through the living room windows. "You're old enough to handle this, Jaycie. One question: are you happy about it?"

Tears welled up in Jaycie's eyes. "Yes. We're ecstatic. We …" She'd almost revealed they'd met their daughter in spirit already. Instead, she said, "We can't wait."

"Then we'll deal with it together." Donna's tone was even, steady, but her eyes, too, were damp.

Jaycie had an urge to go to her mother and hug her, but she restrained herself. Her mother had never been the touchy-feely type. She disliked people hugging her, even her own children.

Sandor cut in, directing his questions at Chase. "What are your plans, then? Are you a student? Jaycie never told us what you do for a living."

Chase squeezed her shoulders, and she put her arm around his waist and squeezed back. "I'm studying to become a master mage, sir."

"Wait a minute," Sandor said. "We're all delighted you found my daughter and brought her home, but you're in Dutch with the council, aren't you? They let you return to your studies?"

Chase hesitated. "I still have some things to sort out, but once everything settles, I'll continue my studies. I'm working part-time right now at a bookstore."

They'd agreed he wouldn't mention his birth father. If her parents asked about his family, he'd discuss only his adoptive parents without revealing the adoption. For now, the pair wanted to keep things simple, and piling Chase's genealogy on top of the pregnancy news would overly complicate things.

Her parents frowned.

"We didn't anticipate this pregnancy," Sandor said, staring at his daughter. "We support your relationship choices, but we figured this one was temporary."

Jaycie froze. "I don't understand. Are you saying you assumed we'd break up?"

Donna spoke, her tone reasonable and implying no one could argue with her logic. "This is your first serious relationship. We didn't expect it to last." She leaned forward, meeting Jaycie's gaze unwaveringly.

"This pregnancy changes things, but you still have options."

"What options?" Chase asked, his voice laced with anger.

"Why, government support for our daughter," Donna replied, as though incredulous Chase didn't understand the obvious. "As a single mother, programs exist she can take advantage of. Naturally, she's welcome to move back home."

"Right," Sandor agreed. "Her schooling can wait. She'll have the baby, and we'll help her raise it. You two can continue to see each other, but you don't have to live together. That's what got you into this mess."

"You won't dictate how I live my life," Jaycie said, wondering how things had gotten so messed up. She'd thought at first that her parents intended to give her emotional support through this, but what they'd meant by getting through this together was controlling her life.

As always.

She turned to Chase and buried her face in his shoulder, unable to stop a flood of tears.

Over her head, Chase said, "I'm sorry you feel this way, but we'll decide what's best for us. We appreciate any support you're willing to offer, but I won't allow anyone to upset her." He gave her a squeeze and then pulled back to look into her face. "You okay?"

She nodded, unable to speak past the lump in her throat.

Sandor stood. "Well, I guess you told us. I think it's time we left. Donna, get your coat."

Jaycie turned her tearstained face to her mother, who met her daughter's gaze with a compassion-filled expression.

"We have your best interests at heart. Consider all your options. We'll discuss this later, when everyone has calmed down." Donna stood. "We'll see ourselves out."

She picked up her handbag and slipped her arm through Sandor's. Together, they walked to the foyer and retrieved their coats from the closet. In silence, they bundled up for the cold outside and opened the door.

Jaycie jumped to her feet. "Mom. Dad."

They halted. Turned.

"I love you."

Her father grunted and nodded. Her mother said, "We'll talk later." They stepped through the doors and shut them tight.

Chase rose and put his arms around her. "Don't worry, baby. They'll come around."

She leaned into him and sighed. "I guess, but I have something else to tell you. Your father called. He's expecting us for dinner tonight. I'm sorry, but I didn't have time to tell you before my parents arrived."

"My father?" His voice telegraphed his disbelief.

"Risto Fina. Are you mad at me?"

He squeezed her close. "I'm not thrilled at the news, but it's not your fault. I have to face him eventually. Might as well do it today. Without him, I won't get reinstated to the mage program."

She swiveled around to hug him. If things had gone so wrong with her parents, what would happen when they faced the master mage?

CHAPTER 37

Nervous energy propelled Kelsey into the living room of their new penthouse apartment in downtown Tkaronto.

"I need to hunt." Her fangs slid out, scraping along the inside of her cheeks. Reflexively, she opened her mouth to avoid piercing her lower gums. She tilted her head back, widening her jaw, and adjusted her mouth to a more comfortable position.

Fangs suck.

She forced herself to calm down and retract them, then eased her mouth closed. This didn't take away the gnawing hunger, but it did make it more tolerable.

Philip rose from the couch and met her at the sliding doors to the balcony.

An inch of snow coated most of the large outdoor area, except where an awning protected the spot in front of the doors. The patio furniture and barbecue were draped in weatherproof polyester coverings.

In the distance, the sun slid toward the horizon. Skyscrapers and the CN Tower, which had been rebuilt after getting destroyed during the species wars, completed the view.

Though Christmas approached, the apartment had no tree and displayed no decorations or lights. The only one to care about the holiday, Kelsey had lost the spirit for it when she became a vampire.

"Have a bottle of donated blood." He put a hand on her shoulder.

She glared at it, and he dropped it, giving her a pained expression.

Josh, ever solicitous since they'd made the deal with Frank Evans, came rushing from his bedroom. He spent most of his time there whenever they were home.

They needed to remain hidden from the authorities until the documents Evans promised them arrived. Once they had those, the deal would truly be sealed. The mob boss would essentially own them, but they'd no longer have to live as fugitives.

Kelsey didn't care, because Philip and Josh were already controlling her life, but she knew it bothered the hell out of Philip. Someday she'd develop enough stakes in the game to resent Evans, but for now, only hunting and feeding meant anything to her.

Her sire put his arm around her. "I'll take you hunting as soon as we're allowed out." He looked at Philip, who nodded.

Josh still hadn't gained enough confidence to guide her through baby vampirehood without input from his maker, and she found reassurance in Philip's presence. His devotion to both her and Josh was evident. Too bad she no longer felt anything for him.

She hissed when her fangs erupted again.

Josh stroked her hair, and it calmed her enough that they retracted.

How did Josh and Philip control themselves? Would she ever reach the point where the thought of hunting or feeding didn't trigger fangs? Even at that thought, they slid out.

To vent her frustration, she raised her face to the ceiling and howled like a werewolf.

"Come on." Josh steered her to the kitchen.

He retrieved a bottle of donated blood from the refrigerator's section that was optimized for storing blood.

The deal with Evans meant they now lived like regular vampires. Vampires populated most of the units in this condo building, and all the amenities catered to their lifestyle. A few humans also lived in the building, and Kelsey wondered if they enjoyed letting vampires feed on them. If so, she planned to make their acquaintance—whenever Philip and Josh took their controlling eyes off her.

Her fangs appeared. She popped the cap with a thumb and began to chug back everything in the bottle.

"Slow down." Josh placed a restraining hand on the bottle. "When you drink too fast, you don't allow it to relieve your hunger. You'll want more even though you don't need it."

Stupid vampire rules. Stupid vampire physiology.

It wasn't all immortality, traveling at breakneck speeds, and super strength. Little things about it drove her crazy. Too many rules and physical limitations; too much burning hunger and craving blood. Sure, she'd always known they drank blood and had to cover up in the sun, but now that she had to do it herself, she resented it.

Nevertheless, she did as he suggested and slowed the gulps to a steady draw. Even so, the bottle emptied before satisfying her need.

She thrust it at Josh. "Another one."

"Tsk. I told you. Now you'll have to wait."

She made a grab for the fridge, but he stopped her with an outthrust arm. "You'll wait."

"I need it." She snarled, and her fangs sprang free again.

"You'll wait because you don't need it. You drank too quickly."

Her hands curled into fists, and an all-encompassing rage seeped through her body. Before she could leap on Josh, arms wrapped around her and dragged her from the room.

She kicked and fought, but Philip's strength outmatched hers. Vaguely she wondered if their building had a gym and if working out could develop her strength enough to beat him one day.

He threw her over his shoulder, and she pounded on his back like a damsel being kidnapped by a troll.

"Put me down."

Silently, he carried her to the master bedroom and dropped her on the king-size bed they shared.

She bounced from the force of his toss and scampered to the side farthest from where he stood. Her fangs sprang out, this time from rage rather than hunger. All thoughts of feeding vanished, replaced by a desire to tear apart this man who loved her.

"Easy, darling," he said.

He dragged a hand across his head and stroked the spot where he'd once had a ponytail. The hair he'd cut off was growing back but at a human's pace. Vampires could grow hair on their heads but not beards if they'd died clean-shaven. None of it made sense.

She eyed him warily, but her fangs retracted. "I want

out."

His eyes narrowed, and he stared at her with more concern than she'd seen in him since her turning.

"What do you mean?" His tone revealed he knew exactly what she meant.

"I want my own place. To go back to my ..." She fell silent. She'd wanted to say store.

"Your previous life?"

"I don't know."

Did she want to return to her old life? To Blair?

She flashed back to an image of Blair bursting in on them at their cabin in Algonquin and Philip mesmerizing him into forgetfulness. Philip had sheltered her for a long time, and she'd fought him over it.

She dropped her head into her hands.

"I don't know what to think anymore. How to behave." She looked up and met his gaze. "I'm a bitch, but I can't stop myself. It takes over. This wildness. This ... hate."

He climbed onto the bed, and she watched him crawl nearer. He stopped short of touching her as he did every time they went to bed.

They shared sleeping quarters so he could supervise her, but he respected her physical boundaries. They'd become nocturnal now she was one of the undead and preferred the dark of night to the burning light of day.

"You're not filled with hate. That's not you."

She shuddered. "Josh hated me when he first turned. It hurt me. I remember how my heart ached." She angled her face toward the window.

They hadn't been up for long. At this time of year, night fell at four thirty. Soon, they'd notice the days lengthening. She understood now why vampires preferred the winter. Cold didn't faze them, and they welcomed the all-consuming darkness.

They must love Alaska.

"You'll get it back."

She shook her head. "You mistake my meaning. I don't want it back. When I loved, it drove me to drink and to destroy my life because I lost Josh's love and couldn't turn mine off."

He edged closer, his knee almost touching her thigh. "What about physical contact?"

"Sex?" She contemplated the idea of just fucking him. It didn't revolt her. It might help her release this desire to run and hunt, to track prey and bring it down.

He sighed. "Sex can help release what's bottled up." He met her gaze steadily, his brown eyes piercing hers.

She remembered the flutters that used to rise in her chest just by looking at him, and something twisted inside her. When she was human, she'd thought he attracted her because that's the effect vampires had on humans. She hadn't trusted she loved him because of who he was. She'd thought she loved him because of what he was, that his vampire charms seduced her.

In the before times, she'd have hated the very idea of sex as physical release. Now, she wanted only that relief from the pent-up energy and tension that constantly knotted her insides. His body, rock hard and cold, would fit against hers. He'd overpower and exhaust her.

The passion rose in her, fierce and feral. She imagined doing wild things to his body. Her fangs snicked out again, and something liquid dripped down her chin. She wiped it with her hand, and when she looked down, she found red-tinged drool.

"I can feel your need," he whispered. "I can smell

your desire."

She sniffed the air.

He, too, had released a scent—primal and spicy and delicious. His yearning for her swept over her like a tidal wave. Her loins ached to be filled, and she wanted him to take her violently. She wanted to ride him wildly.

Kelsey lunged, and he met her fierceness with his own ferocity. Together, they tumbled into the bed.

CHAPTER 38

Her wildness as she claimed him—and he viewed it as Kelsey claiming him rather than the other way around—fueled his passion and his love.

Philip had held off suggesting they get physical even though he knew it would alleviate her burning hunger and lust for blood. Unlike Josh's early days as a vampire, their current situation meant baby vamp Kelsey couldn't use hunting and gorging on animals to work through her feral inclinations. Sex remained the only alternative.

It'd been days in coming, her rage and tension crescendoing into the howl of pain and frustration she'd released in the living room earlier. He'd realized then he'd have to suggest this even as his conscience nagged him that he did it to meet his own selfish needs as much as hers. The moment she pounced on him, however, all his doubts, all his reservations, and all his guilt vanished. Lust and love twined together, sweeping him away so that all he knew, all he saw, all that *consumed* him, was Kelsey.

They bit each other—that was nonnegotiable considering her state—and he reveled in the exchange of blood.

Since two vampires couldn't procreate the traditional way, they needn't worry about contraception. Because the only infection vampires spread created new vampires, STDs or any other diseases also didn't concern them.

So they bit. They licked. They sucked and touched and pleasured one another. Her delight and enthusiasm, and his abiding love for her, took him to heights he'd never experienced in any other coupling. He concentrated on her needs. Because she remained in that baby vamp stage, so did she, but he didn't care if she focused solely on herself. Certain he could regain her love, he gave and gave while she took and took.

He watched her, and his excitement built when her eyes rolled back in her head and she cried out in triumph as she climaxed under him. He felt as though he'd won a prize, but if he thought she'd finished with him, he was mistaken.

She spun them around, swapping out their positions so she straddled him, anchoring herself to him. Human Kelsey would never have behaved with such reckless abandon. Part of him missed the gentle, self-conscious aspect of her, but he reveled in the animal part becoming a vampire had unleashed. When she regained that portion of herself she'd lost in the turning, he'd treasure it all the more.

His body took over, and his thoughts floated away in a heady release. Now his eyes rolled back, and he cried out, his masculine sounds obscuring her soft, feminine sighs. When he lay boneless and spent beneath her, she flopped forward onto his chest, closed her eyes, and slept. Not daring to disturb her, he gave a contented sigh and followed suit.

***

Vampires slept infrequently and never for long. Kelsey opened her eyes and took in her surroundings. Philip lay under her, his muscled chest and broad shoulders providing a firm bed for her satiated body.

She felt energized but no longer tense and frustrated. *Sex. Who'da thought it worked like this?*

Why hadn't he proposed this sooner? But she knew why. He loved her, but she didn't love him, and this had cost him. Recognizing that surprised her, but she'd drawn the knowledge from her human experiences and not from genuine empathy.

He muttered something she didn't catch even with her acute vampire hearing and opened his eyes. "I felt you stirring."

She met his gaze with lust, her loins burning in response.

"You've stirred me again." She practically purred the words.

He grinned, but she sensed a sadness in him. It dampened her desire, and she stroked his cheek to soothe him. It pleased her that she wanted to make the effort.

"Let's get a drink." She licked her lips, and her fangs slid out in anticipation. To prove to him, and herself, that she controlled the urge, she steadied her breathing and retracted them.

"Well done, darling," he said. "A bottle of that donated blood sounds great."

Instantly, she shuddered and the fangs reappeared.

"I get one for myself, right?"

"Show me you can wait."

She wanted to cry from the want building inside her, but she breathed out the tension and breathed in the fangs. Giving him an exaggerated grin that showed her teeth, she said, "See?"

He stroked her hair. "Yes. Perfect." He closed his eyes, and she sensed his sadness bubbling up.

Her presence hurt him. No, it was her indifference that hurt him. *Am I a sociopath now? How long will this last?*

At first, she'd thought it a blessing. A life of indifference to others' suffering had appealed to her. Eat. Sleep. No pooping. It sounded like heaven. Just take and devour. She'd watched Josh go through it, and he'd reveled in it, too. He'd changed over the months, though, until he exhibited random acts of kindness or compassion. Would that happen to her? Did she want it to?

She climbed off Philip and searched for her clothes. She didn't remember removing them and found their shirts, jeans, and underthings strewn about the room. They'd torn their shirts, and her jeans had lost the button over the fly. The frenzied image of them tearing the clothes from their bodies to get to the goodies beneath flashed in her head.

Her fangs popped out, and she pushed all thoughts of ferocious sex from her mind. They retracted. Pride at her self-control made the gnawing hunger bearable. Perhaps learning to feel again was the reward for regaining the social graces she'd lost to vampirehood.

A hunt through her dresser produced a clean T-shirt and jeans, and she threw them on over a clean pair of panties. She didn't bother with the bra. Not only had her body firmed and grown more youthful after her transition, but ever since she learned they'd be stuck inside for a while, she'd dispensed with wearing bras. Comfort meant more to her than style if she had to suffer through forced isolation.

Philip, too, rolled out of bed and riffled through his dresser for clean clothes. He slipped on a pair of briefs, then jeans and a dress shirt. They both left their feet bare. She'd always considered his feet sexy, and the sight of them made her want to toss him on the bed again.

"Come on. None of that now." He led her from the room.

***

When Kelsey and Philip emerged from the bedroom, Josh was watching television. They strolled past him, hand in hand, but he barely looked up. Kelsey giggled at something Philip said, and he responded with another humorous rejoinder.

Josh was grateful his mom and father were getting along and that his mom appeared calmer and free of the childish rage dominating her personality since she'd turned. Hopefully, the relationship didn't become too saccharine. He wasn't sure he could stomach all that sweetness.

Suddenly, all three vampires froze and then turned toward the door. Someone stood outside it. A human male, from the smell of him.

Philip growled low in his throat, and his fangs slid free with a soft snick. "You two stay put." He waited until the doorbell rang to move in its direction.

Philip zipped over and threw it open, startling one of Evans's goons.

The man held out his hand, offering Philip a large manila envelope. "You've been waiting for this."

Philip nodded once, snatched the envelope from the man's hands, and slammed the door in his face, locking it for good measure.

Josh grinned. Evans might force them to work for him, but they didn't have to be polite about it.

"Open it," Kelsey prompted when Philip remained standing there.

He gave his head a shake, as though she'd awakened him from a daze, and tore off the top flap. He removed the documents and the two lapel pins inside it, letting the envelope glide to the floor.

Both Josh and Kelsey nipped to his side and looked over his shoulder as Philip shuffled through the papers, one page at a time.

"Looks as if you're both officially vampires," Philip said.

"That didn't take long," Kelsey said.

Josh picked up one of the lapel pins Philip held in his upturned palm and examined it.

All identification pins were simple, and this one was no exception. Where his Human pin was a white circle with a blue "H" inside, the Vampire pin was a white circle with a yellow "V" inside. From now on, he'd wear it whenever he left the apartment.

"We can go out now?" Kelsey asked.

Philip threw her an annoyed glance and said, "As soon as I verify the papers are all in order."

Josh shifted, uneasy. "Evans can call on us now, ask us to do stuff for him." He still had difficulty accepting Philip had agreed to Evans's terms simply to get them their papers. And to remove them from the police department's search list. Part of that would involve an interview with the Tkaronto police chief. Since the man was on Evans's payroll, Josh expected it to go smoothly.

"We can hunt tonight?" Her fangs slid out.

Philip growled, but he didn't argue. "Fine, but do as I say or we return home."

Kelsey's fangs retracted. "Of course."

Josh looked from one fellow vampire to the other, a plan forming in his mind.

"Count me out," he said. "I've got other things I want to do."

Philip shot him a look of suspicion. "Such as?"

Without missing a beat, Josh said, "A visit to the lake. Is that a problem?"

His father shook his head. "Keep away from humans. We're still not free and clear until after the interview."

"No worries," Josh replied. *Because I'll be visiting the fae.*

CHAPTER 39

The long hallways and many doors in the vast house disoriented Jaycie, and she was glad they had a guide. She followed Chase, who followed Risto Fina's butler, into a formal living room. The furniture had a Victorian feel, with hand-carved wood accents and portraits of what she assumed were Chase's ancestors on his father's side.

Fina sat in one of the floral-patterned padded armchairs across from the couch, a martini glass in one hand. He waved his other hand at the matching sofa opposite him.

"Thank you for coming," he said. "Please, have a seat. Dinner will be ready soon. Meanwhile, we'll have drinks." He smiled indulgently at Jaycie. "We have nonalcoholic options for you, my dear."

Chase frowned, and Jaycie hoped he wasn't planning to start a fight when they'd just arrived. She clasped his hand to reassure him and stave off any display of anger. Gently, she towed Chase to the couch, and with a glance, she requested he sit beside her.

Chase took the indicated seat. He looked miserable, but he'd have to work things out with the master mage and the consortium or give up any hope of returning to school. When he opened his mouth, she feared what might come out and put a restraining hand on his shoulder.

"It's fine," Fina said. "Relax. I've planned a pleasant evening, but I agree with Chase that we should first clear the air." He checked his watch. "We're awaiting one more person, so Edward will take your drink order."

He nodded to the butler, who moved to the bar cart stocked with various bottles, glasses in different shapes and sizes, and a bucket of ice with a pair of tongs hooked over the side.

"I'm good," Chase said.

To ease the tension, Jaycie said, "I'd like a glass of ginger ale, please, if you have it."

The butler picked up a rocks glass, used the tongs to drop in an ice cube, and topped it up with the requested fizzy drink. He brought it to her, along with a napkin, and set the drink on a coaster on the coffee table.

"Welcome, children. So happy to see you again." The familiar voice came from the doorway.

Jaycie turned startled eyes toward the entrance.

"Hello, Cora," Chase said, tension lacing his voice. "What are you doing here?"

***

Chase's heartbeat accelerated as his mother strolled into the room as if she owned the place. Was she living here? Were his parents together? They hated each other. Didn't they?

She no longer wore her familiar goddess gown. In fact, she looked every inch the mortal woman. She'd twisted up her lustrous curls into a coiled bun at the back of her head. She looked as if she'd visited a makeup artist, and her clothing reflected the luxurious surroundings. Her wrap-top shirt draped across her chest into a V-neck, the bright blue color contrasting with her pale face and rosy cheeks. Black dress pants flowed down her legs in a fall of soft, rich-looking fabric. Black high-heel pumps peeked out from under each pant leg. The attire she'd chosen made her appear wealthy and youthful. Of course, goddesses didn't age and always looked young, but Chase couldn't help admiring her beauty. His father would've appreciated that as well, but, even more, her power would've influenced Fina's decision to unite with her again.

No surprise my father wants her on his side. But had they struck an alliance or formed a romantic relationship? Both? While most children of divorce—or whatever this was—wanted their parents back together, the prospect of such a union made Chase shudder.

Cora turned her piercing gaze on her son. "You don't approve?"

She sashayed over to the chair where Fina sat and perched on an arm. He draped a hand over her thigh. She gave Jaycie a slight smile and then returned to staring at Chase.

He hooked a finger around his collar and gulped.

Jaycie removed his hand from his T-shirt and clasped it in both of hers.

"I didn't say that." Could she read his mind?

"You didn't have to," Cora replied. "Your face says it all. Honestly, your poker face must improve if you plan to play the politics game."

Beside him, Jaycie went rigid and emitted a soft gasp.

"Politics? Politics doesn't interest me. I'm interested in becoming a master mage," Chase replied.

Cora chuckled. "Life is politics. You'd better learn that fast, or you'll fail at everything."

He frowned. "How are you even here? It's winter. Shouldn't you be in the south or in Hades?" If she'd broken her agreement with the god of the underworld, it could endanger them.

She gave him a broad smile that livened her typically austere expression. "You're right; I've got places to go. Gods to see." She laughed. "But I can spare a few moments of my time. Consider yourself privileged. If you weren't my son, you'd be on your own."

"If I wasn't your son, we wouldn't be at risk."

Her grin vanished. "Be careful, child. Your ancestry comes with a lot of privileges. Danger is a small price to pay. If you don't show gratitude, the risk might be all you have left."

Chastened, he said, "I'm sorry. I didn't mean to offend."

She nodded. "Forgiven."

Relieved, he turned his attention from his mother to his father. "Tell me why you wasted my time trying to raise Persephone rather than going after Jaycie."

Fina shook his head sadly. Giving Cora an affectionate glance, he took her hand in his before returning his gaze to Chase. "You needed to work with Persephone to open the doors when you returned from Hades, correct?"

Chase brushed aside the question. "Did you know Cora was Persephone?"

"Not then. I found out when I raised her myself."

Chase jumped on that. "You raised her yourself? After I entered Hades?"

Puzzled, Fina said, "What choice did you leave me?"

"That means you could've raised her when I was still on the physical plane and opened the doors from here."

Fina scowled. "You needed to learn your place and your position."

"That's what it was to you? A teaching opportunity?"

"You're a student, boy. You need to learn. I'm a master. I teach. You're my son. I expect much from you."

Chase leaped to his feet and stormed across the room to the large bay window. He stared out into the garden beyond, remembering the spell Risto Fina had cast to summon Persephone. It'd failed. Had he staged that? He spun around to glare at his father.

"You called her and she didn't come." In an instant, he turned his fury on his mother. "Did you hear him call? Did you ignore him to spite him? Or because you worked together to manipulate me?"

Cora smiled serenely. "The doors were shut, so I was stuck. I never heard him." She gave a delicate shrug. "Magick might appear supernatural, but it follows laws within the natural world. Why do you think it has consequences when abused?"

She raised an interesting point, but now wasn't the time to contemplate the physics of magick. Something in their responses nagged at him. They might insist Fina couldn't have called Persephone the goddess forth, but Chase doubted it. Fina's power eclipsed

Chase's. This raised another question from past events.

"Why'd you both act as if you hated each other?" His gaze turned first to Cora and then to the master mage.

She stood and tiptoed her way to her son in her ankle-breaking shoes. She sidled close to him, her head back, which allowed her to meet his gaze three inches above her. One of her hands touched his face and smoothed a strand of hair off his forehead.

"I needed everyone to believe we hated one another. I made your father hate me. He now knows my reasons and understands them." She broke their visual contact long enough to glance in Fina's direction. "Isn't that right, Risto?" Without waiting for a reply, she faced Chase again and stroked his cheek.

His heart squeezed, and he clasped her wrist, then took her small hand in both his large ones.

"Correct," Fina said. "She hid you from me, not out of spite or malice, but to protect you. When I learned I had a son, I was furious. I didn't understand why she'd never told me about you. Why she'd disappeared. What you witnessed was my rage at confronting her after she'd caused me years of heartache. She simply wanted to continue to protect you—not from me but from Hades. My anger was genuine, but hers was a charade and used to protect me as much as you. How can I hate her for that?"

Chase dropped her hands. "You accused him of rape!" He'd hated his father when she'd said it. It'd taken Fina a lot of protesting to raise the doubt in Cora's claim. "Gods, Mother, women are accused of lying whenever they cry rape, yet you lied about something so serious."

"I wasn't going to have him charged, but I wanted

you to hate him enough to keep your distance." She flicked her gaze to Fina. "I regret doing it, but Hades's reaction if he found out Chase existed could've cost you both your lives. Learning about Jaycie and the child she carried would've endangered them both as well."

"Don't you think telling us the truth would've served our needs better? Especially since it was knowledge we needed to protect ourselves?"

"Are you second-guessing a goddess?" She quirked an eyebrow, and her lips curved into an amused smile.

"You're my mother." Even to his own ears, he sounded like a sulky child.

She linked arms with him. When he tried to shake her off, she held fast.

"Calm down and listen. We have better things to do than argue about the past. You know where we stand now. Forgive your father. We have work."

Chase allowed her to lead him back to the couch and ease him onto the seat beside Jaycie.

Cora sat down on his left and leaned her head against his arm. "Tell him our plans, Risto. We need to get on with this."

"Very well." Fina rose, walked to the open living room entrance, and peered into the hall as though checking for eavesdroppers. Satisfied, he slid the pocket doors closed.

"Here's what our family will do." His gaze covered each of them, settling last on Jaycie. "The child will be a welcome addition to Team Fina."

CHAPTER 40

Music floated from the great hall inside the castle where Dakota Lawson lived with her fiancé, Culain Shiels. Josh had once again disguised himself as one of the fae with vampire illusion and magick enhancements. He'd dressed as an upper-class member this time but not too flashy. He wanted to blend in, and he wanted to dance with Dakota.

Blending in wouldn't be a problem, but getting that dance would require guts. Cutting in on the pair would either get Josh an intimate moment with his first love or get him arrested. Rather, they'd attempt the arrest. He'd make sure they didn't succeed even if he left bodies in his wake.

Part of him wanted them to try. He'd been a coiled spring ever since he'd stepped through the faerie ring and could use the tension release.

Best to focus on getting time with Dakota.

He pictured himself whirling her around the dance floor, her sunny smile lighting up his life. Anticipation building, he hurried to the great hall's grand entrance.

The double doors stood propped open, their carved wood polished to a shine. Inside, couples already floated around the dance floor. Large mullioned windows splashed golden light onto the dining area in front of the dais where the prince and his family would sit. The king already sat in his ornate chair, his pale, delicate face gazing out over the guests. Silver thread lined his gold robes, and the jewel-encrusted cup he raised occasionally to his lips was also gold.

Josh had researched the Shiels family prior to making the trip the first time. The king's wife wouldn't be occupying the seat beside him—she'd died when the two princes were young boys. The king had never remarried. Perhaps he'd found no one suitable, or perhaps he continued to grieve for his wife. She'd died during the species wars, and since then, the fae, who'd ventured from their lands only to get entangled in the wars, kept to themselves.

Except for kidnapping my girlfriend. The thought brought a sneer to Josh's face, and he quickly continued his survey of the hall to recover his equilibrium and neutralize his expression.

Brilliant, colorful tapestries hung on the stone walls. All of them showed gorgeous fae in various historical events. The darkest one illustrated scenes from the species wars and included the death of their beloved queen. A huge spear through her chest pinned her to a tree, blood staining her white gown red.

The tables in the eating area were thick wooden slabs surrounded by long wooden benches for the guests, but this wasn't a typical medieval castle. The enormous fireplace, carved into the middle of one of the long walls, still used logs as fuel, but giant chandeliers, powered by electricity, hung from the high, ornate ceiling. A wide area in front of the rows of tables served as a space for dancing. Tables along the room's perimeter held urns for coffee and hot water for tea and the fixings to go with them. No food had yet appeared except for baskets of dinner rolls on the tables and small dishes holding pats of butter. Place settings organized the seating. To Josh's relief, none of the tables were numbered, and he saw no seating lists or place cards.

He wove through the gathering throng and parked himself halfway between the dance floor and the dais—not too close to give himself status but not too far away to make him appear inconsequential in the social hierarchy. He scanned the hall, searching for Dakota or her fiancé. Neither had yet made an appearance. Most guests danced or wandered around or chatted in groups. A few sat at the tables, but Josh found a spot without anyone nearby so he could relax and observe.

He'd left the apartment at dusk, figuring Kelsey and Philip wouldn't notice him gone for a while. Now they'd consummated their relationship, he expected them to spend more time in the bedroom. That his mom and his father had transitioned to a physical relationship didn't bother him. Both were consenting vampires, and the relationship would keep them occupied and away from his personal business. Despite that, as a precaution, he'd left a note explaining he'd gone hunting in a forest outside the city limits followed by a visit to the lake. Philip trusted him, and Kelsey was still too self-absorbed to care what anyone else did.

Before Josh went through the faerie circle, he'd visited an apothecary and used some of his share of the money Frank Evans gave them to buy potions and enchantments to create his disguise. He'd also visited a clothing store that sold faerie fashions and outfitted himself appropriately though the tights made him feel exposed. To cover up his junk, he'd bought a tunic that hung below his crotch. The only one he wanted checking out his package was Dakota.

His vampire abilities enhanced the desired effect, and he appeared as a pointy-eared, dark-haired faerie lord. His attire blended in perfectly with that of the other guests.

On his last visit to the fae, he'd learned the royal schedule for feasts and celebrations. This particular feast recurred the first Saturday of every month—fae time. He'd had to calculate when that would happen in relation to the physical plane's calendar. Visits to the faerie realm made math a necessity, but Josh had a knack for it, and his vampire brain boosted his already superior capabilities. He'd arrived precisely when he wanted to.

"Is this seat taken?" someone with a soft feminine voice said.

Josh looked up to find a young fae woman standing beside him. She smiled as she awaited his response.

He gestured to each side. "Either is all yours." He'd kept his tone detached and offered only a polite smile. He didn't want to encourage her, but if she sat with him, it might help his cover—as long as he said nothing crazy. *Remember, you're fae, not vampire.*

"Thank you." She took the seat on his right, lifting her skirts enough to step over the bench. After she smoothed her dress into place, she faced him and offered that friendly smile again. "I'm Alina Lawrimore." She held out her hand, palm down, and he clasped it in his and gave it a soft kiss.

"A pleasure to meet you. I'm Eoin Morphew." He'd done an online search to create his fake name. The Morphew clan was huge in this realm. She'd have met some members, but not all.

"I haven't seen you at our feasts before. Where do you live?"

"Southern Realm." The fae kingdom was divided into five realms: Northern, Southern, Western, Eastern, and Central. The king ruled over them all from Central Realm. Each realm also had a lord who saw to the more local governing needs. Josh had selected Southern Realm as his fake address, as the southerners had darker skin and hair, the opposite of his normal coloring.

"Are you visiting family?"

"Yes, but I'm staying at a local bed-and-breakfast." Time to switch the focus to her before she asked him a trick question. "I assume you live in Central? Did you grow up here?"

That got her going as he'd hoped it would. For the next while, they chatted about her life and family. She avoided politics, which relieved him since he had a sketchy knowledge of fae politics.

Suddenly, he sensed a shift in the air. He sniffed, his vampire nose picking up a familiar scent.

Dakota.

He stared past Alina's head to the dais, and there she was: the love of his life. The one who got away. He almost stood but caught himself in time.

She walked with her arm hooked through her fiancé's as he led her to her seat. Culain would sit to the right of center, so he escorted Dakota to the seat beside that one. She smiled at the prince, ripping Josh's heart out. Culain pulled her chair out for her, but before she sat, she paused and scanned the room as though searching for something. Her gaze floated from table to table, from seat to seat.

Frozen in place, his gaze refusing to shift from her face, Josh held his nonexistent breath. Their eyes met. She paused, and the seconds stretched out between them until she averted her gaze and continued to scour the room.

Culain leaned over to her and whispered something in her ear. She gave him her golden smile again, kissed his cheek, and sat.

Josh remained seated, afraid if he stood, he'd kick over the table.

CHAPTER 41

Feasts happened monthly for the entire realm and weekly for the locals, and Dakota slowly adjusted to the necessity of attending them. The people mainly wanted to see Culain, but her absence would've hurt him. Fae from all the realms gathered at these events, some traveling great distances, and it would've disappointed them if she missed one. The half-vampire princess on their future leader's arm became a curiosity from the moment the Shiels family had announced the engagement. Few dhampirs lived in fae country, so attention always focused on Dakota when she entered a room. Gradually, she grew accustomed to that.

She'd met only one other of her kind here—a servant who looked like a purebred fae but carried a vampiric scent. She'd assumed he was one of the mixed breeds of fae and dhampir Culain had told her existed. Perhaps he'd had a dhampir mother. If so, she'd love to meet the woman to query her about life here and learn if her family had sold her to the fae, too. She'd almost questioned the man but reconsidered. She wasn't sure if it was appropriate to ask the help about their personal lives. What if he resented her for it? She still wasn't used to having others waiting on her, even dressing her. It just felt wrong and exploitative.

As Culain walked Dakota to her seat, she sensed a vampire presence in the room. She scanned the area but saw no one who might be a dhampir.

Culain had explained the fae wanted only dhampirs, not full-fledged vampires, for breeding. She didn't understand why they needed that human-vampire mix—after all, vampires were once human, and a vampire woman could conceive if the father wasn't a vampire. However, two vampires couldn't conceive. The blood exchange during a human's turning was their way of creating a child. Sometimes the intricacies of species social conventions and physiology made her head ache.

Culain put a hand on her arm. "Everything all right, sweetheart? You seem awfully pensive for someone attending a celebration."

Every feast to these people was a celebratory feast. She struggled to keep track of what they celebrated and when. She still had to ask Culain to explain it to her before each one.

"I'm fine. I thought I sensed ..." She shook her head. "Never mind."

"What is it?" His brows drew together, and he tilted his head, meeting her gaze with a concerned expression.

"I thought I sensed another dhampir. Is that possible?"

He smiled and leaned in close to whisper in her ear. "Could be. I told you they live here. Not many, mind you, but they exist, and they're welcome to attend the feasts like anyone else. Are you lonely?" His tone hinted at worry. "You never mentioned you wanted to meet other dhampirs."

She shook her head. "Not at all. How can I be lonely when I have you?" She meant that. He'd not only helped her settle in, but to her surprise, she'd developed feelings for him and wanted to spend time with him. A good thing, too, because their wedding was less than a month away. Part of her attraction to him, she knew, was that the fae had selected her specifically because, out of all the potential candidates, they'd deemed her the most compatible with him. What had happened to the other girls? Were they sold to other fae who desired dhampir wives? So far, she'd neglected to carry out her vow to find the mermaid girl she'd met before arriving at the faery realm. What had happened to the poor creature? She'd been so frightened.

King Shiels cleared his throat, interrupting their private conversation. "Son, you have a duty to mingle. You both do."

This wasn't the first time Culain's father reminded them of that during a feast. Both Dakota and her fiancé disliked large gatherings, preferring to spend as much time as possible alone together. Like lovers but without taking it to the physical level. *Yet.*

Dakota's desire for the handsome prince was growing uncontrollable. One of these days, they'd settle on the sofa in the den to play chess or watch some fae television and she'd jump his bones. She smiled at the thought of how shocked he'd be. The fae prided themselves on propriety and chastity before marriage—except for the males. *Patriarchal hypocrites.*

When she became queen, she'd make changes. They'd then either be sorry they'd kidnapped her or she'd improve their lives. She wasn't sure which scenario she preferred. *Improving their lives. That's why I'd do it.* She had to keep reminding herself so she didn't grow bitter. *What's to be bitter about? He's a great guy.*

Culain sighed. "Yes, Father."

His every move signaling reluctance, he rose and held his hand out to her.

"Come. We'll mix and mingle until the servers bring out the food." He checked his watch, which looked anachronistic in this medieval setting, much as the other modern conveniences did. The presence of technology in a place that looked like it shouldn't have indoor plumbing still startled her even after living here for months.

She took his hand and allowed him to help her up, savoring the contact.

He led her out onto the dance floor, and they took up the waltz in progress. As they whirled among the other couples, she kept her gaze fixed on Culain. His green eyes mesmerized her, and his pretty-boy features made her want to stare at him simply to take in his beauty.

Other women in the room also glanced his way, appreciating a handsome man when they saw one. His body was well muscled but not so he looked like a bodybuilder. She loved to stroke his biceps and lean her head on his powerful chest. His lips were made for kissing. As always, her physical attraction to him triggered desire, and she wished they could sneak off alone.

And do what? Their customs forbid it.

"Penny for your thoughts." His eyes sparkled, and

his tone dripped with mischief.

She grinned and tried to keep the lasciviousness out of her expression.

He must've noticed her struggle because he chuckled, low and deep. "One more month, my dear." He kissed her lips, and the teasing look left his face. "I can't wait either. You're so ... I love you." He'd choked up on that last bit. He'd said the "L" word to her before but made it clear she needn't reciprocate. His understanding and compassion for her difficult situation only made her love him all the more.

She'd always held back, but this feeling of love and affection had grown so much that she had to acknowledge it. "I love you too, Culain."

Someone tapped her shoulder, and a male voice said, "May I cut in?"

Culain and Dakota paused mid-step and faced the newcomer. The scent of vampire overwhelmed her, and when she moved her gaze from Culain to meet the man's eyes, she was face-to-face with the faerie whose gaze had caught hers when she'd scanned the room.

He must be a mix of dhampir and faerie, but then why does he give off such a vampire vibe? If she danced with him, she'd find out. She met Culain's gaze and waited for his response.

Her fiancé stepped back and gave a slight bow. "Be my guest." He smiled affectionately. "We'll talk later."

Dakota returned the smile and allowed the stranger to take her into his arms.

CHAPTER 42

"I don't like it." Chase paced between the desk and the hope chest at the foot of Jaycie's bed. They'd returned from dinner at Risto Fina's, and Jaycie now dealt with a worried and close-to-panicking boyfriend.

"He wants us to work with them? How can we work with them? He's manipulative." He halted and stared into her eyes. "They're both manipulative. You see that, right?"

She hurried to stand before him and then hugged him. "Yes. We'll have to be careful. Play along. We're in a difficult position."

He squeezed her tight. "I promise we'll get out from under it."

"You can't guarantee that. Your birth parents are powerful."

"They are," he admitted, "but so are we." He shook his head. "I didn't even attend the wedding."

"What wedding?"

"The one I made that stupid tux for. The thing that

triggered all this. I missed it."

Puzzled, she put a hand on his arm. "Does that upset you?"

"No. I just … it's ironic. All that mess because I wanted a tux for a wedding I didn't even attend."

She shook her head. "Whatever you conjured that day would've triggered the demon."

He shrugged. "I guess. It shouldn't have happened, though. Fina caused the dominoes to fall. We need to stay ahead of him in the future. How are we supposed to do that?"

Hope sparked in Jaycie. "Let's draw a card."

The tarot always helped her center herself when the future looked uncertain. The cards gave her a direction to take, reassurance things weren't as bleak as she imagined. If they heralded a warning, she'd prepare and avoid or cope with it.

She extricated herself from his embrace and strode to her bedside table. From the top drawer, she retrieved a deck of tarot cards. She eased her hip onto the bed and removed the cards from their box. She shuffled, focusing on the future she'd share with Chase and the baby. *One card.* She only needed one to enlighten her.

A card flipped out and landed face down on the floor. Whenever a card jumped out of the deck, it held particular significance. It meant the universe wanted to relay an urgent message. She picked up the card and flipped it over.

The Empress.

Both studied it.

A pregnant woman in a green gown sat on a gold throne. Everything about this card spoke of fertility, growth, and nature's power. Isis, Demeter, and Gaia asserted influence on the situation.

"I'm pregnant. That's the obvious message," Jaycie said.

"We can't ignore that Cora's my mother, and this card represents the mother goddess. I drew the High Priestess not long ago. The Empress follows it."

Jaycie met his gaze, and for a moment, neither spoke. Finally, she broke the silence. "The heart-shaped shield is love." She took his hand. "The message can mean we need to protect our family, our home."

"Are you interpreting it as a warning? That we have something to protect our family from?"

"That's not how I want to interpret it, but with everything that's happened, what else can we think?" Her face fell, exhaustion and despair overwhelming her. "I'm not up to his."

He tugged the card from her fingers and set it back on the deck. He took her hand in his. "That's why I'm here. Whatever happens, we're in this together. I saw you back there, Jaycie. You're more powerful than you think."

She recalled her escape from the dream world in Hades, which she'd accomplished all on her own, and her spirits lifted. She squeezed his hand.

"I think you're right."

***

A deer raced past them, and Kelsey's killer instincts kicked in. She tore after it, her pace so rapid the wind streamed her long and once more straw-colored hair behind her. The chase grew more and more exhilarating—so much so that she allowed the animal to run longer than necessary.

"Take it down," Philip said in her ear. He matched her speed and gave her the freedom to continue the chase until the animal's fear scent grew overwhelming.

She leaped, landed on the animal's back, and bit its neck. It staggered and dropped to its knees. She jumped clear when it collapsed onto its side.

"Finish it. Never allow an animal to suffer."

She swiped drops of blood from her lips and licked the resulting smear off her hand. Dropping beside the deer, she mesmerized it and then bit into its neck.

When she finished drinking, she removed a packet of moist towelettes from her jacket pocket and cleaned her face. She deposited the used tissue into a baggie to take home. Philip insisted they leave no refuse behind. The camper's pack it in and pack it out rule. This time, he'd take the carcass, too. They'd brought a pickup truck with them and parked near the hunting grounds. Philip had purchased the vehicle with his own money. Now they were free to live as citizens again instead of fugitives, he could access all his accounts. This gave them breathing room and luxuries Kelsey hadn't even realized she missed.

He'd promised to teach her everything about living as a vampire, including where to sell the carcasses they had no further use for. He'd also promised to care for her and Josh, to help them amass the wealth they'd need to survive through the coming centuries. She didn't know what that might look like, but she was okay with it.

After they transported the carcass to the Skanadario Food Terminal and sold it to the guy Philip always dealt with, they returned to the apartment. Dawn was close, and Josh still hadn't returned. Kelsey noted the absence, but she didn't panic or even experience a twinge of worry. She'd grown attached to him, the way she'd grown attached to friends or extended family growing up, but she also trusted he looked after himself. Vampires were powerful. They feared nothing. Yes, they could be killed—the vampire Josh had slain proved that—but Josh had only gone to the beach. He could cross the entire lake without coming up for air, and he still wouldn't die.

She'd fed well on the deer and had satiated her hunger for blood, so instead of raiding the fridge, she sauntered to the sofa and sat. She set the television to the news channel as background noise.

Philip emerged from the bedroom. "Shall we set up a game, darling?" He meant chess. They'd played almost every night since moving into the apartment.

"Sure. Later." She wanted to do something else first—something she hadn't done as a vampire—something she'd feared when she was human but feared no longer. "Let's draw a tarot card. You got a deck?"

He smiled indulgently. "Of course."

He retreated to the bedroom, and when he returned, he held a pack of tarot cards aloft in his hand. "Here you go. You want to draw the card yourself?"

"Yes. Might as well learn magick. If I've lost my soul, what does it matter if I delve into the occult? As long as I'm damned, I might as well enjoy it."

He chuckled as he handed her the deck. "We'll work on that attitude. Let's see what you get."

She shuffled the cards awkwardly because they were larger than playing cards and she wasn't accustomed to handling them. As she shuffled, she focused on what might influence their future. One card popped out and landed face up on the floor.

"That's your card, darling. If one jumps out, the universe deems it important."

"The Empress. What does it mean?" She bent down and picked it up.

The picture's subject was a pregnant woman dressed in an emerald-green gown trimmed with gold. She held a scepter in her hand. The gold throne on which she sat stood outdoors, wheat growing in the foreground. A rabbit huddled at her feet.

"Look at the symbolism and tell me."

Some things never change. He still insisted on forcing her to interpret the meaning herself, only this time, the directive didn't frustrate her. She wanted to learn, and she had centuries to do it. From habit rather than an ability to draw breath, she sighed, then focused on the card.

"Twelve stars float around her head. Does that represent the twelve months of the year?"

"Good guess, and it's an option. If that's what your instincts tell you, run with it. Twelve zodiac signs exist, too, so that could apply."

"I've never studied astrology," she said. "We're almost in January. That's the first star."

"The first zodiac sign, though, is Aries, which covers the end of March 21 to April 19."

She frowned. None of that seemed relevant, but then, the cards had never made sense to her. *Why even bother with them?* But ever since Chase had asked her to pull a card all those months ago at the bookstore, she felt drawn to them.

"The woman is pregnant, so she's obviously fertile, and don't rabbits represent fertility?"

He gave her a broad, proud grin. "Yes."

"I don't want to get pregnant." Her tone was emphatic.

"As a vampire, you can't—or, rather, it would be difficult. We can't reproduce within our own species unless you count turning someone into a vampire, but that's not creating life, is it?"

"No. Just the opposite. It takes life. We consider it rebirth, but the new vampire is undead." She contemplated for a moment. "But we call the new vamp a baby."

"Makes us family, turning someone," he said. "Josh is my son—not in the same way he's yours, but he's my family."

"Blair will hate you for that." Her ex-husband had already started the hating-Philip process when he'd tracked the trio down in Algonquin and discovered Josh was a vampire. Philip solved the problem by erasing Blair's memory of the event. Unfortunately, he'd learn the truth again eventually. Some journalist would figure out they'd returned and report the story, which might trigger memories.

Philip shrugged. A human's hate wasn't high on his list of things to care about. He hadn't cared what her ex thought then, and he wouldn't care now—not because he lacked empathy but because he could do nothing about it.

"Keep going," he said.

She examined the picture, trying to remember anything she'd learned about symbolism. It didn't amount to much.

"She's sitting outdoors and has a shield."

"What could that mean?" he asked.

"We need protection, or we have something we need to protect? Do you know?"

"Yes. I'm trying to make you think."

She laughed. "That's dangerous."

He chuckled in response. "It's good to see your sense of humor." He studied her until his scrutiny made her squirm.

"Nothing seemed very funny after Evans's men shot my son." Her tone wasn't accusatory, but he cringed.

"I'm sorry."

"I'm only stating a fact." She shook her head. "They did it, not you. We don't need to revisit that argument. I no longer blame you for it."

"Then who do you blame?"

She stared at him, surprised he had to ask. "Evans. It's all his doing. His men started it when they kidnapped Dakota."

He shook his head. "It goes back further than that, I'm afraid. Dakota's mother sold her to them. She seduced me, had my child, and offered her to the crime syndicate here in Tkaronto as if she were a commodity."

"Will you take revenge on her?" Dakota's mother, Annabelle, deserved payback for what she'd done. If Kelsey's ex had sold their child, she'd make him pay.

As if reading her mind, Philip said, "I think we've done enough vigilantism for now. If she stays out of my life, I'll let her leave it."

With a burst of intuition, Kelsey said, "We have to protect us. Our love and our little family. You, me, Josh."

Pain flashed across Philip's face.

"What's wrong?"

"I'm sorry," he said. "It's difficult to hear you talk of our love when I know you don't feel it."

She touched his arm. "I remember it, and if this card represents growth, fertility, our future, then perhaps it's telling us I'll get that back."

He smiled. "I'd like to believe that's true."

A reporter's excited voice cut into their conversation. Kelsey and Philip both turned to watch. Their pictures, along with Josh's, splashed across the scene. The reporter continued in voice-over. "... were found safe. The trio, who disappeared during a murder at the Crossroads Books & Café, turned themselves in to police."

The story continued, providing context with a summary of the events that unfolded in the bookstore and everything that followed: the arson at Blood Shots, Philip's bar, which he co-owned with Dwayne Rathburn; Frank Evans's arrest for the crime; the search for Philip, Kelsey, and Josh—and Dwayne. Kelsey wondered what had happened to him, but she didn't dwell on it long. The news report ended with the announcement that the police chief planned to interview the trio the following day.

"I hoped to at least get through that interview before they caught wind of this story," Kelsey said.

"These reporters act quickly, and they monitor police chatter or get tips from insiders. This wouldn't stay quiet for long."

"What'll we do?" Now she worried about where Josh might have wandered.

She rose and went out onto the balcony. Philip followed, and together, they gazed out over the city. What if the media already had people watching the building? They might catch Josh as he returned, and he didn't know the news had broken.

"Call him," Philip said. "Warn him."

Kelsey nodded and went back into the living room to get her cell phone from the end table. She called Josh's number. From his bedroom came the tune he used as his ringtone.

Worry in her expression, she ended the call without leaving a message and faced Philip.

"Now what?"

"Now we wait. I don't sense he's in danger."

She reached out and felt from Josh only triumph. Perhaps he'd found the quarry he hunted. She shrugged. "I guess he'll find out when he gets home."

CHAPTER 43

"I've never seen you at one of our feasts before," Dakota said as Josh whirled her around the dance floor.

He'd introduced himself using his fake name, and she'd accepted it without hesitation. He forced himself to behave as though they were strangers and she was his better when all he wanted to do was throw her over his shoulder and run off with her.

"Never had the opportunity to attend." He'd have to keep his responses short and to the point. No embellishment or she'd catch him in his lies. He'd prepped for this mission—as he thought of it—but his research wasn't comprehensive enough to cover every contingency. If he turned the focus back on her, it'd keep him in control.

"I understand you haven't lived here long. How do you like it?"

She hesitated, which gladdened his heart, but her response deflated his hopes. "I love it. Everyone is kind to me, and Prince Culain treats me well."

He tried to detect a note of fear or any sign that duty or fear of reprisal motivated her words. Nothing in her voice or manner betrayed anything other than sincerity. Josh gritted his teeth to keep his fangs inside his gums where they belonged. His plan hinged on gaining her trust and then revealing his true identity and his vampire status to her. Once she knew that, she'd want to be with him, not this faerie freak who'd traded cash to possess her. How much did someone like that truly value her? *Not much.*

"It must be strange. A culture shock for you." He searched her eyes for any hint she hated her life now and found none.

"Yes, but I'm learning about the fae, reading as much as possible. I ... I want to make the people proud to have me as their queen." She smiled shyly, and he fought the urge to throw his head back and howl out his grief.

"Might I ask you a personal question?" Her voice was low, conspiratorial, giving his heart hope once more.

"Yes, Your Highness."

Her gaze flicked to his lapel, but, of course, he wasn't wearing an identifying pin. In fae country, laws from the physical plane didn't apply. The fae balked against wearing the pins, and in their own realm, no one did. "I sense you're not entirely fae. You have vampire blood in you. It's strong. Are you ... dhampir? Or fae and dhampir?"

Grateful she'd provided him options she'd accept, he nodded. "My mother was dhampir, my father, fae."

Her steps paused, throwing him off-kilter and forcing him to focus on the waltz for a moment. Inside, he panicked. What had he said to throw her off?

"Was? You speak as though your mother, at least, is no longer with us."

Damn. He portrayed himself as an orphan so she wouldn't search for his family, but now he recognized the glaring flaw in his plan. How would an immortal die? He blurted out the first thing that came to him.

"Yes, they died in the species wars." Many had. It seemed to work because she nodded knowingly.

"Prince Culain's mother died then as well. The wars cost the fae many lives. It's understandable they'd want to return to this plane and refuse to open to the physical realm. I'm not sure any of us should've revealed ourselves, but I guess that's all in the past. What do you think?"

"If the curtains hadn't parted, revealing the hypernaturals, neither you nor I would exist." He smiled at her.

She returned it, her full lips curving up sweetly, her beautiful eyes sparkling with joy, and it took all his will not to lean in and kiss her. His mind flashed back to past kisses they'd shared, and he lost himself in the memories. When someone tapped his shoulder to cut in on their dance, he almost whirled around to punch the interloper. Instead, he stopped dancing just as the music paused and passed her back to her fiancé.

After exchanging pleasantries, Dakota and Culain wended their way through the couples surrounding them, this time to chat with those sitting at the tables. Josh followed their progress with his gaze for a few minutes and then decided he'd had enough. He'd elicited enough information about Dakota's life with the prince to return home and strategize for the next visit.

While the revelry continued, Josh slipped from the

great room and headed for the faerie ring.

***

That night, Dakota sat in front of her vanity after returning to her room. She'd already washed up and wore a nightdress. She brushed her long blonde locks. The brush caught on a hairpin. They trusted her with them now, with good reason. Her thoughts no longer turned to escape, and her behavior reflected it. She removed the trinket and placed it in a drawer in the vanity where she kept her other pins. As had become her habit now, she rooted through them, searching for the one she'd lost. The frustration at its disappearance always puzzled her. It wasn't an expensive piece, though it wasn't cheap, either, nor was it an ornate one. It had sentimental value. Culain had given it to her as a gesture of trust after she'd signed the agreement to marry him.

When her search once again proved fruitless, she gave up, and her thoughts returned to the stranger who'd asked her to dance: Eoin Morphew. Something about him seemed familiar, but she couldn't identify what. His presence had awakened something in her, made her restless. Oh, he hadn't shaken her world and didn't crowd out her longing for and attraction to Culain, but there was something ...

Whenever this sense of angst overpowered her, she turned to the comfort and reassurance of the tarot cards. She set her brush down and strode to the bookcase at the other end of the room.

Her quarters were large, luxurious, comfortable— filled with everything she enjoyed or needed. When she'd first arrived here, that fact had enraged her. It implied they'd researched her, consulted her mother before the kidnapping. Before the deal closed. Even now, irritation rose when she thought of it, aimed mostly at her mother.

Annabelle had never loved her daughter, and the knowledge still stung Dakota. What kind of mother treated her daughter as an object to be bought and sold? Anger rising, Dakota snatched up the deck of tarot cards she kept on her bookcase and relocated to the couch in the sitting area. By the time she sat down, she'd calmed down. She was free of her mother and in the home of the man she loved, who loved her in return.

Things could've gone much worse for her, but she knew that wasn't because her mother had ensured her safety and happiness. That had been incidental. Her mother cared only about the money she got for selling Dakota.

Drop it. You'll tie yourself into knots. She's out of your life for good. Focus on the cards.

She removed the cards from the pack and started shuffling. What should she ask?

Tell me what I need to know. That was a good question: open-ended enough to allow the universe to guide the response but specific enough to ensure an unambiguous answer. As she contemplated the request, her hands sped up and shuffled faster. Before she stopped, a card popped out and landed on the floor, face up and upside down.

She picked it up. *The Empress.*

Experienced in using the tarot, Dakota scanned the image, picking out the various images and symbols. Fertility was the card's key message. She set it on the coffee table and selected two more, placing each one face down beside the Empress.

She frowned, worried. The Empress had appeared spontaneously—a clear message from the universe—but it'd landed reversed, which gave it an opposite meaning to the usual one. Would she have fertility problems? Problems with her marriage? The reversed card could also signify domestic problems.

Culain. Her heart wished he were there with her. Suddenly, she longed to have him in her bed. Wouldn't it be nice if they could climb into bed together, make love, and hold each other? She'd never experienced that.

She and Josh had never slept together. Sure, they'd kissed and cuddled, but they'd never had sex and never shared a bed. No long nights holding one another for comfort. Part of her regretted that. She'd loved him. Truly. Not sure why he'd popped into her thoughts, she flipped over the two other cards.

The first was reversed, but the second faced the right direction. The first card was the Ace of Wands and displayed a hawthorn wand wrapped in ribbons and flowers. A butterfly hovered nearby, and a castle stood in the distance. The positive meanings, had the card landed upright, indicated success and, since it sat next to the Empress card, a conception or birth.

A lump caught in her throat. Her wedding approached rapidly. Did this forecast a failed pregnancy? Or disappointment? She'd be disappointed if ... she didn't want to finish that thought. The Ace of Wands, reversed, also implied denying joy from failing to recognize the blessings in front of you.

But I know how lucky I am.

She set down the ace and picked up the third card: the Nine of Wands. She gulped.

The image showed a woman holding a hawthorn staff in front of her as though ready to fight. Behind her, eight more hawthorn staffs formed a barrier. Even upright, this card foreboded trouble. Whatever was coming, she'd have to prepare to fight, to stand strong. It didn't imply she'd lose, but it meant she'd have to draw on courage and even magick to see her through the time ahead.

Dakota collected the cards and put them away. Part of her regretted consulting them—she'd done so to boost her spirits, not deflate them. Nevertheless, this provided useful knowledge as long as she remembered the messages she received.

She returned the deck to the bookcase. After turning out the lights, she went to bed, but sleep eluded her for hours.

CHAPTER 44

Bells jingling heralded the arrival of what Kelsey expected was her first customer of the day on a frosty January morning. She stood behind the counter at Crossroads Books & Café. Her mouth opened in greeting, but the words never came out.

He spoke first. "Kelsey."

She gave him one slow nod. "Blair."

"Good to see you."

"You too." She meant that in all honesty, but seeing him for the first time since he'd barged in on them at the hideaway in Algonquin still shocked her.

They'd talked on the phone since her return, of course. Her conscience had recovered enough since her turning that she called him after news of their return went public. They didn't speak of his visit to the cabin, and she assumed he still didn't remember it.

"I wanted to talk in person." He reached the counter and waited.

"Coffee?" When he shrugged, she said, "Lemme grab Chase."

The young mage had returned from wherever he'd disappeared to. He worked again at the store while he waited for the next school semester to begin.

Blair liked his coffee black and strong, so she poured him a large mug of it and passed it to him. He accepted it with a thank you and walked it over to a table. She poured one for herself, adding plenty of cream and sugar since vampires didn't worry about nutrition. She carried it to the table, then waved a finger to signal he should wait. Walking to the back room, she stuck her head inside and asked Chase to come out front.

He set the books he was busy unpacking down and followed her out.

"Morning, Blair."

"Hi, Chase. Glad to see you're all right. I was worried about you."

The young man paused at the table to shake Blair's hand and exchange pleasantries, then continued to the counter. He poured a coffee and waited for customers. It didn't take long. The bells jingled steadily as the morning rush triggered.

Kelsey took a seat across from her ex-husband. "I'm sorry we didn't get together before now. You saved my store. I'm grateful."

His tone accusatory, he said, "Why didn't you—"

"We've been over that. We were in hiding. Contacting you would've put your life in danger. Are you here to rehash what we already said on the phone?"

"I want to hear it from you. While you look me in the eye."

She sipped her coffee. Couldn't tell if it was hot or cold. For vampires, everything was lukewarm except blood, which felt deliciously hot. The thought of it, and the steady thud of Blair's and Chase's heartbeats, almost had her fangs gliding out, but she controlled them. She'd had enough hunting and sex over the weeks to ease her hungers and had practiced controlling her fangs. All warm-blooded creatures were safe around her.

Kelsey sighed. "How can I help you?"

She'd dreaded this confrontation. She knew him well enough to anticipate he'd want to hash out the details, and she expected they'd clash. He had a controlling nature—not abusively controlling, just annoyingly controlling. His childhood issues caused him to want to direct every part of his life, and that included anything involving his son and his wife, even if she was now his ex-wife.

"What really happened? Not what the papers report or the story you told the cops. Not the bullshit you told me over the phone." His voice had grown a touch loud—or it sounded loud to her vampire hearing. Any vampires in the store would hear him, too. Having this discussion in the café suddenly seemed like a bad idea. She scanned the store to see if anyone paid attention, but everyone around them appeared involved in their own business.

"Let's go to the staff room."

He blanched and looked uncertain. Fear wafted from him in thick, gooey waves.

"You're afraid of me." She almost laughed. Tears would be more appropriate, but sadness eluded her these days.

End of an era. She felt it in her bones. Things had taken a regrettable turn. He'd fear Josh now, too. A rift in the relationship between former spouses was one thing, but he didn't deserve to lose his son this way.

He jabbed a finger at her lapel pin. "What did you expect? You can attack me. New vampires are feral."

She shook her head. "You're safe. Philip trained me well." As soon as the words were out, she regretted them. *Should've said "taught."*

"Trained." He sneered at her. "Like a dog. You his pet now? Is Josh? That why he turned you?"

She ignored the questions and made a come-with-me gesture. Without verifying he complied, she strode toward the staff room. Behind her, his footsteps kept pace.

Inside the staff room, she offered him a seat at a table with four chairs around it. The room also contained a kitchenette and staff lockers. He declined, choosing instead to pace the room. His fear had vanished, annoyance and frustration replacing it.

"Calm down." Another poor choice of words, but what else could she say?

In his typical fashion, he overreacted.

Why must every little thing require me to talk him off the ledge?

"Calm down? Are you serious? After you disappear for months and return as a vampire? With my son, who's also a vampire? How do you think that makes me feel?"

"Have you held all this in ever since you learned we were back?" *Typical.* He could've aired it over the phone, but no, he had to keep it inside and nurture it until it grew bitter and unreasonable.

"Answer my question, damn it. I have a right to know what happened to my son and my wife."

"Ex-wife."

He whirled on her, threateningly enough that her fangs slid out. He recoiled, and a stink of fright so thick she almost gagged wafted through the room. She retracted the fangs, and the aroma of fear eased but didn't disappear. He took a step backward.

She capitulated and told him but only as far as the story meshed with what they'd revealed publicly. He might believe he was entitled to the whole truth, but she wouldn't give it to him.

"Philip turned Josh at my request. We surprised thugs who'd broken into the store, and they shot our son. You know that."

His brows drew together and his face tightened. He pressed his lips into a thin line.

Since he remained silent, she continued. "Josh turned me because I fell through the ice and drowned." She stepped close to Blair, and when he didn't flinch, she put a soothing hand on his arm. "That's what happened. We submitted the forms after the fact, but they're all in order. A lawyer helped us."

"You wanted this?" He reached a hand out, and even though it shook and the fear stench returned full force, he placed it on her cheek. He gasped as if startled but didn't remove it. "I loved you. Even after you divorced me, I still loved you." His use of the past tense was a good sign. He needed to move on.

"Blair, I don't feel love anymore. Not since I turned. I might never get that back."

He removed his hand from her face, his arm dropping to his side and dejection in his eyes.

"Sometimes I get traces of emotion. Philip"—she'd almost offered Philip's love for her as evidence but changed her mind—"has loved since he turned. Someday I will, too, but it may take years. Decades."

He shook his head. "You never had room for me anyway."

"That's not true." She said it matter-of-factly with no hint of defensiveness. "We had a good marriage. Until we didn't. I changed and we grew apart. That wasn't anyone's fault, especially not yours."

"What do you want from me?"

Her jaw dropped. "From you? Nothing."

He scowled, making her wonder if they were about to have another of their classic fights. Why didn't he let her go?

"What about Josh?" he asked.

"What about him?"

His expression grew agonized, his eyes full of pain. "I love him, Kelse. He's barely spoken to me since he returned. I understand he's a vampire, but he's my son."

She'd have to dance around this carefully and keep from him that Josh considered Philip his father now. "Give him time. He's remembering you. I lost him too, so I understand. Before he turned me, I ..." The despair and loneliness from those long, miserable days came crashing back, first as memories and then as nudges of emotion—the first she'd experienced since becoming a vampire.

Her voice grew gentle. "He'll come around. Right now, he's growing out of that selfish baby vampire phase." She met Blair's gaze. "So am I."

He swallowed his anguish and stared into her eyes, opening himself up. If she wanted to, she could hurt him irreparably with one word. She remained silent.

"I hope everything's fine with the store."

She wanted to take his hands in hers, but, afraid he'd recoil at the touch of her cold, dead flesh, she refrained. "Yes, thank you. I appreciate everything you've done here. Chase said you were like a father to him." Silently, she thanked the boy for being like a son to Blair. They both needed it, though from what Kelsey saw, Chase had plenty of fatherly role models.

Blair averted his gaze. "He was having a difficult time."

Chase had explained everything to her when she returned, and she promised he could work at the store as long as he wanted. At least his life had improved these past few weeks. The mage council had given him permission to return to school next semester. Kelsey suspected that was because Risto Fina was Chase's birth father.

"I'm glad you were there for him. He's a great kid with a lot to contribute." She risked asking about Blair's life now. "How are you?"

"Fine. Focusing on my photography business again."

"Are you seeing anyone?" If she were human, she'd have held her breath.

"Not really. Sometimes. A lycan woman, but we're just good friends." His brows drew together. "You've met her. Laura Growley?"

"Yes, of course. She's nice." The part of her that had once been human twinged with disappointment. Blair was the type of man who needed a romantic partner. She'd hoped he'd found someone who'd love him the way he wanted.

What's love, anyway? Two needy people clinging to each other until one of them gets over it. Was it the vampire in her that made her this cynical? Whatever it was, she doubted she'd ever want to love again, but at least she and Philip could cling to one another for a while.

They stood staring at one another in silence until Blair stepped forward and hugged her. She almost reacted with fangs and violence, but she reined in her baser urges at the last moment. Instead, she put her arms around him and squeezed gently. He'd never know how close he'd come to feeling her bite on his neck.

She sensed what was coming, and this time, a hint of sorrow nudged her.

"Goodbye, Kelsey." He meant for good. Finally, he was letting her go.

"I'm here if you need anything, Blair." She released him, and after he gave her one more squeeze, he also pulled away.

"Thank you. I'll need my space for a while. If Josh needs anything, have him call me."

She understood. "I will. Good luck." It sounded so trite, but she meant it.

He nodded and walked past her to the door. As he opened it, he glanced back once, giving her a small, sad smile. Then he was gone.

CHAPTER 45

"Jaycie Nevil, please remain after class," Professor Abassi said. "I'd like a word."

She waited for her fellow students to file out of the lecture hall before she rose from her seat and approached the professor. He wore a stern expression, but that was his regular face, so it didn't intimidate her.

Getting asked to stay after class would've terrified her once. She'd have feared she'd done something egregious or humiliating or stupid. Now she simply wondered what he wanted.

She reached the desk, where he packed papers into his briefcase.

"What can I do for you, sir?"

He met her clear, unwavering gaze and gave a slight smile. So, she amused him. It couldn't be all that bad. She returned the smile.

"Welcome back to class. I'm happy you've returned." His gaze shifted to her belly and back again.

Jaycie hadn't yet made the news of her pregnancy public, but her growing belly was making it difficult to overlook.

"Thank you, sir." She waited. He hadn't invited her down here just to welcome her back.

"I notice an improvement in your abilities, in your self-assurance. I'm pleased you've discovered your capabilities and recognize your power. You've always had the potential; you simply lacked confidence."

Her eyes widened, and she opened her mouth to protest. She'd always believed she projected assertiveness.

He guessed what she was about to say because he patted her arm and said, "You might've fooled your fellow students, but you didn't fool your professors. We read students. It's our job."

"Yes, sir."

"Is everything all right? I understand you had a difficult time during the weeks you were gone. How are you coping since your return?"

She hesitated. Some of her ordeal had hit the news. Most of it hadn't. No one besides Chase knew what had happened in Hades, and she intended to keep it that way. "I'm fine."

He glanced at her belly again. "I don't mean to pry, but you can come to me if there's anything in your personal life preventing you from meeting your educational goals." He shook his head. "I didn't intend to sound clinical. You're one of my top students now that Chase is taking time off." He studied her face. "How is he? We spoke on the phone after he opened the gates, but I haven't talked to him since he registered for next semester."

"Chase told me you coached him when he crossed into the veil to find me. Thank you for all your help." Chase trusted Abassi. Perhaps she should too.

Hesitantly, she added, "I'm going to have his baby, so I'll take the summer off from school."

He leaned in to examine her more closely, and the scrutiny made her flinch.

"How does it make you feel?" Understanding dawned on his face, and he stepped back from her, giving her welcome space. He framed his next question carefully as though certain of the answer but wanting to verify. "How did Chase react to the news?"

"Fine. We're both happy." She gave him nothing in that response except the verification that both this baby's parents wanted her.

He placed a hand on her arm. "How's your health? The baby's health?"

Here's where it would get dicey. Did she trust him with her secrets? *Chase did. We might need someone outside the family on our side.*

But that also risked exposure. Betrayal. She and Chase hadn't even trusted her parents or Chase's adoptive parents with their secret. Was it even her call? Chase might resent her for letting Abassi into their inner circle, but something was coming. Something powerful she'd need all her resources to tackle.

"Sir ..." She stared into his eyes, taking his measure, letting her intuition guide her.

The energy radiating from him held compassion and a quiet, understated strength. Abassi had power that might match Risto Fina's but tempered with kindness and altruism. An image flashed into her mind of a man in dark robes standing atop a mountain, wisdom flashing in his eyes. Alone, but shining lantern light to guide others in their quest.

"What is it?" he whispered.

"Sir, this child, she'll be powerful. I'm worried

others will want to use her when she's born. What if I can't protect her?" She'd told him without giving him the details, but once again, he understood.

He didn't ask her permission, but she silently granted it as he placed his hand on her belly. Abassi closed his eyes, and his expression smoothed out, wiping away the typical gruffness and sternness. He grew peaceful, and a smile that radiated joy appeared.

"I don't think you have to worry about this girl."

A lump grew in her throat, making her unable to speak. She waited for him to continue.

"We can sense it, can't we, Jaycie?" He opened his eyes.

"What?" Neither of them noticed she'd left off the sir. At this moment, they were equals, colleagues.

"She's a Moon Child. When she joins with a Sun Child, they'll create a new world together." Their gazes held, locked.

Jaycie sighed. "It's an enormous responsibility. What if I'm not up to it? There's so much in between. It's too hard."

"My dear," he said, "It's always hard." He took her hands in his. "You're not alone in this. We're coming together. Don't you feel it? All the little fools who started along this path will gather, and we'll complete the journey together."

The lump in Jaycie's throat vanished along with the knot in her chest and the ache in her gut. They'd been her constant companions since she'd returned to the physical plane.

"Thank you, sir." She returned them to the student-teacher dynamic, but their conversation had changed it. He no longer seemed like a cold stranger but a warm friend.

She stepped forward, and despite the look of surprise on his face, she embraced him. "I think we'll be all right." She released him, gave him a heartfelt grin, and strode from the room, confident in her ability to face whatever the future might hold. *If what doesn't kill you makes you stronger, I can fight dragons now.*

Can't wait to dive into more tales from the unmasqued world? Watch for the next exciting installment, *The Empress: A Promise of Rain*, coming in late 2023.

If you enjoyed *The High Priestess: Persephone's Return*, won't you please take a moment to leave me a review?

ABOUT THE AUTHOR

Val Tobin lives in Newmarket, Ontario, with her husband, Bob, and Scully, their cat. After ten years in the computer industry programming web and software apps, she now spends her days writing, reading, and searching for the perfect butter tart. Her educational background includes a diploma in Computer Information Systems from DeVry Toronto, a B.Sc. in Parapsychic Science from the American Institute of Holistic Theology, a M.Sc. in Parapsychology from AIHT, Reiki Master/Teacher certifications, and Angel Therapy Practitioner® certifications.

I really appreciate you reading my book!
Visit my website for contact information and to sign up to receive my newsletter: www.valtobin.com

OTHER BOOKS BY VAL TOBIN

Fiction

Paranormal Sci-Fi Thrillers

The Valiant Chronicles Series

Earthbound (prequel): A spirit becomes earthbound after refusing to cross over in order to solve her murder and prevent more deaths, some of which might be predestined.

The Experiencers (book one): A black-ops assassin atones for his brutal past by helping an alien abductee escape capture.

A Ring of Truth (Book Two): A rogue assassin triggers an apocalypse when he attempts to rescue a group of alien abductees.

The Valiant Chronicles books are also available as a complete set in e-book and paperback.

Romantic Suspense

Injury: A young actress at the height of her career has her personal life turned upside down when a horrifying family secret makes front-page news.

Gillian's Island: A socially anxious divorcée confronts her greatest fears when she's forced to sell her island home and falls for the dashing new owner.

About Three Authors: Poison Pen: Three wannabe authors suffering from various mental disorders find love in unexpected places when they interfere in the investigation of a colleague's murder.

Forever Young: You Again: Complications arise when an accounting tech is assigned her former lover as a client and his company's previous financial controller is found dead.

Paranormal Romance

Walk-In: A young psychic woman fights an attraction to a handsome but skeptical novelist while she battles a power-hungry sorcerer determined to make her his next conquest.

Horror Suspense

The Hunted: A Storm Lake Story: A monster hunter revisits her terrifying past while helping a reporter uncover the origins of Storm Lake's creatures. A stand-alone sequel to the short story "Storm Lake," *The Hunted* takes place twelve years later.

Urban Fantasy

Tales from the Unmasqued World Series

The Fool: New Beginnings (book one): A newly divorced woman suffering a midlife crisis gets involved in the search for a missing half-vampire teen.

The Magician: Infinity's End (book two): After getting expelled for setting a demon loose on campus, a student mage searches for the real culprit and finds his troubles have only just begun.

The High Priestess: Persephone's Return (book three): Stuck in the spirit world, Jaycie struggles to find a way out. But others want to keep her there forever. Will she make it out of Hades alive?

The Empress: A Promise of Rain: Dakota Lawson seems to have it all: beauty, intelligence, wealth, and a prince of a husband. But her past just won't let her live happily ever after, and when it comes calling, she risks losing it all. Available in 2023.

Nonfiction

Angel Words by Doreen Virtue and Grant Virtue
Val contributed a story to Doreen and Grant Virtue's *Angel Words: Visual Evidence of How Words Can Be Angels in Your Life*